WE WERE THE NEWMANS

BEVERLEY LESTER

Beverley Lester was born in London and grew up in South Africa and Israel. She studied law in Johannesburg, worked in publishing in Tel Aviv, and trained as a psychotherapist in London. Beverley currently lives in London with one large and muddy dog, her husband and three children, where she works as a psychotherapist, clinical supervisor and as a lecturer. Beverley has a particular interest in trans-generational trauma. She has written three children's stories, and a collection of short stories. *We Were The Newmans* is her first novel.

We Were
The Newmans

BEVERLEY LESTER

Published in 2021 by Beverley Lester

Copyright © Beverley Lester 2021

Beverley Lester has asserted her moral right to be identified as the author of this work under the terms of the 1988 Copyright Design and Patents Act.

This book is sold subject to the condition that it shall not, by way of trade or otherwise, be lent, resold, hired out, or otherwise circulated without the publisher's prior consent in any form of binding or cover other than that in which it is published and without a similar condition, including this condition, being imposed on the subsequent purchaser.

All rights reserved. no part of this book may be reproduced or transmitted in any form or by any means, electronic or mechanical, including photocopying, recording, or by any information storage and retrieval system, without permission in writing from the author, except in the case of brief quotations embodied in reviews.

Printed and bound by Kindle Direct Publishing

For
Jake, Ella, Noah
May your lives be filled with beautiful stories

To
Steven
The wind beneath my wings

ACKNOWLEDGEMENTS

With deep appreciation and gratitude to:

Shelley Weiner – for hearing Ruth's voice when she was still whispering in my ear
Luis Munoz – for the generosity of your story, and especially for your time
Sam Gilbert – for your expansive, incisive thought
Simone Landau – a great first reader
Hannah Greenwood – for knowing I could get to the finish line even when I didn't
Sue Schraer – for the push and for Ann Kronsberg for the sharing of how to do it
Anne Newman – for the calm, sound, advice
West Camel – for being that wizard with those commas
Aah – lovely Faberites, for our writing adventures – I wonder who will be next?
Bookclubbers everywhere, but especially to mine: Gaby, Karen, Linda, Mel, Silvia, and Stephanie
Jeri Onitskansky – for the encouragement to take up the space to play

Families – they make us who we are, and I am all the richer for my special families:
The women from 7 Haven Road – for being the haven in the storm
My parents – for embracing each adventure

Jake, Ella, Noah – you hold my heart

And

Steven – because you are my unicorn

'Ubuntu … speaks of the very essence of being human. When we want to give high praise to someone we say, 'Yu, u nobunto'; 'Hey so-and-so has ubuntu.' Then you are generous, you are hospitable, you are friendly and caring and compassionate. You share what you have. It is to say, 'My humanity is inextricably bound up in yours.' We belong in a bundle of life."
– Desmond Tutu, *No Future Without Forgiveness*.

We Were The Newmans is the product of this most African of concepts, Ubuntu.

Glossary

Ag:	oh (Afrikaans)
Amado:	beloved (Spanish)
Arpillera:	tapestry/burlap cloth (Spanish)
Arpillerista:	tapestry artisan (Spanish)
Biltong:	dried meat (Afrikaans)
Blerrie:	damn/bloody (Afrikaans)
Bobba:	grandmother (Yiddish)
Boerewors:	sausage (Afrikaans)
Braai:	barbeque (Afrikaans)
Buenos dias:	good morning (Spanish)
Caravan of Death:	appointed by Pinochet: Chilean army death squad in helicopters that flew from north to south Chile between 30th September and 22nd October 1973 after the Chilean coup of 1973. Executed total of ninety-seven victims
Cariño/a:	love (Spanish)
Chicha:	alcoholic drink (Spanish)
Ciao:	hi/bye (Italian)
Dagga:	marijuana (Afrikaans)
Desaparecidos:	the disappeared (Spanish)
Empanadas:	Chilean pastry (Spanish)
Graçias:	thank you (Spanish)
Haai	good heavens (Xhosa)
Haikona:	no, not at all, by no means (Zulu, Xhosa)
Hamba Kahle:	goodbye (Xhosa/ Zulu)
Howzit:	hi/howdy/how ya doin' (South African slang)
Ja:	yes (Afrikaans)
Koeksusters:	piece of dough in shape of plait deep-fried in oil and dipped in cold syrup (Afrikaans)
Kwela:	penny-whistle based street music with jazzy underpinning and skiffle beat (South Africa)
La bienvenida:	welcome (Spanish)

La Cuenca:	a Latin American couples' dance
Lamb tomato bredie:	old South African Cape name for dish of meat and vegetables stewed together
Limey:	a derogatory term for British person. Origin: British sailors who came to New World prevented scurvy by sucking limes. (South African slang)
Maravilloso:	marvellous/ excellent (Spanish)
Melk tart:	milk tart (South African version)
Mi amor:	my love (Spanish)
Mi bello:	my beautiful (Spanish)
Mielies:	corn on the cob (Spanish)
Mma:	mother (Zulu)
Muti:	traditional medicine/slang word for medicine in general (Zulu)
Ndebele:	Nguni speaking people of South Africa
Nkosi sikelel iAfrika:	God bless Africa: South African National Anthem (Xhosa)
Ouma:	Grandmother (Afrikaans)
Pan Amasado:	bread (Spanish)
Pommie:	person of English origin or heritage. Derogatory term used in South Africa, New Zealand, Australia
Querido/a:	darling, sweetheart (Spanish)
Rhodesia:	what is now Zimbabwe
Sala Kahle:	stay well (Xhosa/Zulu)
Sangoma:	witch doctor (Zulu)
Sec:	one moment/one second (South African slang)
Stoep:	veranda (Afrikaans)
Swaziland:	landlocked country in Southern Africa where gambling and pornography was legal, unlike in South Africa where they weren't legalised until 1994
Tokolosh:	evil spirit (Xhosa in origin but widely used and understood in South Africa)
Umqombothi:	African beer made from maize
Varsity:	University (South African slang)
Veldt:	field (Afrikaans)

*'Injustice is like having an eye gouged out,
but looking away is losing both eyes'*

RUSSIAN PROVERB

Part One

CHAPTER 1

I think I've killed him, my father.

I've dragged him into the bedroom and left him there. Not easy on account of his being such a dead weight – although I don't think he is completely dead, yet. He's leaking onto the wooden floors. With my father there is always mess.

'Come on, Ivor, do us both a favour and die, there's no point in hanging on. It's not like I'm going to save you or anything,' I mutter.

'Ruthie, Ruthie. Patience, my girl – that's your problem. You want everything yesterday. What's the matter with you? Take it easy.'

I know it's not really coming from the mouth of the man who is prostrate in the next room. I know it's Daddy's voice that I carry in my head. Damn him for being right, I need to be patient.

Also, I need to make a phone call.

'Where the hell do you keep your phone, Ivor? Kitchen? Dining room?' I mutter.

There is silence. Of course there is. I think I've just killed my father. 'Fine, I'll just hunt around myself then,' I say into the quiet. What if he doesn't have a phone?

I find a telephone lead trailing along the hall floor and trace it into the entrance of the unlived-in living room. The phone is on the floor. Slowly I sink down until I too am on the floor, my back pressed against the wall. I cradle the phone in my lap for a few moments. My hands are trembling, which makes it difficult to use the phone.

'William speaking. How can I help you?'

I am so relieved to hear his earnest voice. My trembling subsides.

'William, this is Ruth Newman, please can you put me through to Liz van der Westhuizen in Psychological Services.'

'Yes, of course. One moment please.'

'You have reached Liz van der Westhuizen. I am afraid I am unable to take your call right now. Please leave me a message after the beep.'

I have to tell her.

'Liz. Was really hoping to have caught you … Thanks for such a lovely evening on Sunday night …' My voice breaks.

I try again. 'I can't remember when I laughed so much … Anyway … well … Liz, are you there? Liz, Lizzie, Liz … Hello? Hello? Are you there? Oh … still your answer phone, I heard a noise, thought it was you picking up, but it's not. You're not answering. I'm talking to myself … Oh … well … love you, you know that, I …'

I have no idea what else to say. I hate crying. Where the hell are the tissues? I hate the idea of rummaging through his home but I need tissues … my nose … my eye. I feel like I'm drowning in my own eye. I hang up on Liz. Pen and paper would be good right now. Maybe I should write a letter to someone.

There's silence from the bedroom. Perhaps he really is dead. I feel a rush of nausea and wet under my arms. I smell damp and sour. Fear, this is what fear smells like. I am aware of my heart racing, and my heavy breath, and then a more odious sensation floods my body. It is the bitter residue of regret.

I scream to drown out any misgivings I may be harbouring. I scream because it feels good to release this overload of energy that is trapped in my body.

I scream because I think I've killed my father.

Chapter 2

The photo is not what I am expecting to see, not on my father's bookshelf. It stands in its shiny, silver frame next to my mother's favourite vase, a traditional *Ndebele* ceramic. I remember her loving its vibrant shades of blue, rust, yellow, black and white dyes. These colours of sky, earth, sun and people are the colours of my South African childhood.

I stare at the vase, willing myself to remember only the sunlight of my childhood, but the photo prevents such delusion. I stretch for the glittering frame, and my trembling hand knocks against the vase. It teeters alarmingly for a sliver of a moment before splintering across the floor. But the silver-framed photo is now mine.

I hunch over my prize, sobbing with exhaustion. I can't bear any more carnage. Slowly, as if I too might disintegrate, I sit down on the yellowwood chair with the frame pressed into my chest. I sit for a long time, until my muscles cramp. The cold silver metal is slick in my sweaty hands.

I open my eyes and look down to see myself.

Chapter 3

The shutter snaps shut and we are captured in Polaroid for eternity. Everything is almost exactly as it should have been, when this photo is taken.

That dark-haired man in the green-orange shirt, that's my father Ivor Newman. He had thick, bushy sideburns and shoulder-length black hair in those days, in the South African sixties. He is so handsome. I stand next to him in my rose-pink dress, only it doesn't look like I remember it, as the colour has faded under the duress of the ageing photograph. I am only six years old but already I know I am beautiful, because my father says so. I love being near to my father.

'Dancing eyes,' my mother often tells me. 'You have your father's dancing eyes, my girl. Better make sure they don't land you in trouble like they did your father.'

There's my four-year-old brother, Jon-Jon, in his favourite orange t-shirt with the smiling red caterpillar. The chaos of his brown, tousled hair means he has just woken up, but I remember him always looking like that. And standing next to him is my two-year-old brother Mikey, round and plump in his nappy, his eyes screwed up in discomfort against the African sunlight. He is holding on to Jon-Jon with one hand and Mommy's floral skirt with his other, while Daddy darts backwards and forwards, fiddling with the tripod. Here's Mommy so pretty and soft, bending down to free her skirt from Mikey's sticky grip while smoothing out her dark hair as it falls in unruly waves over her face.

'Honestly, Maureen, leave your hair. You look gorgeous as you are,' Daddy says.

The shutter snaps shut. Intense sorrow lands a dirty and unexpected left hook, leaving me winded and raw. I am overwhelmed by the memory of my love for my father, my mother and my brothers.

The photo captures us in the moments before the long journey in our mustard Valiant, my father's first and most-prized car. We are preparing to drive from Johannesburg, city of gold dumps and swimming pools, to Cape Town, the jewel of Africa, which nestles between the Indian and Atlantic Oceans, and Table Mountain. This is the first family holiday I can remember. Or perhaps this is the first photo of a family holiday. Either way, it's an accurate portrayal of how we once were, when we were the Newman family from Johannesburg, South Africa.

Maureen Glass and Ivor Newman met at a dance. Maureen's parents, Yetta and Ziggy, had fled anti-Semitic Lithuania in the late 1920s, determined to build a better life for themselves in South Africa. They became one of Jewish South Africa's founding families; they were civic- and community-minded and swiftly rose to influence, with some varying interludes of affluence. Their only misadventure was Maureen's unexpected and premature birth on a Union Castle liner as it docked at Southampton. Yetta and Ziggy had not anticipated a problem with Yetta being six and a half months pregnant. They had sailed out of Cape Town harbour heading for an adventure on the fashionable streets of London to celebrate Ziggy's most recent successful business deal. A three-week vacation suddenly became an extended sixteen-week winter season, while mother and baby recuperated and Ziggy counted down the days until they could board the huge ship that would return them to the welcoming embrace of South Africa.

The night when Maureen accepted Ivor's hand to jive, she believed she knew exactly who she was and where she was going. She was focussed on the golden future that surely lay ahead of her and concentrated solely on what she wanted to see in order to have what she wanted. And she wanted Ivor. She wanted his dark, dancing eyes to gaze adoringly at her, she wanted his strong, firm hands to guide her, at first across the floor in time to the music, and later in all manner of lust and love.

But enough of that – I know this is a no-go area. My parents' sexuality belongs to them and them alone. Really there is no place for me in my parents' bed. But I can allude to it, for certainly there was a powerful physical connection between them – there must have been or they would not have lasted as long as they did, and, of course, if they had not lasted as long as they did then Mommy would have lasted a whole lot longer. This is a sobering thought. Because then none of what happened would have happened, and I would not have happened either, which makes it even harder to ponder my own painful existence. So, sex, sex, sex – yes, sex between Ivor and Maureen, between Mommy and Daddy, was there from the start, until the end.

Ivor's family, Jewish immigrants running from harsh Russian persecution, was very different from Mommy's family. 'The Russians', as Mommy liked to refer to her in-laws, Lev and Ida Newman, arrived in South Africa at the beginning of the 1900s. They were penniless, desperate for freedom, and keen for opportunity in spite of Lev's Bolshevik propensity. By the time that Ivor was born, the Newman desire for prosperity had become the new family religion. While there was never any money there were plenty of dreams about it, and dreams about property, the deals to be had and bargains to be made.

My mother was four months pregnant with me when Lev and Ida were killed in a car crash. They departed much as they had arrived in South Africa – penniless. At their funeral, diminished and chastened by his grief, Ivor vowed to himself to conquer the free market, in a mark of respect for all he had learned from his parents. He was determined not to repeat their mistakes. If only he had – I could have lived with their mistakes, we all could have.

Perhaps there is a photo capturing the first moments between Ivor and Maureen at The Dance. I have never seen it, and never heard tell of it, but I am sure it would have had the quality of an old-fashioned Hollywood love story. Ivor was tall and handsome, and Maureen was shapely and raven-haired. From the outset they were drawn to each other's intensity.

'Dance?' he'd have said, already sure of the answer. In the beginning, it was always 'yes' to Ivor.

The juke box belted out the latest and most popular Chubby Checker, Elvis and Jerry Lee Lewis rock 'n' roll songs, which became their songs, to be played at their wedding six months later, and so often at home, a home filled with music.

Mommy loved to dance, and to dance with me. One of my earliest memories is of the two of us spinning round and round. My chubby arms and sticky fingers clutch at her dark hair as it swings around and over me, our faces pressed to each other. Her spicy smell and her laughter spill out and over me as we sway and turn, her soft and welcoming body enveloping me in a world that is only for us two. I am terrorised and delighted when she throws me high and spins me fast and never drops me, not once. I love dancing with my mother.

My first nursery rhymes were all courtesy of Paul, John, Ringo and George, and in particular, 'She Loves You'. Maureen and Ivor, yeah, yeah, yeah. He loved her, and me, and both my brothers, until, a certain moment, on a certain day when the world stopped turning.

It breaks my heart when I think about how it must have been between Mommy and Ivor – a marriage of exquisite compromise for her, which Ivor never suspected. He was a real romantic. For him, love was the beginning and the end.

My mind is distracted – it is painfully hard to stay with us Newmans. But, there is no escaping that we were the Newmans, smeared all over the newspapers in the days and weeks that followed the 29th October 1976.

CHAPTER 4

'Two damn hours, Ivor, that's all it would take to fly to Cape Town by plane. Why do you need us to go on some big driving adventure in your damn car? Why are you forcing us to suffer the Karoo desert in the boiling heat? I can't believe you're so selfish and self-centred,' Mommy shouts. 'Why do I always listen to you?'

This is what I remember as the shutter snaps shut; my mother's dark anxiety, so easy to engage, is now in full flow.

But Ivor can't afford five seats on a plane to Cape Town, or anywhere else. To be truthful, they can't afford it, but in matters of money it has become Ivor who can't afford.

When it comes to affluence, there is a clear division in my family. Ivor is poor: he is inflamed by his rich Newman heritage of poverty that fuels his hunger for wealth. He is focussed on finding the momentum and the moment when he can grasp what always seems to be just out of his reach. My mother is rich: she has an inherited sense of entitlement and the security of an eventual inheritance, both of which sit uncomfortably alongside her socially uninspiring and financially disappointing life with Ivor. She knew from the outset that she had married a dreamer, but she had not anticipated that she would have to pay for his dreams by giving up on hers.

Their honeymoon period is brief as Ivor is in the middle of a once-in-a-lifetime deal that needs him to concentrate on work rather than on his bride. Maureen accepts this and accepts his promise that once he has clinched the deal, or the next one, they will have a honeymoon to challenge all honeymoons. She is happy enough, initially. She has Ivor. And his next big deal is going to be the one that will set them on their path, the one she knows is waiting for both of them. But as each of Ivor's deals melt away she sees her assumed golden future begin to fade away too.

Resentment and self-entitlement, in equal measure, accompany her as she packs and repacks the cooler bag. Even the reassuringly brightly coloured container of frosted treats will let her down when it is inevitably overwhelmed by the heat and unable to contain the limp and unappealing mess of warm, sweating foods and liquid icepacks.

'Are you sure you've calculated the time properly?' Mommy asks Ivor again.

'Yes, doll. I wish you'd relax. It's a good ten hours until we reach the Karoo. It'll be about eleven pm when we drive through.'

'Yes, but do you think that will be cool enough?' Her voice is shriller now. 'Ivor, I can't go through the Karoo in the heat, I can't do it, and it's too hot for the children too. Maybe we should cancel. Maybe we should stay at home for Christmas. The Gabriels are staying at home. They've planned *braais* every night, and midnight swimming parties, and rowing on Zoo Lake on Christmas Day.'

'Time to go,' he replies, and walks out of the kitchen.

I start crying. I hate it when they shout. I particularly hate it when Mommy gets upset. It gives me a sore tummy.

But back then, love was as simple as 'I love you' and safety was an enveloping hug from my Daddy's firm arms. Back then my Daddy was lovely and cuddly and smelled of trees and had a scratchy night-time face.

There is a loud hooting from the car. Jon-Jon has scrambled into the driver's seat, impatient to be off. But some ten minutes into the journey he has already had enough, and soon we are crabby and bored, and start fighting over who is sitting where and who has more space and who sat in the middle last time and who can't see properly if they are not in the middle. And then Mommy starts fretting again about the heat, about the drivers, about Daddy's driving. She seethes with rage both at herself and at Ivor, at not being able to persuade him to let her pay for the two-hour flight from Joburg to Cape Town.

And then, miraculously, as though to prove that my father is a miracle maker, 'She Loves You' wafts from the radio. First Daddy starts singing in his rich deep baritone. I love Daddy's voice. It makes me feel all warm and light inside. Mommy sings sweetly, tunefully, the laughter and pleasure evident in her voice and on her face. I join in 'yeah, yeah, yeah', and Jon-Jon warbles away. Mikey claps his hands.

We love him, 'yeah, yeah, yeah'. We love our daddy. We are on holiday now and driving from Johannesburg to Cape Town in the Marvellous Miraculous Mustard Couch on wheels, the Mustard Motor Machine. Mommy's earlier hysteria adds a wonderful and mysterious anxiety to the proceedings that both terrify and titillate us.

I think that every family has a subtly unique culture, formed of shared memories. They can be triggered by something concrete, like a piece of music that uplifts and transports you to a particular summer, or sensual, like spilling the cinnamon and finding yourself longing for your Grandmother's apple pie, which you last tasted thirty-five years ago. I think there are other memories too that sit heavily in the gut, when you recall a certain look that can pass between siblings to warn one another that you-know-who is on the warpath, so all heads down and eyes sharp, or else. And for families with traumatic, life-defining moments, a catastrophe becomes the powerful bond that connects you in a manner that is impossible to sever, despite geography or time – which of course is why no amount of therapy or passage of time can separate me from Ivor – from my father.

Some of the textbooks, and certainly some of my esteemed mental-health colleagues would have a problem with this – after all, we therapists believe in the powers of therapeutic intervention. And I get that, I do. I'd be a useless therapist if I didn't practise what I preach. I'm just saying that therapy cannot be the panacea for everything – it has its limitations.

I am as much my father as I am myself. I look so much like him. It is his eye that I see in the mirror when I'm washing my face in the morning. I am my brothers when I laugh with reckless abandon, my humour forged from all that amused us in the years we had together. It is Jon-Jon in particular that I hear each time – we always found the same things funny, and we have the same laugh. It is a bittersweet experience for me that makes the humour of any given moment somewhat disturbing and lonely. I am my mother in physical grace, hairy arms and my love of the *kwela* township jazz that I absorbed from my cradle, when my father was not around. I love onions and garlic in my food, as she did. I too enjoy the sound of my own voice and I am deeply moved by acts of bravery, courage and suffering. I have the same soft spot my mother had for dignified elderly widows. These women reminded her of her grandmother. Unlike her, however, I do not crave excitement. I have no desire to be fawned over.

This, then, is how I come to be myself. I have devoted energy and time on trying to cast off this heart-breaking blend of nature and nurture, but it is no more possible than ripping out my remaining eye. I must make a quick confession: there have been moments when I contemplated this – ripping out my eye – as the only way to avoid confronting him in myself. But that would have meant complete blindness and certain martyrdom. I am a great many things, but I am not a martyr. I am the living monument, the witness, the victim and the heroine, of that final moment.

She loves you, yeah, yeah, yeah, and we did. Of course we did – Daddy was lovely, he was our hero. He was Daddy. We were the Newmans and nothing could be finer.

This photo. It is an instrument of pain and pleasure.

Despite Mommy's anxieties about driving through the desert in the heat, we arrive in the cool of the night on the outskirts of the Karoo, the 150,000 square miles of flat, barren land in the middle of South Africa. The many droughts have wreaked havoc here. The earth is cracked. Farms have been abandoned and population growth has stagnated due to little economic opportunity. Most middle-class South Africans regard the Karoo as an irritating obstacle between Johannesburg and Cape Town that is to be endured. I think they see only a vast expanse of nothingness, ignoring the earth's largest variety of plant life. By day, a weary, hot wind rakes up a dry and choking dust. When the dust settles the depleted and sporadic rural towns feel rundown and desperate. It is because of the oppressive daytime heat and my parents' typically urban prejudices that I have little experience of the Karoo by day.

But I remember the desert nights – a majestic sky – diamonds sparkling in an infinite blackness. My childhood is rich with these memories of speeding through the midnight desert, where breathing is so light, so effortless, it is without desire or intent, it is as if I am the sky, the sky is me, so seductive is the space, the air, the land. If only we had not been fixated on speeding through the night I would have loved to lie on my back and stare up at that wondrous sight. Perhaps I'll still do that, one day.

Where the desert terrified my mother, I feel inspired by the vast expanse. It is under the northern sky that I endure claustrophobia. I suffer from the impossibility of breathing in a grey air that is laden with the damp, fetid bones of aristocratic succession, scarcely a ray of sunlight between monarchies.

My father belts along the straight, empty roads until his drooping eyelids force him to a shuddering stop in some small-time nowhere place of a town that lies between gold mines and the mercurial blue oceans. The scratchy blankets and sour-smelling beds in roadside motel rooms are where Mommy reluctantly allows us to stretch out for a brief rest.

'Don't get under the sheets,' she mutters, 'you never know who's been here.'

I can't understand why Mommy is so bothered by this. Her anxiety provokes my curiosity – now I too want to know who has been in these rooms and what they have been doing here, if only to understand what makes my mother so jumpy.

The Valiant's spacious interior shrinks the longer we are in it; we wriggle and squirm and bicker in the cramped confinement of the endless car journey. Our ordeal is rewarded by our arrival into Cape Town and the sight of the sun's dramatic rising over the sea. Now that the journey is over, perhaps Mommy will be smiley and good-natured. But when we arrive at our rented holiday accommodation, either the key doesn't fit the lock, or the apartment doesn't match the description in the newspaper, or the area is that bit too far from where everyone else is.

'Ivor, it's all wrong, it's all wrong. I can't believe it, after all we've been through on this wretched journey!' my mother says through clenched teeth.

Somehow Daddy manages to negotiate the front-door locks, the disappointing sea view, the less than ideal accommodation. Mommy goes for a lie-down on the bed that is 'too terrible for words' yet manages to find many words to let us know how terrible the bed is.

Daddy goes for a walk to stretch his legs and we amuse ourselves by running amok in whatever way we can. When he returns, his arms are filled with buckets and spades and the promise of ice cream. We throw ourselves at him, clamouring for the ice cream, already imagining the mix of sand and sticky fingers, desperate to feel the hot sand on bare feet as we hop our way across golden beaches. Mommy takes several days to recover from the overwhelming disappointment of how her life is panning out.

On our third family holiday to Cape Town, when I am nine, Liz van der Westhuizen and I meet and discover that she is going to be joining my school back in Johannesburg at the start of the next term. We meet on the beach, colliding in the spot that lies somewhere between where my brothers and I are digging the world's biggest hole and the encroaching small, neat, singular castle that she is building and decorating with ice-cream sticks. We are dark-haired, dark-eyed and smallish yet solid. Liz is flaxen-haired, blue-eyed and skinny. Newmans are never skinny.

Liz is intrigued by our camaraderie and intricate sibling rivalry, and I am entranced by her privilege of solitary preoccupation. I end up with the best of both worlds on that holiday. Lucky me – I get to keep my gang, to gain a school friend, and to make believe that I am the girl who doesn't have to share while Liz tries out being a sister to Jon-Jon and Mikey. The boys are oblivious to our contriving.

I think that holidays can conjure up what is missing within the family, while at the same time possibly highlighting where we come together, where we join – at best families are a bittersweet ideal. And for us, the Newmans, so long as we don't engage with the 'everyone else' who has also temporarily migrated from Johannesburg to Cape Town for December, the perfect month for summer school-holidaying, we are lovely as we are, even Mommy. It is only when we are with 'everyone else' that Mommy suffers most from what she cannot bear not having and what she might have had/could have had if only Ivor had a different kind of job with different kind of money, or was from a different kind of family where perhaps their money carried more weight than his job.

'If only' … those two little words have the weight of a whole lifetime, two words that have haunted me ever since what happened did happen. If only it hadn't … but it did. If only my mother had married someone else, but she didn't. If only Daddy … well … if it was down to 'if only' I wouldn't have needed to kill him.

Chapter 5

On my seventh birthday my parents buy me a new bike. I am ecstatic. I am also overflowing with anxiety as it means I now have to ride my bike without fairy wheel stabilisers, because this is the condition of getting the bike, my father's condition.

The day after my birthday we go to the park for my maiden voyage. My hands are damp with fear, my excitement a faded memory. I stare miserably at my pretty bike with its hard, shiny, pink plastic seat and silver bell. My legs are rigid with terror and my father is not in the mood to cajole me.

'C'mon, what are you waiting for?' he says. 'We've discussed this a million times already. Just get on the bike and pedal like mad.'

'I think I need the toilet,' I say.

'C'mon, my girl, just get on the *blerrie* bike.'

There is no way out. I sit down on the seat. My shaking legs won't hold me up.

'I've got a headache, Daddy.'

'Okay Ruthie, here we go, three, two …'

'Daddy.'

'One …'

Fat, hot tears slide shamefully out of my eyes because I don't know how to ride my beautiful new bike.

'Ruthie, no tears now. C'mon, doll. Let's do this like we said, okay? Let's do it together.'

'Okay,' I whisper.

I feel easier now that he is next to me.

'Okay Ruthie, just like we practised,' he says.

His firm hand grabs at the back of my t-shirt to balance me. He starts to walk, pulling me alongside him. I pedal and he is running now, his grip yanking my t-shirt under my arms until it cuts into my skin. Faster and faster I pedal. And then he lets go. My legs rotate independently from my fear, trees and people and park rush past me like a streaky smudge of paint. I am cycling on my own.

The path rolls out in front of me, a blurring streak of brown, sandy ground with furry-green mossy edges. I ring my pretty bell. Up ahead of me the path wobbles to the left. I have never cycled this far away from the grassy fields of laughing children and parents. And I no longer remember how to stop my bike. I don't know how to look behind me to see where my father is, he hasn't taught me that yet.

Tears fill my eyes again. Now the path darkens under the canopy of long, leafy arms that jut out from the gigantic trees looming overhead. I definitely can't see my father. I can only grip the handlebars in slippery terror. I speed past the trees and then thankfully the path brightens once more as it opens up under a clear blue sky. I am alone.

Cycling and crying is not a good combination. I can't see properly and I don't see the two boys laughing and joking as they cycle with look-no-hands and no-cares and no-cautions about the seven-year-old girl who is riding her bike alone for the first time, who is crying and confused and lost, and does not remember how to stop.

I am thrown into the air and for the briefest of seconds I experience flight before landing hard on the grass, knees and chin first. But then I am scooped up into my father's strong arms, suspended over the boys, who lie stunned and sprawling on the ground.

'You *blerrie* idiots, why didn't you look where you were going!' growls my father.

'I didn't see her, she just appeared like a ghost, sorry, sorry.'

'Sorry, *ja*, she just came from nowhere. I didn't see her.'

'You came from nowhere, and you better disappear before I send you back there!' he snarls and turns his angry face to me.

'And you, my girl, what the hell was that? I need eyes in the back of my head with you. You've got to look where you're going.'

'But I couldn't see you, and I didn't know how to stop,' I sob.

'It doesn't matter if you can't see me. It doesn't even matter if you can't find the brakes. Why didn't you just turn away from them?'

'But I didn't see them,' I cry.

My hands sting, my knee is cut. I hate my bike.

'That's right. You didn't see them. They were on your blind side.'

'I'm not blind.'

'Not blind, doll, blind side. Listen to me. Your blind side, it's what you can't see. So just look for what you can't see, doll, it's easy. You just must see what it is you can't see and then you'll be fine.'

'I want to go home.'

'Sure, doll, after we cycle one more time.'

'No, I want to go home.'

'*Ja*, of course, once we've checked out this blind side of yours. C'mon, let's go.'

I am placed on the bike once more. Now we face the direction I long for – the path that will take me home to Mommy.

'I want to see Mommy, I want to go home.'

'Sure, doll. I know that. So get on the bike, pedal those legs and we'll go home. What're you waiting for?'

I am pulled back and upright as my father balances me once more by grabbing at my t-shirt.

'Faster, Ruthie, faster,' he commands me.

'Don't leave me, Daddy, please, please,' I beg him.

'I'm not going anywhere, I'm right by your side, doll. Now, pedal those legs and sit up straight and steer in a straight line and look out. Oh, for God's sake Ruthie, you're pedalling like a baby. Use those legs, girl!'

I can see the light shining through the trees. Just beyond is the short path that goes past the playground, and then the car. My mother is waiting for me. I want this horrible day to end. I pedal as fast as I can. He is shouting at me, but I can't hear what he is saying. The wind rushes over my face and ears, and my breath is loud and uneven. I can't hear him. I pedal fast, very fast towards the car park. I can't remember which is my blind side or what he wants me to look out for. Whatever it is, I can't see it. I can only see what is straight ahead of me.

* * * * *

My father pursues my development with commitment and focus. For him it is personal. I am going to be all that he might have been. I am a very lucky girl.

'Now remember, my girl, tomorrow when that gun goes off, you run as fast as you can. Don't even think about stopping. Pump those legs and arms, and think of me, and run.'

'I don't like the gun noise. It hurts my ears.'

'Listen, doll, I don't care about that nonsense. Do what I tell you.' 'Okay, Daddy.'

'Where's your mother? Where's dinner? It's 8.30pm already. This is ridiculous. I've been out working all *blerrie* day and she can't even be bothered to be home with some food, man. Where is she, Ruthie?'

I hesitate. I can't remember if this is something I am supposed to say or not, and I also can't remember where she is. Fortunately he has become side-tracked by my athletics event again.

'Who else is running tomorrow?' 'Dunno. People. Everyone, like usual.'

'Hey, don't look so anxious, doll. I'll be there to watch you win, like always. Have to be there to see how my girl is doing, to make sure you've listened to everything I'm telling you. Do you know, when I was a boy I could outrun everyone, absolutely everyone? There was one time when…'

My father is the best storyteller ever. I don't care that I've heard the stories before. I love listening to his rich, deep voice. Absent-mindedly he strokes my hair. I move in closer, and he picks me up and lifts me onto his lap. I snuggle into him and inhale his musky smell. He makes everything feel perfect, when we are together like this, the two of us.

'Come on then, sleepy girl, it's bedtime. Can't have you falling asleep on me.'

'But I haven't had supper.'

'Well that's Mommy's fault. Come on, your brothers have been asleep for hours.'

'That's cause they're babies. I'm hungry.'

'You can have a bigger breakfast tomorrow.'

'But I'm hungry now,' I sniff.

'Ruthie, we both know I can only make pancakes and chocolate sauce.'

We look at each other. Suddenly I recognise that this might be a game I know.

'Whatd'ja think your mother would say if she came home and found you eating that at this time of night, for your dinner, huh?'

I say nothing.

'Huh, Ruthie?' he quizzes me.

'Huh?' I grunt.

'Well that's it then. There's no other solution. You've nagged me until I have no choice but to give in to you. Pancakes and chocolate sauce it is – but you made me do it, it's your fault,' he scowls.

What can I say?

Solemnly he grabs me and hoists me onto his shoulders.

'Oh no! Pancakes and chocolate sauce for supper …' he moans.

Relief floods through me. Now I am certain of where we are in this game. I start to chortle with delight.

'*Ja, ja,* pancakes now, chocolate sauce now!'

My father is a magician. He can make bedtime disappear. He can bend all the rules until there are none. He can smile through the cloudiest, gloomiest moments of not knowing where Mommy is. I find myself no longer caring about where she is, so long as I can keep him.

'Now, who on earth can help us lick the bowl with the chocolate sauce?' he wonders.

I chortle all the more. My father is the best.

* * * * *

Every Sunday is a *braai* with some or all of the Gabriels, the Bloustshauns, the Aarons, the Lazars, an endless stream handpicked from the social whirl for Mommy, women from her girlhood and the men they have married.

'Hey Maureen, doll, have you remembered to get enough beer this time?'

'There's always enough if you don't start on it so early, and if you don't drink so much.'

'*Ja*, okay, whatddya expect, these people are so stuck up, man, it's all I can do to get through my steak.'

'Oh Ivor, if only you tried a little chatting, you know, it won't kill you.' 'Sure, sure. "So Ivor, what do you think about the sports boycotts?" It's killing me, man. How'm I suppose to respond to that jerk?'

'Actually Alan has some very interesting things to say, if you listen.'

'I'd rather listen to the meat sizzling on the flame.'

'Well, that's your choice.'

'No, it's yours. If you invited some fun people, instead of all this intellectual rubbish …'

On and on they spar. The blue sky is clouding over. The sun seems to cool a little. I don't know what my parents are talking about and I am bored.

'Daddy, Daddy, can we play tennis? Can we play tennis now? Eileen Schneider said we could use her court this weekend as she's away. She said she would leave some balls in a basket on the court, just for us, she told me she would do that. Please, please.'

'In a minute, my girl, I'm just doing some sorting out with your mother. Where are your brothers?'

'They're so boring, Daddy, they're being really babyish. I want to play tennis with you. I want to play with you now.'

'You see, Maureen, a man's gotta go where he's wanted. What's that you say, Ruthie, my girl?'

'I want you, Daddy.' 'Louder, I can't hear you.' 'I want you, Daddy.' 'Again please.'

'I want you, Daddy,' I yell.

'Okay, my girl, okay, let's go play tennis.'

'Ivor, the meat, what about the meat?'

'Hey, Maureen, my girl needs me, didn't you hear?' 'We'll only play for a little bit, Daddy, I'm hungry too.'

'Sure thing, doll, let's go hit a few balls first, get the appetite working.'

I give Mommy a quick glance. She smiles reassuringly at me. She always looks so pretty, I love Mommy. But she is so boring, so full of rules, especially when Daddy is around. And all those Gabriels and Bloustiens, and all the rest of them, are pretty boring, and so are their boring children.

Daddy scoops me up onto his strong shoulders and rushes me through the gap in the fence that we share with the Schneider family. I whoop with delight.

Everything my father does is charged with excitement. I want a whole life of Daddy. Maybe after tennis Daddy and I can sneak off to the corner shop for ice cream.

It's hot playing tennis in the midday sun. Now that I'm on the court I want to lie on the ground and pant like a dog. I hit a few balls apathetically.

'I'm hot.'

'I can see.'

I hit a few more balls to him and practise my serves. They all land in the net. I am not very good at tennis.

'Have you got water?' 'Something better than that.'

I catch the light in my Daddy's gleaming eyes as he eases my swimsuit out of his pocket.

'In the mood for a little river swim, my girl?'

The river runs behind the back of our garden. My brothers and I are not yet allowed to go down to the river alone without our parents, but seeing as Mommy is uninterested, the river is Daddy's domain.

'Let's be quick.'

'What about Mommy?'

'She can come if she wants to.'

'But she can't, she's with the Gabriels and all of them.'

'Well then, I guess she doesn't want to go swimming with us.'

'What if she sees us?' I try once more.

'Hey, who's in charge here?' 'You are, Daddy.'

'That's right, so I say let's go swimming.'

I hesitate only for seconds between the pleasure of the icy water that is waiting for me, and the ice that will be in my mother's manner on our return. But perhaps if we leave it long enough the guests will arrive and she will be too busy chatting to remember to be fed up with me or disappointed with my father.

'Coming, Ruthie?'

'*Ja, ja.*'

My father smiles and holds out his strong hand to me. We abandon the court, squeeze back through the fence and head for the bottom of our garden. I am the self-appointed lookout. Mommy will be inside the house, freshening up, or fixing stuff, or sorting out the boys, or greeting guests, or anything other than remembering me.

'In we go,' Daddy says, grasping me, and we jump into the water.

It is only waist deep for him, but I need him to help me fight the sharp, stony floor and tugging current.

'In we go,' he says again, and ducks us both under the water. I come up, gasping for air, slick as a seal, in my father's strong arms. He laughs with pleasure. I laugh because he laughs.

The pleasure comes at the price of a late-at-night muffled shouting behind my parents' closed bedroom door.

Chapter 6

I love Fridays. My mother's parents always arrive in the late afternoon with an armload of chewing gum and comic books for us, and stay for dinner. They ask me about my day, they vie for my attention. They are only interested in my successes. I am a princess who can do no wrong in their eyes. It is a delight to be so worshipped and adored without expectation. This must have been how my mother grew up.

When my grandparents visit with us Daddy talks louder, and Mommy gets quieter, and it feels like she is not in the room with us. I love having my grandparents visit, but also I hate it because of the arguments that it causes between my parents before my grandparents arrive. I never understand what the arguments are about, but they seem to revolve around Mommy always shouting the same things at my father:

'Don't you dare do that.'

And Daddy shouting back, 'Why not? It's a once-in-a-life-time opportunity. No risk, water tight ... You can't stop me from—'

The intervention of the doorbell always interrupts the he-said, she-said business, leaving me desperate to know what my parents are so divided over.

Sometimes Mommy has red-rimmed eyes when she comes out of her bedroom, and Daddy is irritable. Dinner lasts forever when they are in their bad moods. But my grandparents are oblivious to this.

'Maureen, you've done it again. Yet another magnificent meal! Yetta, I think her chicken soup is even better than yours,' says Pappa Ziggy.

'Well she can cook for you every day then,' says Granny Yetta.

'Ma, he's only joking, aren't you, Pop?' says Mommy.

'No, I think your chicken soup is better than your mother's. Can't a father say this about his own daughter and his own wife?' says Pappa Ziggy.

'No,' says Mommy.

'Let's do charades,' I announce between the chicken course and the upside- down pineapple pudding, apple crumble and chocolate mousse. Mikey and Jon-Jon are at my side, jumping up and down with excitement. We are hopeless. We giggle, we fall about, but my grandparents smile encouragingly at us. Mommy and Daddy are silent for most of our performances until my father clears his voice.

'I have a charade.'

'Go Daddy, go,' we cheer him on.

'Well …' He looks sideways at Mommy. 'See, there's this father, a really good father, who works hard and tries to earn the best he can for his family, but it's a charade because the money is slow, so one day he has an absolutely brilliant idea, a great business plan, only he needs to borrow some money. Now, he knows some people who could lend him the money, but he also knows someone who won't let him ask those people if he can borrow some of their money, and that's the charade, the charade of hard work and good ideas, and, especially, supportive wives.'

'Daddy, that's not charades. You don't even know what charades are. He doesn't know what they are,' Jon-Jon shrieks, falling about with laughter.

'Hush, Jon-Jon,' Mommy says quietly.

'So, anyways Maureen, before we get to the pudding I thought I'd be clear about this charade.'

'Thank you, Ivor. Mom, Pop, some crumble? Chocolate mousse with or without ice cream?'

Mommy is smiling. She smells lovely. I want to be like her when I grow up, but not as grumpy.

'I'm still talking about charades, Maureen.'

'Yes Ivor, I know, and I'm talking about apple crumble and ice cream. Ma, would you like to take your coffee now or after dessert?'

'Now is good, doll, now is perfect.'

'How about you, Pop?'

'Look, Maureen, well … I think I've lost my appetite. I think you also have Yetta. It's time for us to go.'

'But I haven't had dessert yet. I love Maureen's crumble. Do you know, Ruthie, my mother taught me how to make crumble, and I taught your mother, and now she makes it better than me. It's travelled all the way from a poor village in Lithuania to Parktown North, a fancy village in Joburg!'

'Yetta, I said we're going home now.' 'Please, Pop, stay a while longer.'

There is some huddled whispering. Mommy has something in her eye. Daddy is clattering in the kitchen.

'I won't be treated like this, not in my own home,' Daddy roars. 'Do you want us to stay, Maureen? What's got into him?' 'Nothing Ma, he's tired.'

More whispering.

My grandparents put their coats on.

'Granny, Papa, don't go, don't go,' Jon-Jon cries out.

'I'll call you in the morning. Bye sweetheart.' Granny ruffles his hair.

Pappa Ziggy is standing by the front door. I rush up to hug him.

'Night, night, my girl. Be good now. See you next week.'

He straightens up, tall as an oak. The front door opens and they are gone. There are crashing sounds coming from the kitchen. Now the real shouting will begin.

'Come, children, time for bed. No backchat, hurry up,' Mommy chivvies us along.

'Yes, Mommy. Coming, Mommy,' we reply.

We know something of what is about to happen when Daddy gets louder and louder, and Mommy gets sadder and sadder. I want my father's embrace. I want to feel warm and safe against him, but when my mother's smiles make my belly ache I know that is not going to happen. The sooner I fall asleep, the better. Mommy lifts up Mikey and helps Jon-Jon to his feet.

'Come, my big girl, you can do this with me,' she says gently.

'Yes I can,' I say proudly.

I know how to go to bed in a house that doesn't feel good and I know how to wake up in the morning and pretend whatever it was that we are pretending. Not even Liz can tell when I am doing that, and she is my best friend, who knows everything about me, except for the pretending part.

* * * * *

Thank goodness for Liz. In the beginning I believed that I was rescuing her from her solitary, quiet family life, but it was in the ordinariness of her home that I became aware of the extraordinariness of my family, and not in a good way. Liz's mother, Esmé van der Westhuizen, is blandly, reassuringly predictable. I like her without feeling the need to compete for her attention. Liz doesn't have a father – a living one. I think she doesn't know how to be around a father, or perhaps it is something about my father that she doesn't feel comfortable with, but she isn't her full Liz self around Daddy. That is confusing for me, for I am my most Ruth self when I am with him.

My parents confuse me. They continue to laugh together, dance together and dream together, and sometimes I am at the centre of their world. They are also sad. They argue and fight. They shout and snarl. But when the sulphuric atmosphere dissipates, Mommy calls me to cook with her, and calls Daddy to put the records on, and they dance the twist and the jive, and just when I think there is no space for me, I feel myself floating up into the air until I am on my father's strong shoulders. I wrap my arms around his head and bury my face in his shiny black curls. I look down to see Mommy's smiling face looking up at me. The cloud moves on, the sun shines once more. I have questions but no words with which to form the questions. I have feelings that I can't understand.

On weekends Liz comes for a sleepover. We build tents out of blankets and write secret letters to each other with invisible ink. We run away from Mikey and Jon-Jon, play dressing-up and have water fights. We read comics and play tennis. We are best friends. When we grow up we plan to live in houses next door to each other with an adjoining garden, and we plan to have exactly the same number of daughters. And we plan to share clothes, and I'll make my mother's apple crumble, which will be even better than the one she makes, and Liz will make her mother's *melk* tart, the one with the delicious smell. Our childhood is filled with fun and laughter, love and colour, excitement and adventure: me, Jon-Jon and Mikey, and Liz. We have a great many sunny, sunlit days, for years and years.

* * * * *

It is only the first week of a four-week school break. We've already spent hours reading comics and playing tennis and running through the sprinkler a million times, and now it looks like the holidays might last too long.

'Ruthie, darling, didn't you hear the door bell,' Mommy calls from the kitchen. 'I'm sure it's Lizzie. You can open the door, my hands are covered in flour.'

'Mmm,' I mutter, deeply involved in my *Archie Andrews* comic that Papa Ziggy gave me last night.

'Ruthie? Are you getting the door?' '*Ja*,' I say, as I flip the pages.

'For goodness sake, Ruth, I'll have to do it myself. Hello Lizzie, how are you? Love your plaits. Did you do them yourself?'

'Hi, Mrs Newman. My mommy did them for me. Are those real diamonds in your earrings?'

'Yes, Lizzie, my father gave them to me for my sixteenth birthday. They're really pretty aren't they!'

'*Ja*.'

'You know where Ruthie is.'

'*Ja*, thanks, Mrs Newman,' she answers demurely.

'Liz? I'm here in my room,' I yell out.

'Hi Ruth. I've got more comics,' Liz bellows down the hall to me. 'Me too,' I yell back.

We read together for half an hour, but our restlessness drags us away from our comics, out of my bedroom and into the pantry, where we sneak a packet of chocolate digestives. We are moody and walk ourselves up the road, on the lookout for an adventure, on the edge of a rare squabble.

'My house is so boring.'

'No, my house is really boring. At least you've got boys in yours.'

'They aren't boys, they're babies, and anyway they're really boring.'

We've not been gone for more than a few minutes when we pass the group of five boys on the other side of the road. We look, and then look away without taking them in – we are deep in conversation about the general disappointment of how boring our school holidays are so far. It's hard to recall exactly what happens next or the order in which it happens, but suddenly we are surrounded.

'Hey, girlies, hey. *Howzit*.'

'*Ja*, lets jus' say hello and be friendly.'

'Hey, chick, I've got something for you that you'll really like. D'you wanna see it? It's in my pants.'

'Yeah, Brett, give her what she wants.'

'Go on, Brett Boy, you can see she wants it.'

I am definitely not bored now. I am filled with adrenaline. I can feel my body trembling. I remain silent.

'Hey, you, I'm talking to you. Do you want a screw?'

They screech with laughter. I know what he is talking about. I try not to let it show on my face. I feel protective towards Liz, who I am sure has no idea what these boys are threatening.

'Hey, you, don't ignore me, girlie. Do you want a screw? Do you want to screw?' says Brett Boy.

I don't like his voice. It is harsh and loud. He sounds more authoritative than the other voices. He is taller and looks older. I don't look at their faces. I look at Liz. She looks like she is about to cry. I stop trying to walk on. We all stop, all seven of us.

'I've got nails in my shoes. I can't give you those, they're fixed in my shoe,' I say levelly.

'I've also got nails in my shoes,' says Liz.

'We haven't got any screws, leave us alone,' I say. The gang laugh at me.

'That's great, that's a classic. Hey Kevin, that's a great one.'

They turn on each other, laughing and falling about, mimicking us and laughing louder and thigh-slapping. This is our chance. I push Liz.

'Run, run. And don't stop. Don't even think about stopping. Pump those legs and arms, and think of me, and run.' I hiss at her in my father's stern voice, in my father's uncompromising words.'

She is no runner, but she does what she is told. We rush at the nearest house and bash on the front door. It opens and we fall into the arms of a matronly woman. We are a crying mess of snot and tears.

'Come in girls, come on in. I'm not sure what all the fuss is about, but come in. You're safe here,' she says.

We are only eleven. Between us we get the words out. I want Daddy. I've done what he taught me, I've run as fast as I can, thinking only of him. Now I want to see him, and want to feel his warm embrace. Our saviour makes some phone calls and gives us orange squash and a few raisins to nibble on while we wait. Mommy arrives in a flurry of reassurance and concern. She holds us close and we both start crying again. I am safe and sound in my mother's embrace.

'My sweet girls, let's go home,' she coos at us.

Daddy comes home as fast as he can, to comfort and protect me. He strokes my hair and gently catches the tear running down my cheek with his finger and brings it to his lips.

'Salt,' he says.

Daddy is here to fight off danger, to keep me safe, to take us out for steak. As it so happens, it is Thursday night, maid's night off and family night out.

Thursday nights taste of steaks that fall over the side of your plate, they're so big, and golden chips, and ribs that ooze juice and tasty fat, and succulent, sweet chops. In a land far away lies Ethiopia – another kind of Africa, quite unlike these South African bacchanalian Thursday nights of carnivorous gluttony.

Despite my pleading, Liz goes home to her mother. She is shaken and tearful, but I am now hungry and can't wait to get that juicy meat between my teeth. And Daddy is always in such a good mood on Thursday nights.

'*Howzit*, Seymour. How're the wife, kids? Really recommend the ribs. They're looking fantastic tonight. When're we going to play some poker? The wife let you out much these days after that little business with the stripper? Ha ha!' he says to a man who looks like he is doing his best not to recognise him.

Daddy is in his favourite mode of backslapping and handshaking. Everyone loves Daddy; he always has so much to say, full of good advice and great ideas.

'Hey, Selwyn, how about a little golf next week? I've got an unbelievable little business thing going on. Happy to cut you in on it. We really should talk about it, you're going to love it. How're the chops? They look excellent, man.'

So many people to talk to, it's no wonder it takes us an age to get seated at our regular table. My father is in heaven with such a captive audience. We always have a lovely time, especially if Mommy doesn't order salad. I sometimes don't like my vegetables, but there is something about salads and vegetables that my father always finds really upsetting.

'Maureen, you've come to a steak house for steak, not hippy rabbit food,' he says as he cancels her salad and orders a steak, medium rare, for her instead.

'Not sure what's going for you, girl, with all this lettuce business all of a sudden. We've come out for meat and that's what we're going to eat. Nothing out of the ordinary or different or European for anyone else here. If it's good enough for all of us then it's damn well good enough for you.'

Mommy smiles at him.

'Sure, Ivor, it's only vegetables, after all, nothing to get upset about – like poverty or illness or war.'

'Damn right,' my father hisses. 'So calm down, Ivor.'

'I am calm,' he snaps.

The chips arrive and we dive on them. Thousand Island dressing too. Now I really am in heaven.

Halfway through our meal Daddy tells us he is going for a walk, and I watch him weave his way through the restaurant, on the lookout for people to shake hands with. Mommy chats away with us about our homework and our friends until he returns. She is often surprised by the number of drinks on our bill, far more than we have drunk ourselves.

'What's wrong with buying a friend a drink? It's the decent thing to do.' 'But Ivor, you haven't seen Seymour in months.'

'Exactly. Now's the time to buy him a drink.'

'Surely Seymour didn't drink ten …'

'Forget it, doll, forget it.'

Daddy is so sweet and generous; he always buys drinks for his friends on a Thursday night. That's why people love him so much.

CHAPTER 7

When I am twelve my grandfather dies of a heart attack, followed six weeks later by my grandmother, who had spent a lifetime at his side. Mommy is subdued and sad, but my father is jubilant, flush with my mother's inheritance.

'Let's go spend some money, doll, live it up a little,' he says. 'Let's go to Swaziland. I've always wanted to do that. It'll be fantastic. Let's put a smile on your face – just what your folks would want for you.'

'Ivor, that money is from my father, for us to use on a rainy day.'

'Well this is a rainy day, doll, and I'm bored with looking at your sad face. You need cheering up, and I've got a great idea for how we can double these bucks in no time at all.'

'Ivor, you can't. Don't, please, that's not your money to spend.'

'What's that you say, doll?'

'Ivor, what I said … What I meant to say was that this money, the money my father left us, this money is not yours for you to spend however you fancy. It's family money. It's our family money.'

'*Ja*, quite right, doll, and, and seeing as it's family money and seeing as I'm head of the family, I think my idea of how to spend it is at least as important as anyone else's. But let's check. Hey, Ruthie, shall we spend some money on ice cream in Swaziland? Wanna go swimming in Swaziland?'

'Ivor, please, please don't involve the children, I'm begging you.'

'Listen, doll, the children are involved. You involved them when you told me it was family money. So let's be clear and fair. Everyone gets to vote. Hey, little guys, d'you want chocolate or vanilla ice cream in Swaziland? Ruthie, what would you like my girl?'

'Chocolate.'

'Vanilla.'

'Chocolate.'

Daddy turns to Mommy. 'Maureen, are you going to tell your kids they can't have ice cream?'

'Ivor …'

My mother needs to improve her tactics if she is going to get better at Ivor's game. We leave for Swaziland the next day.

The five-hour journey becomes a mad dash when my father suddenly remembers that the border crossing between Johannesburg and Swaziland usually closes at 8.00pm and we aren't due to arrive until 9.30pm.

'We'll just have to sweet talk our way in, that's what we'll do,' he says.

'I'm not spending the night in this car, Ivor,' my mother hisses at him.

We suffer an anxious and uncertain journey to the background music of their sniping at each other until we finally arrive at a long and slow-moving queue.

Fortunately our luck is in; in celebration of the king's birthday the border is open all night long, and we join the throng of party revellers come to celebrate. The Marvellous Mustard Motor Machine with its overheating engine and overheated passengers eventually splutters through the crossing at 11.00pm.

'A good omen, doll, a good omen,' Daddy chortles.

My mother is sullen at his triumph. 'What's so special about Swaziland anyway?'

'You'll see tomorrow, doll. It's really beautiful here. Very green, great hotel with a casino and pools and …' He leans forward to whisper something in her ear.

Her eyes widen. 'Really Ivor, how disgusting. How do you know about that?'

Once more he whispers to her.

'That's why we're here? Ivor, I can't believe you've dragged us, me and the children, into something so sordid.'

'Relax, Maureen, it's going to be great. The money will come pouring in. I already have orders, plenty of orders. These guys don't even care what it looks like so long as they can get their hands on something … Ha, ha, ha!'

'Pop would never have given you the money for this. Never.'

'A man's a man, doll. To you he may be Pop, but I know he was a regular guy, like the rest of us, so don't get all high and mighty with me.

And we both know you'll be keen for a peek as well, which I'm looking forward to. "Oh! Oh! Oh Ivor!"'

My mother is scarlet. She does not speak for the rest of the journey.

Our trip is a mixture of swimming in the pool, trying to prise open the mini-bar and tasting all the breakfast jams. Daddy has lots of meetings and comes back to the room with several wrapped parcels, which Mommy insists he 'sort out immediately'. By the time we leave Swaziland the parcels are no longer to be seen. I know exactly where they are though, seeing as the Valiant's huge back seat is now a mysterious several inches higher on the drive back home to Johannesburg than it was on the journey out.

* * * * *

My mother works hard to create and hold on to the idea that we are a happy family, at least to the outside world, and my father holds on to the fantasy that one day his ship will come in. I believe in him, I love him; it is my mother who I struggle with far more. It is to the Gabriels, the Blousteins, the Aarons, and the Lazars, that she offers a whitewashed and more acceptable version of who we are, and in her doing so I become unrecognisable to myself. I overhear my mother telling her friends that apparently I have my father's creative streak and I am good with people, exactly like her. To myself, however, I feel awkward, my cheeks frequently flushing with embarrassment. This does not strike me as compatible with strong people skills.

'You know Ivor, he's such an ideas man,' my mother tells her Tuesday evening bridge-playing friends when she thinks that I am asleep. I watch and listen from the darkness of stairs, trying to understand this confusing adult world where you say one thing and do another.

'He's so creative, Maureen. It must be wonderful living with such a creative mind. Alan is such a predictable type. He's even sorted out Lauren's wedding fund, and she's only nine.'

'Yes, he's so creative. I am really lucky like that. I shouldn't boast but …' Certainly this does not sound the same as the 'pipe-dreamer, nothing but hot air, lazy, good-for-nothing, scrounging bastard' that my mother shouted at my father most recently, while 'suffering' the headache from which she is 'still recovering'.

'Alan sounds so reliable and steady.'

'Yes, he is, and dull.'

'Well, things are never dull around here,' Maureen laughs.

Does dull mean peaceful and quiet? There are so many words with so many subtleties. I want to ask my mother what she means, but I know I can't ask her. I can't let her know that I am eavesdropping on her conversation. It is a difficult home to grow up in. My disquiet is a conclusion I arrive at as a result of how uncomfortable and anxious I feel when I walk through the front door.

By the time I am a teenager I accept that I can never be sure of what to expect from either of my parents when I come home. Sometimes I find Mommy huddled over the phone in whispered conversation, or laughing loudly in an unfamiliar way until the moment she notices me. She hurriedly ends the phone call and reaches out for me, reassuring and familiar once more. Sometimes I come across my father sitting in the darkened lounge, alone and cut off. At least he doesn't scramble back into a more acceptable way of being a father, but stays as he is, looking at me through his deep sad eyes.

'Hey, Daddy.'

'Not now, Ruthie. Not now, okay.'

'Okay.'

I slink off. He won't explain, and I won't ask. I think I prefer this unvarnished feeling.

When I am fourteen my mother enrols at university 'to complete the education I abandoned in order to look after Ivor', she laughingly tells her bridge club.

'Does this mean Ivor is more grown up now, Maureen? I would hate to think of him settling down like Alan.'

'Oh no, not my Ivor. I can't say he's grown up, and I can't say he's any different from how he ever was, but I'm done with waiting. It's my turn,' she says.

'But Maureen, university is filled with kids and radicals and communists.'

'And now it'll have me too. Deal the cards, Glenda.'

White suburban South Africa of the early 1970s is broadly successful in suppressing its political anxiety about a black danger. The spoken order of the day is the belief in preserving the status quo through the binding powers of state and church. The anti-apartheid rumblings that dominate world news do not feature in South Africa. Our news is not for our ears. The political activists are either locked up or in self-imposed exile, which serves to suppress and stultify aggressive activism. Instead of resistance we have sunny skies, steak and rugby.

There are also general thuggery and everyday anxieties. We are a divided family. My mother is liberal and wishy-washy, according to my father. My father's politics don't warrant a comment from my mother's sanctified lips.

I know that it is understandable that my world will feel upside down because of my hormones. But my world really is upside down. My mother is a student. She studies philosophy, sociology, and English literature. She is happy and preoccupied. She grows her hair longer and wears less make-up. She reads and writes a lot. My father is bad-tempered when she chooses her books over him. Sometimes she chooses her studies over my brothers and me, but she is also kinder and more gentle and patient with us than I ever remember her being before she became a student. She looks beautiful. She wraps African beads in her hair, and she does the same for me, when I let her. She wears multi-coloured bracelets and brilliantly coloured scarves, and encourages me to share her exciting, exotic wardrobe. I mostly reject it in favour of my jeans, which are so tight that they can only be done up if I lie on the floor and Daddy pulls my zip up with a pair of pliers. He has to help me to stand, as bending is not an option in my modern corset. I wear platform shoes and whatever make-up I can get away with.

My father now travels several times a month to Swaziland. He always returns with heavily sealed boxes, which sit in our garage while he makes his phone calls. And then our doorbell rings incessantly and only he is allowed to answer the door, and holds muffled conversations with male voices we can hear but not see as he blocks the doorway between him and the outside. Daddy is glued to the front door until the contents of the garage are emptied once more and the house can breathe again. He crows his success like a cockerel.

'Look babe, lookatmycashlookatmybigbucks.'

For some reason my mother continues to be inflamed by this money that she has always seemed so desperate for. My father is oblivious to her discomfort.

'I told ya it'd pay off. Those horny bastards,' he laughs, waving wads of money at her.

If my mother throws him a warning glance, he ignores it.

'Hey, doll, go shopping tomorrow, get your hair done, get some new shoes,' he tells her.

Here my mother chooses the path of least resistance and takes the proffered money, silently. There is no joy in her face.

'Let's go get some steaks,' he says.

'I've got a paper due this week. Why don't you take the children, and then drop Ruthie off at running practice?'

'C'mon, doll. I'm doing this for all of us,'

'Aren't you done yet, Ivor?'

'I told you, the demand is endless. Of course it is, those horny bastards.' He pumps the air victoriously.

'What's a horny bastard?' Jon-Jon asks.

'Yes, Ivor, why don't you tell him?' Mommy says.

'Well, my boy, it's a guy who's kind of itchy in a grown-up kind of way.'

'I'm itchy. I got bitten by two mosquitoes yesterday and I scratched and scratched, and then it was bleeding, and Mommy gave me a plaster.'

'*Ja*, Jon-Jon – what a lovely Mommy you have. Now, let's go get steak. Let's go, let's go,'

On this night my father wins my mother round, yet again.

Chapter 8

I can still smell Liz's childhood home. The first time I was confronted by real difference was when I crossed the threshold of her home. She is so different from me even her house smells unlike mine. At first I find the unfamiliar smells exotic, and then I find them uncomfortable, and eventually I mostly stop noticing them, as I am too busy trying not to notice what is starting to really stink in my home.

Her house smells of unfamiliar foods cooked in unfamiliar ways – certainly no Russian or Polish influences. And incense, there is always the smell of burning incense. When I think of incense I think of her, and also of her long, angular, frumpy, sweet-natured mother, who likes to be called Mrs van der Westhuizen. I have never called any of my parents' friends, or parents of my friends, by their surnames. I have also never met a person who is so quietly spoken and as even-tempered as Mrs van der Westhuizen. There is something intriguing about her because of the vast differences between her and my mother. Do I envy Liz her mother? I know she envies me mine, that she aspires, like lots of the other girls, to be like Maureen, my mother. I don't really want Mrs van der Westhuizen as my mother, but she is more available than mine, and that's what I envy. I want Mommy, like everyone else does, only I am her daughter, her only daughter.

I am a self-conscious and self-obsessed teenager with an exciting mother, which is very embarrassing for me. In her earlier adulthood Maureen had been drawn to South African imitations of European fashion, but now, through her increasing involvement in student life, she develops far more bohemian, ethnic tastes – swirling skirts, dangling earrings and a distant gaze in her eyes. When she hugs me I feel her arms embrace me, only without concentration. I am not her whole world, or even a significant event. In spite of my teenage preoccupation with myself I realise that it is not just me that she is pulling away from – this is not about me; she is no different with Jon-Jon and Mikey. But I do not remember to think about what this might be like for my father. I think only of my brothers and myself – they are a useful, loving, amusing and irritating extension of myself that I can compare myself with, to envy or gloat over.

Although I can't articulate how I experience my mother's growing absence, even when she is with us, I am aware of a building sense of unease, which begins in the pit of my stomach and sends out long tendrils of anxiety throughout my body. It is not clear to me what I have to be anxious about, but I know that when I am in the incense-filled van der Westhuizen home, I feel fuller, more settled and less uneven.

By the time we are sixteen, Liz's shimmering fair hair is bobbed and sharp, and my dark hair falls halfway down my back in unruly curls that show no respect for my attempts to tame them. We look like each other's negative. Liz has slender, shapely legs and boyish hips that I long for; I have a nipped-in waist and plump breasts that she wishes she had. I know that my father enjoys me looking like a blend of his mother and my mother, because he tells me so. I am good at art, which apparently I get from him, and I am poor at maths, which no other family member is prepared to own up to. There are boys, of course, and Daddy and I argue about the hours I keep on a Saturday night and the boys who try to get away with kissing me on the front door step of my father's house. Liz's boyfriends are always big, butch and play rugby, and mine mostly wear glasses, talk a lot and are not known on the sports fields of our school.

Aah – since then how my tastes in men has broadened. But I remain alone. My childhood fantasy of solitude has become my reality. And now it is Liz who is the loved, the beloved, the belonging-to one, with her tightknit family, and I am the only one, the lonely one, a finality brought on a short while ago, when I severed my only remaining familial tie: Ivor. Like a kite cut free from a taut, restrictive string, I can now extend to my full capacity, where the sky is my limit. If only this was all it took to set me free. I am not sure what I expected to feel, but I feel no different. Surely I should feel different now?

* * * * *

I have confused feelings about my mother. My dates blush when she speaks to them, and my girlfriends prefer her to me when she is near. But I feel sad around her. It seems to me that she is wearing a mask behind which she hides herself and her true feelings.

One night – the first night that my mother does not come home because she is 'working in a soup kitchen' – I am filled with an unspeakable dread. But when I come down the stairs in the morning, she is there, in our kitchen, laying out our breakfast. She looks weary, beautiful and sad, and she doesn't meet my eyes.

'See you later, sweeties, I'm going to get some sleep now. So tired,' she says.

My mother is an affectionate, demonstrative person. On this morning however, she doesn't come too close.

The 'soup kitchen' evenings become a random and sporadic occurrence – every ten days, then once a week, followed by nothing for three weeks, and then for two successive nights, during which time she returns home to catch up, check on us and change her clothes. She is rapidly slipping away from us, from me, and I can't speak it, to anyone.

If only … if only … if … only.

No matter which way I try, no matter how many years I try for, I cannot stop thinking, if only she hadn't, and if only he hadn't.

If only … if only … if … only.

I can't breathe an untarnished breath. I can't block out the need to create and recreate, and ruminate over what I remember, and what I have had to make up in order to make sense of what happened on that day, the day that we Newmans came to our sticky end.

* * * * *

29th October 1976

I can't believe I'm running all the way home in this heat just to get my tennis racket. And my school shoes kill. They're just so shit to run in. Liz'll kill me. She hates waiting. Oh good, Mom's car. Maybe she can give me a lift back to school if she's in a good mood. Where are my keys? Where are my keys? Where are my keys? Shit. Shit! Oh here. Ha, just where I put them. So desperate to make a wee. Quick, door, open, open. Yes! Finally …

'Hi, I'm home,' I shout, and rush to the toilet.

No one ever answers you in this house. Why are people never where they are supposed to be?

'Can you give me a lift back to school?' I shout again, as I race upstairs to grab my tennis things and change my shoes.

It's so hot out, I must get a cool drink. Icy coke – that's what I want. Shit. My feet are killing me. Shouldn't have run in my school shoes. Dad'll kill me.

'Hey, Mom, Jon-Jon, Mikey? Where are you?' I shout as I run back down the stairs.

Peanut-butter sandwich. Must eat that now. Absolutely starving.

'Mom, please … I've got to go back to school. I'm playing tennis with Liz. I had to come home for my tennis racket. I'll be home for supper.'

I bet she's on the phone again, always on the phone. Who the hell is she talking to, anyway? Liz'll kill me. I've been so long.

I go into the kitchen

'Oh, Dad. *Howzit*. What time did you get in? I thought you were in Swaziland until next week,' I say as I reach into the fridge. 'I just popped home to grab my tennis things because I'm playing Liz at tennis. Do you know where Mom is? I'd love a lift back to school.'

Shit, now he's going to see my love bite from Craig and stop me seeing him Friday night, which will be so awful as we were gonna do 'it' again, and I can't stop thinking about doing 'it' with him. Dad will know, he'll just look at me and know. Shit. Shit! Definitely can't ask him for a lift back to school.

'Dad, see you later, okay?' I say, still in the fridge.

He's kind of quiet. If I can get out of the house without a million questions, that'll be good. I close the fridge door and look at my father.

'Did you drive all the way back without stopping? Mom'll go mad if she discovers that you didn't stop … Dad? Dad? Hey … Dad?'

Whatwhatwhat gungungungunthinkthinkRuththinkgungunohmyGodMommyMommyMommy

'Who did this, Daddy?'

Uuuuuh … OhmyGodblood … Daddy …

Chapter 9

I have created so many possible scenarios for what happened on 29th October 1976, but none appease me in full. The only appeasement would be to ask Ivor himself what happened.

If only … Maureen
'Maureen, it's me or him.'
'Ivor, what are you talking about? There is no one else.'
'Don't lie to me. I can smell him on you.'
'Ivor, I'll not stand here and listen to this rubbish. Are you here for dinner?'
'You're not going anywhere.'
'Don't be ridiculous. Ivor. Get off me, Ivor. Ivor, stop. Stop, please …'
'Ivor, I'm begging you, put down the gun.
'Ivor, what do you think you're doing?
'Stop, Ivor, I'll do anything you ask. Please, please … don't shoot.
'Oh my God … Ivor. No. No. No.'
'… Tell Ruth I love her …'

There is no comfort in imagining my mother's last words before my father shoots her down. But seeing as I will never know what she said, I have only my fantasies to draw on, with me as her final declaration of love. It is extraordinarily painful but reassuring to imagine that perhaps her last and final thought is of me, her daughter.

But perhaps it is worse than that. Perhaps she didn't realise she would never see me again …

If only … Maureen
'Oh … Ivor, what're you doing home? I wasn't expecting you until Monday.'
'Hey, doll. Great to see you too.'
'C'mon Ivor, I'm in a hurry.'

'Seems like a hurry to get away from me. I've only walked in and you're off.'

'We need to talk, Ivor.'

'So, talk.'

'Not now, I'm running late. I have to take the boys to football. But we really do need to talk.'

'I'm done with talking, Maureen. It's time for doing.'

'That's what I think we need to be talking about.'

'Mm, not so much talking as much as bag-packing.'

'Ivor, there's no rush. You don't have to be hasty, I really think we should sit and talk!'

'We'll talk, we'll talk in the car. In the meantime let's pack so that we can be gone by the time Ruth gets here. Take the most basic things – and that does not include your hair dryer or curlers or make-up or hippy books. Grab the passports, the diamonds from Ziggy, and cash – whatever cash you have stashed around the house. Hurry.'

'Ivor, what are you talking about … curlers, cash, Ruth … you can't leave Ruth. That's ridiculous. She needs me, she needs a mother.'

'Let's pack a few things and the rest we'll get later.'

'Ivor, honestly I've no idea what you're talking about now. Please, I'm begging you, let me sort out the boys, and I'll cancel my other plans and we can talk as soon as I get back.'

'Maureen, there is no later. It's too late for later. We need to be gone in the next hour if we're to have a head start.'

'What are you talking about?'

'Maureen, have you not been listening to a word I'm saying? Have you gone soft in the head or what?'

'Okay, Ivor, you win. No football for the boys. Just you and me, talking now, about our marriage, now, about how impossible it is for us to talk to each other, like now, when we don't understand a single word the other is saying. Do you understand me? Look at us. You and I, we're no good for each other, not anymore.'

'Maureen, what the fuck are you talking about now?'

'Me? Me? What are *you* talking about?'

'They're after me, Maureen. I can't pay them back. The cash. It's all gone. They're coming at seven-thirty to collect. I told them I'd have the cash all *ready for them and that we'd have a little drink and shake hands and sort it all out, but I don't, I don't have a fucking penny. So we're out of here. We're history. No goodbyes, no last hugs and tears. We need to be gone if we want to wake up tomorrow morning. They can have the fucking house, it's only a pile of bricks. But we need to be gone before they get here. Do you understand now, doll? Do you understand me?'*

'Ivor, what are you talking about? What have you done? I'm not leaving my house. I'm not running anywhere. Let's call the police.'

'Maureen, I don't think you get it. We're leaving, as a family. So no fucking football today, no fucking university for you, no fucking vegetables or hairy-legged demonstrating.'

'Ivor, you run if you need to, if you want to. I'm not part of it, and neither are my children.'

'What do you mean your children? You mean our children.'

'Yes, our children, Ivor. We need to be thinking about them.'

'Maureen, no more thinking. I'm done with thinking. My head aches with blerrie *thinking.'*

'I'm not leaving. I've finally got a chance to do what I want. I won't let you ruin it for me.'

'It's time to get going. Pack the bags, now!'

'No, Ivor.'

'Yes, it's time to go. Do what the hell I tell you or else!'

Mommy, whatever happened, I hope you fought him back, the bastard.

Part Two

Chapter 10

I am someone else. I am someone that I don't know.

If you had asked me how I defined myself during the period in my life when I was ignorant of what lay ahead, I would have offered a response to try to impress you, and to try to relieve myself of my teenage ordinariness. But now, in my altogether out-of-the-ordinary status, I am defined by the shock and trauma of what I no longer am and what I no longer have. I no longer have a family, I no longer have a home.

I am flown to London, a place I have never been to, for some ground-breaking medicine, and apparently I am met off the plane by a team of medical staff, and my mother's cousin Janice and her husband, Neill, neither of whom I know.

I am no longer.

Where my relocation might have seemed like a self-imposed exile, it is nothing of the kind. I do not have a self to exile, my self is lost and the fragments of what was once me now find themselves forced by both nature and nurture to reform in this new damp and grey country. It is a struggle for me of immense proportions. Even my words, my very language, taste foreign on my tongue.

Now, when I say 'me' or 'I' or 'us' or 'we', it all means something different from what it has always meant, from what it was meant to mean. I do not have the energy or the articulacy to make this clear to anyone else. And the anyone-else team are involved primarily with how well my body is doing, how well my system is tolerating food, and how well I appear to be holding on to my sanity, under the circumstances.

I soothe myself with the only thoughts that I can tolerate – my memories of the place of my birth, with its abundant sunlight, hot, red earth, slow sunsets and long dusks. I wallow in my recall of the sounds of the street sellers who hawk their *mielies* in the late afternoon, and the sounds of the dogs barking in the gardens, the splash of the pool in the summer and the clatter of summer hail as it crashes onto the metal roof of the cricket pavilion where I huddle with my friends until the storm passes.

I have lived my life with the background chattering of the maids in the back yard behind the kitchen, and with the sound of the Zionist church congregation singing in the *veldt* on Sunday afternoons – such a beautifully lyrical sound I never realised I knew, let alone would miss now I can't hear it. If only I had known how ephemeral the sounds of my South Africa were, I would have listened harder, longer, with intent. I would not have dived under my blankets to drown out the guttural accents of Breakfast Radio and the voice of my favourite DJ as it blared from my clock radio first thing in the morning. I am no longer able to breathe in the sweetness of September honeysuckle, the sizzle of the meat on the *braai*, and the smell of Coppertone suntan cream Factor 2 in the time before skin cancer existed. How can this be true? And yet it is. How can I exist like this? And yet I do.

There is a moment where I hear the unmistakable sound of boyish laughter – life is spilling over outside my ward. Ignoring it is not an option. I can hear nothing else but this fat, life-affirming amusement between two teenage boys. I don't have to guess their ages. I know it. I know boys. I knew boys, once. I feel my heart stop – not just miss a beat, but actually come to a stop. The earth does not spin on its axis for these moments of pure, penetrating pain. Nothing else exists. I am only this pain. My heart is stopping, my heart is stopping. I am dying of pain, a deep and all-consuming pain. I want to yield. But I am not the master player here. My monitor kicks into action and emits a shrill shriek, and flashes a disturbing light that initiates a chain of command from nurse to consultant in order to resuscitate my cardiac arrest. Once more my heart begins to beat, again the world spins, and I continue to be alive. Now I know it is impossible for me to think about what I have lost, about whom I have lost. In order to live I dare not think.

I am in transition. That's what my consultant tells me, that's what my physiotherapist tells me, that's what my psychiatrist tells me. I am not so sure about this transition thing, as it implies I am moving from one state to another. I feel terrified of any further movement. I have so many new things to learn, so many emotional and physical adjustments to make.

Sometime after my rehabilitation begins I realise that what I can see with my left eye is what is left of my life. My right eye, like so much else, is dead forever.

Apparently my vision returned to my left eye in those first recovery weeks in South Africa, but my emotional brain could not acknowledge it as there was nothing that I wanted to see. But now that I am in London, where the grey northern skies are absorbed by the greyness of my soul, I accept that what I experience as my inner world is my outer world as well. It takes me many months to understand that what I am seeing and what I am experiencing is my new reality.

Janice visits me every day. She is a solid and reassuring presence. She is a stranger.

'Here I am, Ruth,' she announces each time she walks into my room. Despite myself I like her. I like that she announces herself: I am never startled by her arrival, and there is no ambiguity between us. She is clear about what she is doing in my room. She is there for me, even when I am unable to be here, there, or anywhere. I cannot remember how she introduced herself to me or how I responded to her in our first conversations, as I only become aware that I am aware of her mid-conversation. I assume she is a senior member of the medical team, until one long and desperate night when I ask for her. It is not a good night – I am struggling and I want her voice and presence to soothe my pain.

'Janice, Janice, where is Janice?' I mutter to the nurses who do their best to pacify my anxieties and sorrow.

'Janice, please can you find Janice. Please get her,' I say. 'No nurse here called Janice, love.'

'Please, Janice. She was here today or yesterday. She's always here, at about four o'clock.'

They confer.

'Janice? You mean Janice Goldstein?'

'Janice, please get her.'

'Janice doesn't work here love, does she?'

'Doesn't she?'

'She doesn't, love. She's a visitor. She's your visitor.'

'I don't have any visitors,' I say.

'Well, you have, Janice, don't you, love. And she's your visitor, so you must have a visitor, and that's her, there's no doubting that. Right as rain, she's here always after ward round, about four o'clock.'

'I don't have any visitors, I don't have anyone.'

'Well, yes, I can see how you thought that, but you do. See, you have Janice. She's your cousin, love, your mother's cousin, to be precise, a lovely lady, lovely lady. Wish more patients had visitors like her. Lucky girl you are.'

Lucky me.

I feel betrayed by the discovery that I still have family. I want to resist. I want to refuse her. I want to burrow into my cousin's lap and cry myself to sleep. I have someone. It is something. I am not alone in the world, not as alone.

'Here I am, Ruth,' Janice says the next day as she walks into my room.

'Here I am, Janice,' I manage.

'Ruth, hello. Ruth, hello,' she says, noting the change. It is the first time that I have said her name in front of her.

'Thank you, Janice,' I say.

'I am here, Ruth,' she replies, and for the first time I really look at her and she can see me.

'I am trying to be here,' I say through my breaking voice.

'Yes, you are. So far, so good,' she replies and reaches for my hand. My tears fall. I like my cousin. She is my rock.

I try not to think about Liz. Some days it is all I can do to breathe in and out without ever daring to think about why it is that I am here and she is over there, over there in the sunlight, still wallowing in our past, which for her continues to be her luxurious, enviable present and ongoing existence. I have not read the letters that she wrote to me while I was in hospital. They have travelled with me from Johannesburg to London; someone packaged them up in brown paper and velvet ribbon. Someone thought that someday I might want to read them, I don't know who it was. Sometimes I think about destroying the letters so that I can forget her more easily. Other days I think that there may come a day when I might want to read every word she has written to me. I might, I hope. I live from fragment to fragment in the aftermath of the day when seconds stood still to form time without boundaries: 29th October 1976.

Inevitable, tedious, repetitive familiarity is the stuff of which my days are now built. I am surrounded by kindly strangers, who become friendly acquaintances, some with the potential for friendship, if only I were able to be receptive to relationships that are not based solely on my most essential need – learning to renegotiate myself in my new world. I am learning to compartmentalise myself and my experiences into what was and is no longer, and what is left. I have no idea how to think in terms of what might be.

Chapter 11

I slowly recover something of myself. I am no longer an in-patient of the famous hospital that has put me back together again. I am free to live with my new family of Janice and Neill. I can turn out the lights when I like. I can eat what I want. I can stay in bed, under the covers all day, if I choose. I am regaled as a heroine for being a survivor by my several medical consultants, physical and occupational therapists, nurses and interns. I am a walking miracle with very few visible external scars, surrounded by a team of people who have only ever known me as a badly wounded survivor of a domestic trauma. I am not known as the daughter of, the sister of, the friend of. I am not known.

Janice and Neill take me as I am. This place, their home that I can call home, becomes both familiar and yet also remains foreign to me. We live in a neatly terraced, rose-covered pre-war house. Mine is the small bedroom next to the cold guest bathroom. I have the great freedom to be as silent and withholding as I find necessary. In the beginning I find silence very necessary. I am beyond words, I have nothing to say. After a while, my instinct to belong to, to be part of, to be one amongst a group of others, is more intense than my need to be left to myself with only my own thoughts for company and distraction. I try some talking but it exhausts me, and I scurry back into the safer, solitary relief of my own counsel, my own silence, my self. I am not ready for the world. Janice and Neill care for me, encourage and support me. It is a harsh, black time, when I am looked after as if a helpless child. They offer me a haven, a new beginning. And I have books, as many as I can read, as many as I can reach out to touch.

It is within this gentle acceptance and quiet, steady companionship that asks nothing of me, where I begin to grow once more. While my life is dull and staid for a maturing young woman, for me it is the best that I can manage.

I learn to play cards, and Neill teaches me Scrabble. He is

incredulous that I am unfamiliar with board games. But I can't recall a time, ever, when I played one.

'It's all the sunshine you see,' Janice explains patiently to Neill.

'Aah,' he replies, unseeingly. Clearly there is something missing from my upbringing that disturbs Neill. It is not the trauma of my shooting or the murder of my mother and brothers or the incarceration of my father. That kind of judgement is unnecessary. Neill's disapproval is with a culture that can't be bothered to instil a sense of healthy competitive energy through the safety of alphabet tiles.

'Not even Cluedo on a rainy Sunday afternoon? There's surely nothing more wonderful than a fire crackling away, fresh tea brewing, and a yeasty cake rising in the oven as you battle it out with a swift throw of the dice. Makes me long for rain just thinking about it. How terrible for you, Ruth, to have missed out on one of life's great pleasures,' he says.

Although I can't remember the last time I laughed, I catch his sense of merriment.

'Rain? Crackling fire? Yeasty cake? You mean sun, swimming, tennis, swimming, steak, swimming, ice cream, swimming. *Ja*, poor me!' I agree.

'It sounds unreasonably sweaty, Ruth,' he says.

What lies unsaid between us is the absurdity of Cluedo, with its possibilities of who might be murdered, where it might happen, and how it might happen. I know who has been murdered, I know the weapon, I know where it has happened. I just don't understand why or how my father became the person who pulled the trigger.

Neill plods on with my re-acclimatisation. He embraces the damp grey of London with a cheer and vision I can't understand. I dare not disappoint him for fear of crushing him.

He insists on art galleries and the occasional warm beer, which I reject.

'Icy beer? You've got to be kidding, right? Janice? Jan, darling? She's joking isn't she? Nobody drinks icy beer?'

Janice shrugs her shoulders.

'What's the matter with that barbarian family of yours?' he hollers in fake outrage.

Yes, we are barbarians. I am the spawn of a true barbarian.

I learn London in digestible pieces, as taught to me with great reverence by Neill. He is from Manchester and loves London with the passion of the newly converted, despite the fact that he has lived in London for over twenty years. Neill is an architect who insists that I too learn to love London's varied architecture, the majesty and flow of the Thames and her bridges, more than two hundred underground stations, the many and varied parks, statues and monuments. Under his guidance I come to accept, after much debate, that Hyde Park is by far the most magnificent park, sublime with the widow's golden shrine to her beloved Albert. I learn to love London through Neill's eyes. And I like him quite a lot, as much as I can tolerate liking anyone. He is a good man.

Janice is a Londoner. She is related to Mommy on the maternal line, but mercifully she takes after her father's family, which means she looks unfamiliar to me. Janice is a concert pianist, and I adore listening to her practise as I fall asleep. I allow her to gently push and coax me out of my tiny kingdom.

'Ruth, I must show you something absolutely wonderful. Are you free to come with me this afternoon?' is how she begins to prepare me for any number of seemingly spontaneous trips that in truth she has planned carefully over several days, as part of my ongoing rehabilitation.

'There's this absolutely divine little boutique in Notting Hill that I want to show you. I need to pop in there to grab a dress for next week's concert, and I'd love your opinion.'

How can I refuse her?

'So long as there's no warm beer,' I retort.

She allows my childish ingratitude, and I find it difficult to be resentful for long. The focus of our shopping trip to Notting Hill is a psychedelic pink boutique, which holds a host of lush velvets and silks, of so many colours and styles, they overwhelm the eye.

'We have to get this hat, it's so you,' she decides and plonks a concoction of mustard, lime green and black confectionary on my head. It is absolutely gorgeous. I look nothing like myself. It is difficult to feel ugly when I look so marvellous – even I know that.

There is a money exchange as she completes the purchase of dresses and trousers and capes for some future music recitals, and my glorious hat.

'Thank you Ruth, thank you for coming with today, I really would have struggled without you,' she says as we leave the boutique in a flurry of glossy bags and tissue paper.

How could she possibly need my help? My tastes and style are ignorant, dull and uninspiring next to her swinging British chic. Where Mommy was bohemian and exciting, Janice is sophisticated and cultured. She teaches me a cosmopolitan sense of grooming and fashion, which is ironic considering how much Mommy had once strived for this London look, in her younger days when she first met Ivor. Janice is a very appealing role model for me. She makes me feel needed and wanted.

Janice spends time and patience guiding me through the process of my prosthetic right eye. My laughing, dark-brown eyes from my childhood have matured into a single unblinking chocolate brown. It is not an easy match. Where I might have rested with a mid-brown eye and perhaps a longer fringe draped over the right side of my face to hide my fury, Janice perseveres with possibilities. We make our peace with a richly coloured prosthetic replica of my eye. I wear my hair however I like, much as I might always have done. With effort and some bravado I learn to look people in the eye so that they can look me in the eye. I am overwhelmingly grateful to Janice, but I can't share my gratitude with her.

Janice and Neill do not match any blueprint that I have of what it means to be a couple. They appear complete both in themselves as individuals, and also as a couple. They don't have children and I never learn the reasons behind this.

I am probably the first person that Janice and Neill have shared their home with. They cope admirably with me. At least I think they do, but of course I don't know what goes on behind their closed doors. I have been left with an undisguised anxiety about what is real and what is pretence. Perhaps they are not as they seem. I know only that their dealings with me are constant and considerate, and wonderfully generous. I can do nothing but accept it.

Chapter 12

Wise counsel. Constant support. Dependable relief. Therapist. Shirley enters my life. I don't want her. I have refused all previous offers and suggestions of therapy until now. But it is Liz who insists in her persistent letters that I contact Shirley, who is apparently 'amazing with people suffering from trauma and also South African'. Mmmm, that sounds so pathetic. I'll be fine as soon as my eye adjusts to the prosthetic and as soon as I can sleep through the night and as soon as I can walk through the house without bumping into ghosts and as soon as I don't fall asleep breathing 'if only … if only … if only' into my dreams. But I am exhausted and I need to get some sleep, and need to let the ghosts go, if only for a little while. I can't remember what it is like not to feel scared of dying and scared of living. It isn't easy being the only one left alive, and it is hard to know what to wish for – I have my days when I wish I too had died. Except that I am a heroine and to die would be to give in, which would be to help him succeed in destroying all of us, which would make me an accomplice of sorts. So I have to live, even if it kills me a little, every day, which it does.

I follow up on the phone number that Liz keeps sending me so that I can finally get her off my back and feel that I have done something for her. Liz never explains how she has come by Shirley's number, but I remember that Liz's mother has psychology training, and also that she has family who emigrated to London after the 1960 Sharpeville massacre. Is Shirley a relative? How else could Liz have the name and contact details of a person she has never met, in a country she has never been to? Liz. She is the only one left who knows me.

My first reaction towards the idea of Shirley, or a Shirley-type person, is one of huge resentment. But despite my desire to make Shirley a bad idea, when I hear her familiar guttural accent over the phone, I feel a lurching wave of nostalgia for all things South African, and Shirley fits the bill. She does not match my idea of a psychotherapist. She is nothing like the austere and proper therapists who have been thrust my way by my consultant, my physiotherapist, my health visitor, my GP, or any other number of spiritual and pastoral carers who have been assigned to me.

Shirley is plump and dressed in Marks and Spencer's finest ordinary clothes for ordinary women with ordinary bodies. There seems no flair or spark of originality in her outward appearance, in the misplaced blusher that falls halfway down her cheek.

Where I am expecting a discreet side entrance into a sophisticated therapy room, I am confronted by the earthy familiar fragrances of home cooking. I cross the threshold of the suburban house in a suburban street into everyday domestic bliss. Those aromas unnerve me. I swear I've been there before. But how can it be possible? My mind, or at least my nose, is playing tricks on me. I can smell Mrs van der Westhuizen's apple pie and possibly the hint of the nutmeg in her *melk* tart. Are these beloved fragrances travelling from the southern to the northern hemisphere only olfactory disturbances of my mind? Perhaps I am having a delusional homesickness that manifests in smells, but it is not homesickness in the usual emotional sense, because the home I think of fills me only with sickness.

Shirley leads me up a flight of stairs, past some closed doors and into a small, sparsely furnished room with two chairs, a small table with a box of tissues, and a clock that faces her. And so we begin.

I can sense, from the moment I enter Shirley's home, that children live here. There is that fug of chaos interwoven with set mealtimes and routine piano practice, a muddy garden with a football pitch of sorts. I can't see any of this but I know it is there. I understand that an everyday family lies beyond the closed doors – doors that are closed to me.

A pink feather boa trailing feathers and bits of sequin has been shoved into the corner cupboard under the stairs. There is a hint of that damned incense wafting around the room. I hate it and love it in equal measure. The door doesn't close properly, the boa never manages to stay completely contained. I feel and smell family love. While that love is not on offer to me, I think there is the possibility that I might be listened to, heard, respected, and even understood by this woman, who sits opposite me, her short legs just reaching the floor beneath her seat. She is serene, she is cerebral, thoughtful and provocative. Above all, it is her sense of humour, and her laugh in particular, that blows through me.

There is a day when I become aware that it is no longer winter in the northern hemisphere. It is spring. On this day something new is in the air, something new that I have access to. I can smell spring, I can feel a certain buoyancy, which gets into my hair, under my skin and between my limbs. I feel uncertain as to what to do with myself, and confused by a slow, creeping sense of a forgotten feeling, which I eventually recognise as optimism, or at least something akin to an expectation that almost verges on excitement.

The possibilities of restoration and reconciliation – all of these ideas seem like real opportunities for me on this day. But the wonderful feeling does not last beyond the first weeks of April's perfumed, blossom-heavy light. Then the rains pelt down, stripping the trees of their beautiful colour. A mulched and rotten residue of the previous week's flowers lies crumpled at the foot of every tree. I am betrayed and I am heart-broken. Relief is not mine. Redemption is not on offer. It is a cruel blow to discover that my expansive exuberance is primarily to do with my sudden awareness of the changes in the seasons rather than a renewed ability to shift away from my intense mourning.

Now, all these years later, I have a sense of how accustomed I have become to living in a country with four distinct seasons. This is so different from the land of my birth, which offers a climate boasting the heat of summer and the chill of winter, with only a brief interlude of spring.

It is only now that I have come to recognise the intense mercurial changes that come over me as the seasons change in the northern hemisphere. With spring I feel euphoric, until it rains. In the autumn I feel both melancholic and yet greatly enchanted by the array and display of nature's colour and plumage. With the exception of the first few days of winter, where hot chocolate, new boots, scarf and coat feel so dashing, I am filled with a heavy loathing of the short days that hardly get going before it seems like night-time again. And summer – both a pleasure and a disappointment of huge proportion. Summer, the time when I dare to feel most like myself, as I once was and would have been had it been possible to stay as me.

Summer, the thrill of heat on my shoulders and down my back, the caress of soft swirling material on my bare skin, and the sensual pleasure I get each time I look down at my feet to see my glossy, painted toenails peeping out at me through my bejewelled and colourful sandals. Summer, the pleasure at the possibility that it is here to stay, and the disappointment when it stays a day and then disappears for days on end. The cheap, nasty, flirtatious slut of summer, tantalising with its hint of carefree abandon, which probably will never come, not in this England that is forever rain sodden.

Perhaps the dramatic change in climate would always have affected me. I can't know what I would have known if I had been able to experience myself through both my eyes, if I had been able to experience the pleasures that London has to offer without my grieving self.

April showers all about me, I turn bleak and heavy with an inconsolable sadness that soaks me to the bone. It is Shirley who helps me to contain my pain and my huge, endless rage. She holds me with her words, she embraces me with her constant support, her consistent interventions and presence. Week after week, month after month, there is Shirley, steady and sure, offering me direction when it seems like my existence is adrift. I struggle to eat, to sleep, to dress, to wake, but with Shirley I can express the unbearableness of my existence. Her voice, her accent, her laughter is a lifeline to my life. I try to focus on what I have left of it. It is a very long time before I am able to verbalise to myself that it is Shirley's belief in my ability to live that enables me once more to try life. The oppressive darkness lightens, lifts and dissipates. A low-level depression is left in its wake, which I am sure I can manage.

CHAPTER 13

I am nineteen. It is my birthday, and I have arranged to meet Janice and Neill in Hyde Park. 'Wear your trainers, wrap up warm,' Neill instructs me.

'Bring a hairband, you'll want to tie your hair back,' Janice tells me.

I am nineteen. I am still here somehow, and over there, in the distance, is my family, my new British family. We fit like three odd socks. Janice is tall and elegant, with fiery red hair that frames her pale, angular face; her eyes are green, her skin generously freckled. In conversation her face is serious and thoughtful, but after several glasses of her favourite red wine she is soft and smiling. Janice is an intensely dedicated musician, wife, and life saver – mine. No wonder Neill delights in being around her. He is lanky, a silver fox with coarse, thick hair and bushy eyebrows. He has smiling blue eyes and laughter lines that spread easily across his weathered face. He has a soft northern accent that I don't always understand. I am small and sad-looking. I am slim, skinny even. I always wanted to be skinny, but this is the skinny that is the look of loss. My muscles have shrunken down. I am not strong. I used to be once, when I ran and swam and jumped for joy. Now I am an old, brittle stick.

Today I am in the park. I am nineteen. It is my birthday. I am meeting my cousin and her husband. We are going to be celebrating my birthday.

'There she is, there she is!' Neill shouts out, jumping up and down, waving his arms at me. 'Look, Jan, there she is!'

'Neill, I can see her, of course, there she is. Over here, Ruth, can you see us? Behind the bench,' she calls out.

I struggle with orientation, uneasy with new environments. My anxiety radar continuously scans my surroundings to try and anticipate and evaluate possible dangers that I can't yet see.

'I'm not blind, you know!' I snap, and then immediately regret my harshness.

'I'm not blind, you know!' mimics Neill. He knows how to manage me. 'How many fingers then? How many fingers?' he demands, holding his hand near the right-hand side of my face.

I turn my head to the right so I can see his hand with my left eye. It is only my ingrained competitive streak that prevents me from ignoring him.

'Three!' I announce.

'Wrong. Wrong! It's eight. You didn't count the fingers behind my back. I'm tired of telling you, you need eyes at the back of your head, Ms Newman,' he says, waggling his fingers at me.

This conversation makes me feel uneasy but I can't put any of my ten fingers on why.

'Enough, you two. Like a pair of babies, honestly,' says Janice in her firm voice. It works. We fall in line.

'Now, birthday time,' she announces.

'We've bought you a great birthday present,' Neill says.

'And we can take it back, if you prefer,' says Janice. 'Really, you can always take it back, and we'll get something else.'

'No, she won't. She'll love it, it's fantastic,' says Neill.

I am silent. I feel uncomfortable with their expectations of me.

'Here. Tadaaah!' announces Neill, and from behind a tree he pulls out a brand-new white-and-silver bike with a silvery bell. Slowly I touch the bell and a tinny tinkle rings out.

'Ruth, give it a go. It's perfectly safe and steady. We'll help you balance,' says Janice.

'On you get,' says Neill and holds the bike so I can straddle it, one-eyed. 'It will be great for you, it'll help you strengthen your muscles. Do give it a go,' says Janice.

Bike. Trees. Path.

I've been here before. I just can't remember when. Can't. Dare not.

Cautiously I sit down on the hard, black plastic seat. I ring my pretty bell once more.

'Go, Ruth, go on,' they encourage me. 'Show us how it's done.'

Riding a bike one-eyed is one thing, but riding a bike one-eyed and crying all the tears in the world through that one eye – that is really challenging.

I am nineteen. It is my birthday. I'm learning to ride a bike, again.

My bike gives me freedom. I am going to get stronger. I can feel it in my limbs.

The following week I watch Janice gliding round the kitchen after her Sunday early-morning yoga class.

'I've been thinking about one-eyed yoga,' I say to her.

'Hmm,' she says as she drinks her coffee and waters her plants. 'Come with me next Sunday then. But you'll have to be ready to leave at six-thirty, you know.'

'*Ja*, that's fine,' I lie. We both know 6.30am is not my finest time of the day, but I am ready for more change.

'You'll like Stefan, he's really hot,' she says in her prim voice.

'What's this? Who's hot? You know you can't talk about me in this sexist, demeaning way. I won't have it, especially if I'm not in the room,' says Neill as he comes in search of a cup of tea.

'Stefan. I said Stefan was hot. Not like you, of course, Neill, not hot in a baggy kind of way like you, but more in a solid hunk of yoga muscle kind of way. I think Ruth would enjoy his class. Lord knows I do,' she chuckles.

'I thought it was all that stretching that gave you such gloss. Now I hear it's called Stefan,' Neill mutters abjectly.

'I thought you liked my stretchiness. Come, darling, let me show you how stretchy I'm feeling this morning, I'm sure you'll find it interesting,' she says with a smile, and leads Neill up the stairs.

I never knew that couples could use their jealousies so positively. It is an eye-opener.

I feel a building pressure to repay their hospitality by demonstrating my interest in glossy flirting with Stefan, the yoga teacher. Will this make me normal?

'I saw a running track in Gospel Oak, you know at the bottom of the Heath, earlier on this week. Do you know anything about it?' I ask Neill during dinner.

'Yes, I know it. Let's go on Tuesday evening. I can meet you there. Let's try it out. Excellent,' says Neill.

'I know something about running,' I say. 'I used to run.'

There is a brief silence. I have referred to a past that precludes Janice or Neill, an unmentionable past I never mention and they never ask about.

'Perhaps I can reshuffle my day and meet you both there,' says Janice. Now I can't get out of it.

'I heard that it is possible for blind athletes to run with sighted runners, that they hold a scarf between them. I don't think I'll really need that, but my balance, you know… it's a little off still, I think.'

'Yes, thanks for the new coffee cups by the way. I've been meaning to mention it all week. Love the blue colour, so much more uplifting than the beige ones that broke,' she says in reference to my most recent smashing of several mugs.

All these years later I still misjudge distance and spaces. My spatial awareness has never returned to what it once was.

I arrive early and stand on the edge of the red-tarmacked track, watching normal people. There are several runners engrossed in their laps and a huddle of people stretching and chatting. Laughing, chatting, stretching, running. Normal. It has been more than two years. Perhaps I might find myself there, on that track.

Neill comes over to me. 'Hi, Ruth, all ready? I'm desperate for a little trot around this field. Been thinking about it all day. I've been talking to the coach, Claire her name is. She's happy for us to try out today and after that to see what's what. Ready?'

'Mmmm,' I mutter.

I do a few lunges and bounce up and down, feeling self-conscious, but no one is watching me. No one is watching me. No one.

'Hello Ruth, hello Neill, love. What a wonderful evening for it,' says Janice, hugging us. 'Looking forward to watching you show us how it's done.'

Janice. Janice is watching me. Neill is watching out for me.

We all walk over to Claire – a robust, stocky woman with ruddy cheeks and lank blonde hair.

'I hear you've not run for a while,' she says. 'Mmm, *ja*,' I manage.

It isn't that I want to be rude, but any introduction makes me anxious about an explanation.

'I understand you're South African. Well, we've heard a lot about you buggers. Let's see what all the fuss is about. I suggest you start with the four hundred metres, nice and steady, then a few hundred-metre sprints, and if you fancy there's long jump, hurdles and high jump in the second field to your left. We'll set up hurdles in about thirty minutes.'

'Okay,' I say.

'Please find me when you're done, and we can chat about how you've got on and what we can offer you. Take no notice of everyone else here, they know what they're about.'

I am fixed to the spot. What if I fall over? What if I don't see someone on my blind side?

'There's some coloured batons in the bag over there,' she says, pointing behind her. 'You probably want to be running with one of those between you and Neill, to get you going, it will help you to remember where your feet are. I suspect once you've got your old legs back you'll not need him,' she says. 'Are you up for it darlin'? Do you reckon you can keep up with a young South African filly?'

'I'm Mancunian,' says Neill, drawing himself up to his full height.

'Oh well, can't be helped. Do your best,' she nods, and walks off while Neill splutters indignantly.

'Oh, very exciting. I'll settle down in the stands. I've a lovely hot chocolate with me, so take your time, take your time,' says Janice. She gives my arm a quick squeeze. 'This is a good moment, a really good moment, Ruth.'

She glides past me and whispers something for Neill's ears only, and he lets out a dirty laugh and winks at me.

'Let's go Ruth, I've got a lot riding on this.'

We approach the start line. I don't know how to do this, to run as a pair, to have my right eye held in trust by someone else. We hold either side of the red metal baton. I feel ridiculous.

'Neill,' I say. 'Yup,' he replies.

'Neill, I'm not so sure about this.' 'Me neither,' he replies.

'I'm scared of falling over or bashing into someone' 'I'm scared we'll not make it round the track,' he replies.

'If I'm too slow then just run without me. I'll stop and you keep going, I don't want to hold you back,' I say, quickly shamed by being such a burden.

'Well, very kind of you to say so, old girl, and certainly I would dump you at the first chance, but that's not the problem exactly. '

'Oh. When did you last train? How long has it been? You didn't say.'
'Yes, well, that's it you see …'

'What?'

'I haven't, I mean, I don't … I've never done this before.'

'Oh,' I say. 'Why didn't you tell me that before we came here?'

Now he is shamefaced. 'Well … see … I thought it would be a good idea. I didn't think I was going to actually run round the bloody track, did I?' he says.

'Oh,' I say, already knowing what to do. 'Well. I'll have to teach you how to run, while you watch out for my blind side.'

'Okay, sport, got you covered,' he says uneasily.

'On my count then. One … two … three,' I call and begin to run, pulling Neill alongside me.

It is like riding a bike.

Don't even think about stopping. Just pump those legs and arms. Don't think. Don't think.

* * * * *

Six-fifteen Sunday morning, and I am slumped over a dark black coffee. Yoga had sounded like a good idea last night. Janice, my marvellous cousin, drifts serenely around the kitchen, drinking hot water and lemon. She is in white, floaty things. She looks ethereal. I'm in baggy black track pants and a baggy black top. I look like a dark, dirty cloud.

'Nice hair,' she mutters and absent-mindedly pats my bird's nest down from its dishevelled position.

'Let's not keep Stefan waiting.'

Stefan. Damn. Haven't brushed my teeth. Haven't engaged with deodorant this morning – too early. Too bad. I am off to yoga, not a date.

Date. A date. It has been a while. Will I ever be normal?

The following Sunday I am slumped over a black coffee. It is 6.15am. Where is Janice? We'll be late if she doesn't hurry up.

'Morning, Ruth, doesn't your hair smell good? Like a meadow. I'll be ready in five minutes.'

'Mmm,' I grunt.

I scrunch my hair into a ponytail then loosen the ponytail. I take the hairband off and shake my hair free.

'We could go out for breakfast after class, if you fancy?' Janice says as she drinks hot water with lemon and applies moisturiser to her creamy-looking skin.

'Yes,' I reply.

I can't think beyond the next hour and a half.

The following Sunday I am slumped over a black coffee. It is 6.15am. I read the note Janice has left for me on the kitchen table: *Ruth, feeling like I need a lie-in today so won't be joining you for yoga. We'll meet up on the Heath for coffee and cake if you like. Have a lovely time. xJ*

I wobble, briefly, and then dash for my bike. Can't be late for yoga.

By the time I meet Janice I am fighting a feisty adrenaline rush, which makes me want to run around, barking like a mad dog rather than take a leisurely walk sipping cappuccinos. Stefan has already indulged me with thick black coffee and buttery croissants while telling me about his wife and young baby back home in Sweden, and his views on open marriage. I don't need seducing, and I am not interested in his moral code. As it turns out, he is not interested in mine either. What a relief. The back of his car requires more dexterity than his yoga class.

'That yoga's certainly putting a glow in your cheeks, Ruth. I might try it myself one of these Sundays,' Neill says as we trudge around the Heath.

'What's the name of the bloke who runs the class? Claude? Kurt? Some foreign bloke who no doubt wears leather sandals and has a beard,' he says with distaste.

'Uhh, can't remember,' I reply. 'We don't really talk much …'

'Come to think of it, there are better things to do on a Sunday morning,' he says, and strokes Janice on the bottom.

Indeed.

Stefan returns to Sweden two months later and is replaced by a new yoga teacher – James from Slough. But James is not married and I am not interested. I will have to look elsewhere for married, unavailable men.

'I think I'm done with early Sundays,' I tell Janice the following Saturday evening. 'I feel a little worn out.'

'I understand. Nothing ventured, nothing gained,' Janice replies, busying herself with her pot plants on the windowsill. 'But it looked like it was a good idea while it lasted.'

I splutter on my drink as I feel a hot crimson flush wash over me. Janice continues to fiddle with her pots. I recover myself and steal a look at her. She looks directly at me, winks, and then returns to her task.

I have rediscovered my body.

I begin an evening course to complete my severed school education. I am becoming a little bit more normal.

Chapter 14

Athletics, sex, school – it's better than not, but it's not enough.

* * * * *

Shirley is my confidant, my confederate. I think she holds the key to who I am, and who I might be. If only I could prise the key from her firm grasp then I would know what it is she knows of me that I can't grasp. I don't tell her about the relentless demands my father continues to make of me, in my head. I can't shut him up, I can't shut him out. I am no more able to separate myself from him than I am to separate myself from my self.

'Go, Ruthie, go Ruthie,' he insists, his voice drumming a solitary beat that only I can hear.

I know these words; they are the same words he yells from the parents' enclosure at my sports day when I am twelve. I know he's going to be angry with me if I don't succeed. I hate it when he is angry. I am running my fastest, I am trying my best. Everything around me is a blur, except for his voice.

'Go girl. For Pete's sake, Ruth, wake up and run. Move it, she's just behind you, damn it. Just do what I tell you. Oh for goodness sake, run, girl!' he roars.

He cajoles my brothers into action, and they also shout out: 'Faster Ruthie, faster. Barbara's behind you, she's catching up, she's on your heels.'

Somehow I win. Perhaps Daddy trips her up – I wouldn't put it past him. I collapse, and my father and my brothers are suddenly at my side, slapping my back.

'You've won, you've won. It's a new world record. You've won,' they triumph, sharing the glory with me.

I can't get their voices out of my head. They urge me on, even when I feel at my most despairing.

'I can't, I can't, it's too much, too …' I sob. 'I can't go on. There is no point.'

'Go, Ruthie, go. Go, Ruthie, go,' they cheer.

'Too much, too much, no, no, no …'

'Go, Ruthie, go. Go, Ruthie, go,' my treacherous father shouts at me.

I am filled with self-loathing. I hate my despair. I find myself intolerable. 'Nobody knows me, not the real me,' I tell Shirley. 'I'm not really like this. This is not me.'

'Well,' she answers in her slow and thoughtful voice, 'this is you, Ruth. This is you now. Who else do you imagine it might be?'

Her response leaves me sulking and resentful for several days. If it wasn't for my competitive nature I'd give up. I'd lie down, play dead. I might think about really being dead. But I won't give in to him. That's one thing I won't do.

* * * * *

Liz: I finally read her letters without stopping to linger over a comma, a phrase, or to consider a sentiment.

1st November 1976

Ruth

I wish I could see you. Then I'd know if you were really in a coma or just pretending not to be here. I'm sure if I saw you I could get you to open your eyes, but the doctors won't let me visit you. They don't understand that you need me.

Love L

PS: Of course you will pull through. Mom has told me you will, except that I heard her weeping and praying in the kitchen last night when she thought I had fallen asleep. I saw her on her knees, with her eyes closed and her hands pressed together.

'Come child, we must be brave. We must hope for the best and prepare for the worst,' she said. She stroked my hair over and over, whispering to me. And I cried and cried like a baby, saying your name over and over.

I went back to school yesterday. The school dance has been cancelled because of what has happened to you, on account of it being in bad taste. There are lots of tears even from people who didn't know you. You would hate how false that is. But at least we have hardly any homework. English was interesting. We had to write whatever we wanted so long as it was 500 words and on the topic of 'how I feel right now'.

Hey, you'll never guess what. While I was waiting for you, Greg, YES GREG ROBINSON!!!!!, and I started talking. I wasn't paying too much attention at first as I was feeling hot and sweaty, fed up with waiting for you, He kept smiling like he couldn't help it. After a while, I started to hope that you wouldn't turn up. Ruth, I'm so sorry I wished that. And now I can't stop thinking about that, about wishing you wouldn't turn up, but I did and then you didn't, and now look at what's happened!

Ruth, I'll just die if anything happens to you. I won't ever be able to forgive myself. Of course something has happened to you, the worst, the absolute worst thing. It's so terrible I can't even think about it for a second, I can't, I really can't. So let's just talk about Greg. So while I was waiting for you and beginning to wish that you wouldn't turn up so that I could keep talking to him and looking at him, he told me a joke (which wasn't that funny). I laughed, obviously. Anyway, so there I was, laughing my head off, and he leaned forwards and brushed my hair out of my eyes and looked at me.

'Jeez, but you've got blue eyes,' he said.

I couldn't breathe. I swear I couldn't breathe a single breath. And then he walked me home and asked me to the dance and then all I wanted to do was rush home to call you, when I saw Mom and she told me what had happened. At first I couldn't believe that I wasn't going to get to tell you any of this, the most exciting and amazing news, and then I realised that of course I had to tell you while I remember every detail, although I'm sure I'll still remember it all over again once you are awake.

Everything is changing so fast – it's like you're not here. If you were here we'd be talking about him ALL THE TIME, until you were sick of it or he was sick of me or I was sick of him.

We haven't even spoken about what happened on Saturday evening with you and Craig, and what it was like to go all the way with him. I can't believe such a life-changing experience has happened to you and we haven't even had the chance to talk about it properly. I'm so desperate to know absolutely everything!

Ruth, I feel scared just thinking about the shooting, about what it must have been like. I can't believe it. I really can't believe that they're gone. I can't believe it. Love L

13th November 1976

Dear R

Your nurses guard you like hawks. Sometimes I feel jealous of them, of Rosie, who has you at night, and Amos, who has you during the day. They get to know everything that is going on with you, and I don't. I left some tie-dyed scarves for you and a note for Amos telling him that if he wanted to tie up your hair that he should at least respect you enough to use the scarves rather than the pompom ribbons.

Hope you enjoyed the melk *tart that Mom and I left you. Mom thought you would feel we were in the room with you even when we weren't if you could smell the nutmeg she always uses – you'd know we were thinking about you ALL OF THE TIME. I meant to come with some incense to make your room feel more comforting and familiar, like my room, but I forgot it at home, and then discovered that it's against hospital policy to light up in the hospital!*

Ruthie, I don't want to put you under pressure or anything, but it's time you opened your eyes and sat up. The longer you stay in this coma the more difficult it will be to wake up. I'm sure it's not that different from trying really hard at swimming or tennis. Focus your mind and wake up from this coma, Just do it. Just go for it. Open your eyes and I swear that I will be there, looking right back at you.

Love L

PS: I will help you, I promise, I swear to you on my pa's grave I will help you get through this. There is so much we need to talk about.

22nd November 1976

Dear R

I'm sorry I cried so much when I saw you, but I was just so shocked. I didn't expect you to turn away from my voice. I didn't know exactly what to expect – or perhaps I expected us to be as we always were before all this happened.

I heard about your left eye, that you can now see with your left eye. That's really amazing news. You can read these letters, we can go to movies and play tennis if we want, but that doesn't matter if you don't want to do that as we're both rubbish at it anyway.

I've thought and thought about what I would want to see if it had been me losing my sight and then getting some of it back. The first thing I would want to see is my mom. I guess if I could remember enough of what my pa was like, or how he would be like now, then maybe I might have thought about him, but for such a long time it has been me and Mom as our own family, so it would be her face that would give me courage.

If I couldn't see her then of course it would be you, but I can't imagine it not being Mom – that's just too devastating to think about. Do you wonder where she is right now? Your mom? I think about her a lot. I wonder where she is or what's she's doing. I try to imagine that she's looking down at us, at you, and will keep you safe, except that you weren't safe before she died when he shot you, so how can you be safe now that she's dead? I don't understand the scriptures, I really don't. And especially that bit about honouring your mother and your father. Seriously! A father doesn't hurt and kill his family. I've been thinking about what happened quite a lot, and I realised that I hate him. I HATE HIM I HATE HIM I HATE HIM I HATE HIM. I swear I will never tell another soul how I feel, not Mom and not Greg – anyway he'd dump me like a shot if he knew how ugly my thoughts are. But Ruth, I can't help it, I want to kill him for what he's done to you. I know that I will never, ever, in my whole life forgive him. He deserves to rot in hell. I will never take these words back. HOW COULD HE? HOW COULD HE? Sometimes when Mom and I pray for you, I also slip in a prayer for myself, asking God to help me stop feeling so wicked. It's true what the Bible says, that good deeds beget good deeds, and bad deeds beget bad deeds. I've never had evil thoughts before, and it is really awful. I just can't forgive him for taking you away from me when we were always meant to be together, through school, and varsity, and travelling, and after that. But that won't happen now, not like it's meant to happen.

Ruth, I don't know if anyone has told you, but your doctors are now talking about some fancy new treatments that are on offer in the UK. They think you're a bit British, which is why they are talking about how you could be treated in a special hospital in London. I can't believe they are serious and yet I think they must be.

Mom and I are desperately worried about the situation.

Going ice skating with Greg later. Just when I think I will never laugh again he does the funniest things, and then, even if I don't want to, I can't help but laugh, and he always looks so proud of himself afterwards. He's so cute!

xx L

PS: I think it's kind of serious between me and Greg. We've only fooled around a little, but I really like him. I really want to wait, you know that, and our church is really big on that stuff, but I could definitely imagine going all the way, and I'm even more desperate now to talk to you about what 'it' was like with Craig – who by the way has only asked once about you. What a creep! Miss you tons and tons.

L

28th November 1976

R

You are, you really are, going to London. I can't believe it. You're leaving. You'll have to learn to drink tea and wear a coat, and eat slimy, disgusting cucumber sandwiches. What will happen to you?

Love L

4th December 1976

What will happen to me?
  Love L

13th December 1976

Ruth. This is it.
The last letter.
I need to tell you some things, before you go, before it's too late.

The first thing is that I am so, so sorry that this terrible thing has happened to you. I still can't believe it, and yet I know it's true.

The second thing is that he ruined everything that you had. And I do not want to forgive him for that. Ever. Perhaps it sounds very un-Christian of me. Too bad. So much for Christians then. I shouldn't say that – there are so many people, and many of them Christians, praying for you, and I don't want to be rude or ungrateful, only, I cannot, will not forgive him.

The third thing is that I will always, always, be here for you.

The fourth thing is that I love every single moment that we have shared – you and me, and the boys. And your mom.

I have been missing you so much and don't really know if it is possible to miss anyone more than I miss you. My world has changed now that you are not in it. It is not the same world.

Forever friends, best friends.
LIZ

The letters put me in touch with vestiges of my rage that I am not yet acquainted with.

I shred the letters.

And then, on a day in May or June, on a Monday or Tuesday, the doorbell rings when Janice and Neill are out. I look through the peephole. I see Liz.

I stalk the front door, like an animal trying to determine whether to fight or flee. I do neither. I freeze in the face of my past.

She rings the doorbell again and again. 'Ruth? Ruthie? It's me.'

'Ruthie, can I come in? It's cold outside, open up.'

'Ruthie, can I come in? We'll just chat for a little bit. Please, let me in.' I hear a sob catch in her throat.

Why is she so insistent? Why won't she go away? Doesn't she realise I might be out, busy with my new life? Doesn't she know I'm not here? I stare at the imprint of her face pressed up against the opaque glass that is set in the wooden panelling. I turn my back to her, ramrod hard against the timber. It would take very little force to bring down that old front door, but an impenetrable world stands between us that won't yield to anything other than time. And I am not ready.

There is silence and then the sound of her footsteps as she gives up and walks away. I look through the peephole and see a flash of her blondness. I call out her name, when I am sure she can't hear me.

What had she expected? How can she come knocking on my door as herself, as she has always been? I cannot tolerate her flaunting her existence in my face. I look again through the peephole and see only an elderly man walking a brown Labrador.

* * * * *

Liz continues to write to me. I continue to read and shred, read and shred. I don't write back.

* * * * *

My first phone call to Liz is about a year after her visit. '*Howzit*, Lizzie, it's me, Ruth,' I say.

It is hard to hold the phone in my trembling hand. It is hard to speak through my thickened throat and hard to think through my thumping head. These five words are all I have on offer – I have dialled her phone number on impulse rather than with thought.

'*Howzit*, Ruth, long time no speak,' she says, without drawing a breath.

'*Ja*, speaking wasn't on the agenda, but suddenly it's come back up,' I reply, noting the old girlish flippancy in my voice.

'I'm liking the agenda,' she says.

'Me too,' I say.

'Me too,' she says.

'Did you hear what happened to Debra Vermuelen last night?' she says.

'Yeah, sure, of course I heard, all the way from Buckingham Palace, people are talking about Debra,' I retort.

'Good, then I don't need to tell you,' she says.

And then I say, and then she says and then I say and then she says and he says and she says and he says and she says and did you know and you'll never believe it but and then …

'Gotta go now. I'm really late.'

'And what else is news? You're always late.'

'That's great, coming from you.'

'Chill out.'

'Chill out.'

'Same time next week?'

'Same time next week.'

'*Ciao.*'
'*Ciao.*'
We hang up.

I stare at the phone. Like riding a bike, some things you never forget. No matter how hard you try to.

A shrieking noise breaks the silence. It takes me several seconds to recognise that it is the phone ringing in my lap.

'Hello?' I manage.
'*Howzit*, Ruthie, it's me, Liz.'
'*Howzit* Liz.'
'Just checking you're still there.'
'I'm here now,' I answer.
'Good,' she says.
'*Ja*, yes, it's good.'

* * * * *

The trusts that my grandparents established for my brothers and me reach maturity, leaving me the sole beneficiary. I have a lot of money. My first thought is that my benefiting from my brothers' deaths makes this inheritance blood money. My second thought is that I am entitled to this money –after all, I've paid in blood, and more besides.

I repay Janice and Neill all the pocket money they have given me since the week I moved in with them. I enrol in university for a first degree. I study psychology and Spanish. I have classmates and running mates and coffee friends and sex options. I no longer need my lovers to be married to other people. I am more sophisticated and experienced now.

There are always men around me. I love the way men feel and smell and laugh and energise me. I laugh at their jokes, and tell dirtier ones in any corner of any kitchen at any party in these years, in any years, with the men. And then there is sex, of course. Sex is the easy part for me.

I am becoming even more normal.

I graduate with honours. I celebrate by going to parties and out for dinner and out for breakfast. I am surrounded by people that I don't mind and there are even a few that I like. They think they know me because of what we have shared over these past three years. But they don't know me, not the real me. I have not shared myself. I am not really on offer.

We – Neill, Janice and myself – celebrate with a quiet cup of tea and a slice of Neill's favourite apple pie with custard. Janice plays Chopin and Tchaikovsky for us. It is a beautiful moment. Janice and Neill. They are a blessing in all that they are not. They are not home, but they are a refuge.

It is time for me to move on. I can no longer justify sheltering with them. I buy a small Victorian cottage with a red front door and climbing roses. It has a real fireplace, wooden floors and whitewashed walls. It is delightful, exactly what I want, only my leaving is not as straightforward as I had hoped. I revert to a frightened and withdrawn self that prevents me from moving into my new home. I have days when I struggle to leave my small bedroom next to the cold bathroom. Neill takes time off from work, and Janice cancels several concerts so that we can drink more cups of tea and play Scrabble and cards and Cluedo once more. I sleep a lot. I cry often. But they wrap me up in scarves and coats and wellingtons, and we walk in wet, windy parks and visit our favourite museums. Janice and Neill pull me back into the light. We set a second date for my leaving. My pretty house is waiting for me.

I don't know how to say thank you. It is so long since I have given anything to anyone. But I bake a delicately perfumed lemon cake that I know Neill adores. It is his mother's recipe and I want to make this cake for him.

'Not bad, not bad,' Neill says, his eyes wet with emotion.

'Neill! It's every bit as good as your mother's. It's delicious, Ruth, really first class.'

'It's not bad,' I agree, with my adopted British understatement. I pull tickets from my jeans pocket.

'Here, these are for you, for us,' I say awkwardly to Janice.

'The Chelsea Flower Show! Oh Ruth, thank you. How splendid. I've always wanted to go. The Chelsea Flower Show. Neill, The Chelsea Flower Show!'

Neill isn't listening. He is staring in amazement at the two tickets I have given him to Wimbledon's Centre Court Men's Finals, bought on the black market. I feel light-headed and giddy. This is what it feels like to give back. I am out of practice, but I am ready to learn.

'Wimbledon Clubhouse, as a building, is not too bad. I think you'll probably think it needs an overhaul, but it's not too bad,' I try.

And then I am crying and Janice is wiping her eyes and Neill is blowing his nose.

'For a bloody foreigner you make a pretty good Brit,' he says. 'A pretty good Londoner.' This is his highest compliment.

'I had a good teacher.'

'Yes, you did, this is true.'

We hug each other and then we drink more tea. I am British now.

I move into my new home. Perhaps I am normal again.

Chapter 15

I graduate as a psychotherapist in the autumn of 1985, after five years of post- graduate training. I divide my clinical work between the National Health Service psychiatric outpatients and the Women's Refuge and Refugee Centre. I love the variety and unpredictability of my two-days-a-week National Health Service caseload. But more importantly, I have been slowly and carefully put back together by the National Health Service and so carry a debt that I can only try to repay, from the other side of the hospital bed.

For three days a week I choose to work with a community of refugees from the Women's Refuge in North London. The status of refugee is not only a service for refugees in the geographic sense. A woman who needs solace, a refuge, is after all a refugee fleeing her home.

A large part of my job is listening to these women tell me their stories of beatings and rapes, abuse and family breakdown. I try to help these women, to think with them about certain unspeakable events that have happened to them 'back home'. I have some understanding of this, of a home that is dangerous. I understand the anguish of feeling you can't go back to where you have come from.

I am good at listening but I struggle to understand why many of these women want to forgive their abusers and reconcile their families, even when the family has disintegrated beyond repair. I don't understand these women. I don't understand how it is that they are willing to forgive the perpetrator responsible for their most extreme anguish. These women do not appear to be interested in revenge and pay little homage to bitterness. They want to buy into a forgiveness that will bring them peace. This is what they repeatedly tell me. This is what I covertly reject. Perhaps my inability to grasp this concept is what keeps me coming back to them, to hear their stories, to try to believe in my heart what my ears hear. But I am not optimistic for my conversion.

I meet Raquel after my first six months at the refuge. Raquel packed her bags and ran from her husband after she had found her passport in cinders on the kitchen table. She was no longer safe at home.

'He was gonna make me disappear. He was startin' with paper work first. No papers, no work, no money. That was big trouble, big trouble for me. And it gonna be my baby he comes for next. He's only three, I can't let him take my baby,' she says.

The purple welts are starting to fade from her arms, but the multiple cigarette burns continue to give her the appearance of lightly charred meat. She is gaunt and haunted by her years of abuse. I am repulsed and shocked by her story. I've heard stories before, many hours of terrible stories, but she is the first person to get under my skin. I know I need to put aside my feelings about her experience and help her to focus on her feelings. But her feelings don't make sense to me. My feelings don't make sense to me either. I want to hurt this man, but Raquel is only focussed on housing benefits and solid locks on her door.

'I won't let him touch us no more. Even if I have to keep on runnin' from him the rest of my life, I'm not goin' back,' she tells me.

I can't help myself. After all it is still during the early years of my clinical work, and I am there to learn.

'What about your anger? I'm wondering about your anger?' I say.

She looks puzzled. I try again.

'I'm wondering how you can sleep at night knowing that somewhere, out there, is this man … this man …' I silence myself.

'Look, lady, you think it's gonna be easy for me to always keep runnin', to always keep movin' in case he catch us? If he catch us I'll be puttin' a knife in his face. But if I'm killin' like him, that be death, a real death of me if my boy sees me like that, sees me same as his dad.'

'What about revenge?' I ask, as unknowing as a child.

'Revenge? Revenge?' She looks momentarily sad. 'That's not my problem. I not got no time for that. I've got a baby, my baby needs me.'

Her eyes are as clear as glass, her face open and responsive. Fortunately for both of us, our fifty minutes are up.

We meet a few more times for form-filling and box-ticking rather than for anything that I might be able to offer her. She leaves the refuge a few weeks later, and I remember her as a brave and intuitive woman who might, possibly, succeed in creating a new life for herself. She doesn't. It takes only five weeks for her husband to find her and give her the burnt-passport treatment. It transpires that he had been intent on her disappearance. I rerun our sessions over and over in my head, wondering how I might have kept her safer. Revenge is all I can come up with. It is difficult for me.

I look for answers from each of the women I work with. It is as if they know something that I don't. Long after these women have left the refuge their stories stay with me. They leave me a legacy of confusion. I like to believe that I have engaged in this work because I want to make life safer for those who have suffered. I desperately want them to have a place to go to where they can say this is what happened to me, so that they might begin to find themselves again, because it is awful to be lost to yourself. I like to think that my focus is on them, but the truth is that it's all about me. I am lost, still. I know that.

Shirley. Without her I would be scrambled egg. She continues to teach me to navigate my own journey by learning about myself, in small incremental pieces. I like an orderly and focussed routine, because it keeps me feeling safely held. Occasionally it works. In my impatience to escape myself I try alcohol, but it leaves me thick-tongued and wild-eyed with dreams that conjure up uncontrollable demons. I smash my wine bottles, enraged that even the relief of inebriation is not available to me. It is many months before I cautiously allow myself a glass of wine – now I know that the liquid pleasure of one tight glass of chilled chardonnay or a sultry shiraz will give me loosened limbs, but any more and I am facing despair. I know my limit.

I learn to run an independent four miles a day, which charges my body with adrenaline, purpose and a tight arse. I don't stumble as much as I used to, I am less unbalanced. I love adrenaline, the health junkie's drug – cheap and easily accessible once you've forced yourself out the door. In my therapeutic practice I am able to be tolerant and supportive, but when I close my clinic door at the end of a day's work I am done with relating. I am learning my limitations.

I'm still very vulnerable to certain situations, like today for example. I can't say that I knew I was going to kill Ivor, but certainly I am not surprised by today's outcome, and only a little confused. I had hoped we would have a chance to get to know each other so that I could ask him all the questions I had been longing to ask, and he would give me the answers that he had been desperate to air – the least he could do, seeing as he had already done the most he could do.

Still, I am free of Ivor now. I'm finally feel free to go to sleep tonight without fear of where he might be and what might happen if we were to see each other. Now I know what might happen.

CHAPTER 16

My professional life is a great success. I have varied and interesting work, and I am becoming recognised as a person who can make a difference to others. My peers encourage me to do a PhD – in truth I am easily persuaded, as I am receptive to academic flattery and the opportunity to be remarkable. But it is when I am only eighteen months away from completing my doctorate on 'Legal and Psychological Interventions for Best Victim Outcome after Violent Crime', that I first read about the concept of restorative justice in a Canadian academic journal on victim-offender programmes. It changes my academic argument in an instant.

I'd never before thought about a justice that encourages victims to share with their perpetrators the impact of their crime, and where perpetrators carry full responsibility for making things right for their victims. This is not something that I have encountered in my clinical practice or my academic learning. I am astonished by the opportunities for healing that this could offer victims. The possibility to restore carries with it the belief that all can, sooner or later, be put to rights.

I enrol at a postgraduate law school to learn more. Those three letters after my name will have to wait. Restorative justice is where I think I want to be.

José. He enters my life stage right, my blind side. I am caught unawares. He is beautiful, brilliant, and utterly foreign to me. He is irresistible.

José Lincoyán.

I meet him in 1987.

José is a Chilean law graduate from George Washington University and is in London completing a PhD on restorative justice in post-revolutionary society and working as a visiting lecturer. I am one of a group of twelve who form part of his thirty-week seminar. When José offers an analysis of *lex talionis*, the law of retaliation, it feels as though I have been offered a reprieve from my uncomfortable desire to avenge

Raquel. It is sweet relief to discover that my base instinct to go for the jugular is not some hideous, violent streak that belongs to me alone. There is a whole body of law that deals with the complexity of vengeful feelings and actions. I am not mad or bad, I am beautifully human. I have been restored.

I am certain that no one else in the room can understand the need to wrestle with revenge like I do. I hear my peers debate the intellectual and political aspects of talionic societies as honour- or revenge-based cultures, but for me it is personal. It is as if these concepts are conceived with only me and my internal world in mind, as if I am the only person in the room with José.

José. I am intrigued by his willingness for controversy and debate. I am intrigued by his knowledge. He is also maddeningly sexy. At the law school end-of- year summer party held for the faculty and its students, José is there with a date, as am I. If I remember correctly, my date is called Andy.

That night then, my first night with José, begins with my dancing with Andy. Despite my efforts, I am not able to stop looking at José. I had not noticed until this moment, on this dance floor, how mesmerised I am by him. This is an unfamiliar experience for me. I feel José's eyes burning into me as he looks over his partner's head. He pushes and grinds into her, he sways with her and caresses her, but he stares at me. I have an unbearable ache in my groin and my breathing is quick. Andy wanders off in search of glasses of cold Pimm's, which I have no intention of drinking. Poor Andy.

José. He is there, at my side. We continue to stare at each other. We don't touch but I feel him all over me, inside of me.

'Ruth,' he whispers.

I give him my hand and let him lead me away. I don't trust myself to speak.

Moan, yes, cry out, most definitely, but speaking is an inarticulate form of communication in these first hours. It is exhilarating. It is exquisite.

He is beautiful. I try to leave several times during our first forty-eight hours. But it is extraordinarily difficult to leave someone while being held and holding on, while being enmeshed with and intertwined with, and by being truly bewildered by the glory of whatever this is that I have never known. I give in, I give up. I stop trying to leave. He never notices as the struggle has been only in my head. He is beautiful.

Whatever this is, I love it. Whoever he is I think I might love … him. José.

At some point I become aware it is time to separate in order to eat, to shower, to see what we might be beyond our carnal selves. I leave him sleeping and drift out of his bedroom to find the shower. I turn the water on full throttle and let it pound over my head, my shoulders, and down my back. I wash myself with soap. My skin feels unfamiliar. I am soft and loose in my body. I turn around and around under the water. Everything feels as if it is a caress. I smell my skin. José. He is in my skin.

'Ruth, do you want coffee with milk? With sugar? Do you want eggs? I have fruit, yoghurt, bread. Come eat with me. We need to eat. I need you to have energy *querida*, we need lots of energy for each other,' he calls and bangs on the bathroom door.

I jump out of my reverie. I am still in the land of his skin and he has now moved on to the everyday banalities of eggs and bread.

'What day is it, José?' I call out, suddenly uncertain at my unfamiliar and reckless behaviour. I am always so careful. What have I overlooked?

'Sunday. Relax, Ruth, no work today. That's good. It's important not to work all the time. Tonight we sleep, yes?'

No wonder I am starving. The party was Thursday evening. He has made several journeys to his kitchen for water and ice cream and small, sweet cakes, but we have not eaten a proper meal in more than forty-eight hours.

'I'll be out in a minute, do you have something I can wear?' I ask.

My party dress is no longer wearable now that we have ripped it off my body in our haste to get to each other.

He knocks again at the bathroom door. I open it and look at the smiling naked man.

'Here, *querida*. I'm sure I have a longer one somewhere, but that would spoil my pleasure,' he says, and hands me a pristine white shirt. I drop my towel and quickly put the shirt on. It rests at the top of my thighs. He stares at me. I stare back.

'Uuhh,' he sighs, 'you're so sexy. You must be the devil herself. I am in such trouble, Ruth, such trouble with you.'

I feel myself melting in his hands. I am also very hungry for food and one of us has to end this madness.

'Let's eat,' I say, and walk out the bathroom. I can feel his eyes on me.

'Okay, okay. You are right. We need to eat. I'm showering and then we eat. Go downstairs, go and be comfortable,' he says.

His home is a bright terraced house with clusters of CDs and hundreds of books that overflow their shelving and are stacked in piles on the floor. He has green plants that spill out of terracotta earthenware, and he has photographs, lots of photographs, clustered around his living room. I pick up a dark wooden frame. It is a group photo of laughing men with dark hair and thick beards and moustaches, and a small dark boy with José's smile. I put the photo down and pick up another. This photo is of an older man between two younger men. I can see what José's face will look like in thirty years' time. It is a beautiful face. The men look straight at the camera, unsmiling, upright, serious. They are the same men as in the previous photos, only older.

'Those are my brothers and my father,' José says as he walks into the room.

I jump anxiously. Have I been caught doing something inappropriate? He comes to stand behind me and slides an easy hand under my shirt. We are pressed against each other once more. He strokes my skin. I can't move. I want to stand like this for always. We fit. With his free hand he points at the photo.

'This is Luis, he was eighteen, and this is Patricio, he was twenty-five in this photo. And my father, Héctor, he was fifty-six. And here,' he says as he picks up a smaller framed photo, 'this is my sister, Adriana, and her fiancé, Jorge. She was twenty-three. They were both twenty-three.'

There is something in his use of the past tense that makes me uneasy. I know this is not good.

'What happened?' I whisper.

'They are dead, they are all dead now,' he says. 'Me and my mother, we are the only surviving ones. My brother, Luis, he was a student at the University of Concepcion in Antofagasta. He was studying philosophy and sociology when the coup happened. He was radical in his politics.

He loved Marx and Lenin, but then Pinochet happened. He destroyed so much, destroyed so many. Luis was last seen on the 3rd of October, 1973.'

'Oh,' I say. 'What about the others?'

'Patricio, he was an engineer. He had spent time in Cuba, in the camps, the military training camps in the late 1960s. He was working in Santiago when he was arrested. His Cuban training meant an immediate death sentence. He never stood a chance. His activities in Cuba were well documented. They had to make an example out of him.'

He is silent. I don't know what to say to this man who has lost two brothers. I have nothing to say. We stand together, our bodies leaning into each other, and I already know I love him. He breathes deeply.

'And my father, Héctor, he worked for the socialist newspaper, *Ultima Hora*, he was a typesetter. He didn't even write the news. But the Pinochet regime didn't care about detail. They were only interested in destroying the enemy. Socialism, Marxism, dissent. That was the opposition. On the 25th October, 1973, my father went to work. He never came home.'

I need to sit down. My body is trembling.

'*Querida*, you are shocked. This is me, this is my story. I will stop talking now. Let us enjoy each other, enjoy ourselves,' he says, turning me towards him.

We sit on the couch. He strokes my face and reaches for my hand but I grip the small, dark frame with the photo of the young woman wearing Jose's face.

'What happened to her?' I ask.

'My sister …' He is silent, his composure now uneven. He closes his eyes. 'Adriana studied sociology. Everyone was studying. It was because of her that I wanted to go to university to learn, to educate myself. It was such a wonderful time for students. We had people come from all over the world to give lectures at our universities, to educate us, and to learn from us about the pleasure of a truly Marxist society. The people could attend for free, without even being enrolled as students. It was a very happy time for her. She met Jorge. He was involved in student politics. She became involved also. My mother insisted that she and Jorge leave Chile. It was too dangerous for them to stay. They escaped to Mexico and managed to get word to us that they were fine. We were so sad and also relieved that they were free.'

He stops talking, silently staring ahead.

'What José? What happened?' I ask again. I know the story is not done yet.

'They were killed, in a car accident a few weeks after we heard from them. It was no accident. It was DINA.'

'Dina? Who is Dina?'

'Not who, but what. DINA – Directorate of National Intelligence – systemic, state-sponsored violence, Pinochet's killing machine. Adriana and Jorge were burnt to death in a car accident with only their papers to identify them. Their death had all the hallmarks of DINA. We could not bury them, there was nothing to bury.'

I can't help myself when the tears come. It is a truly terrible story, such a waste.

'And you?' I ask, 'How did you survive?'

'My mother was a teacher. She managed to arrange for me to be seen by a contact of hers who knew of a man at the American Embassy who could help us. This man, he was in charge of handpicking bright, young right-wing Chileans and placing them in American universities in Chicago on scholarships where they would study economics. The plan was for them to graduate and return to Chile to help implement Milton Freedman economics, another form of attack on the legacy of Marxist Chilean politics. But this man – El Riojo we called him because of his red hair, and secret left-wing politics – he also handpicked a few radicalised left-wing students and gave them scholarships to Ivy League universities to study whatever they wanted. He was a cold war all of his own. I was one of them, one of his scholarship students. He created the paperwork and funding for me to study in America. That's how I ended up at George Washington University. I left Chile at sixteen. I go home to see my mother every nine months, but really that is when I left home. I lost my family at sixteen.'

I could free myself now, I could pour my heart out, I could take this chance. But we only have effect in common, not cause, and that divides us. I feel the burden of my own impossibility.

'Your mother, she has suffered so much,' I say.

'She is a very determined person. She did not want to lose me, and she knew that she had to get me out of Chile on legitimate grounds or she would never see me again. My mother, she and I, we lost our family in 1973, but we still have each other, and of course we are not the only family to have suffered like this.'

'Yes, there are many families that suffer,' I say.

'And you, Ruth, what is your story?'

'Mine, well …' I am unprepared. 'I can't, I mean, I'm not … It's soon, too soon for me to talk. I don't like to talk outside of my therapy. It's not you, it's talking, I just … I can't … I need some clean spaces that aren't contaminated by what happened, and I would like, I would really like for this to be a clean space, here with you,' I manage.

He holds my hand. 'It is bad, yes? I can see it in your face.'

'My face,' I say. 'Yes, my face. My eye. It is bad.'

'A beautiful face,' he says. 'A beautiful eye. I am sad for you that you have only one eye. Does it bother you?'

I blink fast with my beautiful eye. This is not a moment for weeping. 'Sometimes, but not today, not right now.'

'That is good. And tell me, please, restorative justice, this is something big for you? I have felt it all along. It is personal for you?'

'Yes,' I say.

'Our countries are different but share terrible experiences of oppression and state-sponsored violence,' he says.

'Yes,' I say.

'We can talk about it, when you want,' he said. 'I understand it is not easy to talk, especially for those of us who are so used to listening, like you are. I too couldn't talk for many, many years. But I found it only made it worse for me, and I didn't have therapy – you know Chilean men are very macho.' He smiles. 'One day you will be ready to talk to me, you will see, and I will listen to you.'

I am exhausted. I am confused by these last forty-eight hours, for which I have no precedent.

'Come *querida*, don't look so sad.'

'*Querida*? You keep saying that. What does it mean?'

'*Querida*, it means you – it means "my darling", "my beloved", it means Ruth,' he says.

I don't know whether to laugh or cry, dance or run, stay or go. The moon is changing shape. The grass is no longer only green, nor is the sky simply blue. I am not what I know myself to be, even now when I thought I knew myself. I have not been called beloved before. I have not wanted to be called beloved, I have not wanted to be loved for a very long time.

'Let's eat, now. I am feeling that I might need more energy very soon. Very, very soon,' he says with a look that is unmistakably lusty.

I am free to become his beloved.

I ram bread into my mouth and into his. 'Hurry up,' I say. 'Hurry up.'

How will I ever get dressed again or eat a full meal or leave this flat? I can't imagine work the next day, my clients, my running, my garden that needs watering. José. He is beautiful.

José is a precious, dark pleasure that I slowly learn to integrate into my life. My preference is to keep him stashed away, my secret treasure. But he is intent on shouting us out from the rooftops of London. He is intent on celebrating us and on celebrating me. He is a talented artist, and draws quick and fluid sketches of me when I am asleep, when I am at work at the kitchen table, when I am fighting with the knots in my hair, because I am beautiful, apparently. It is not the first time I have been told I am beautiful, but I push that out of my mind. I introduce him to Neill and Janice over lunch.

'Not bad, Ruth, not bad at all,' says Neill while José is in the kitchen, cutting up fruit.

'Gorgeous, he's absolutely gorgeous Ruth. I can't understand how you two ever manage to dress yourselves,' says my sultry cousin in her prim voice that I have come to love. Love. Yes I am brimming with it. I love Janice, I love Neill. I love London. José.

José is an active member of Amnesty International, and despite my discomfort with groups, I too join up. Restorative justice remains an ideal of ongoing work in progress, for me. There is plenty of opportunity for me to think about it within the impersonal political context of Latin America, my newly adopted culture. I postpone my thesis and let José teach me the tango. With only one seeing eye I have uneven perspective and balance, I also have two left feet, but it doesn't matter when the music is loud, and your clothes lie in a tangle on the floor. I take an advanced Spanish course and wonder about how my life has become so *maravilloso*. I forget myself. I am becoming *maravillosa*.

Am I now complete?

* * * * *

Do you see the couple on that bench? The man is clearly not British. He is the colour of nutmeg and has dark curls that dance across his head. He is hard to ignore. He seems entranced by the woman he is with. There is no mistaking the intensity of their connection. Their bodies are touching almost from shoulder to ankle. The woman is striking. She has long dark hair that tumbles over her shoulders and down her back. She also does not look British, although her skin is pale. Her eyes are dark and softened by laughter. She looks like a woman who laughs a lot, perhaps especially when she is with the man. She is captivating. I don't recognise her, and yet this is the woman I meet when I look in the mirror. This is the man I see when I am held by love. The couple on the bench, they are us.

* * * * *

José and I are sitting on our favourite bench at the top of Parliament Hill. The sun is warm and soft, the kite fliers competitive. We drink our iced coffees as I enjoy looking at the glistening purple nail polish I have applied to my toenails, it is the ultimate in luxury for me to take pleasure in my toes.

'Ruth, we need to talk,' José says.

I take a delicate sip of the coffee. I don't want to talk. I know what I want to do, and it is not acceptable on park benches in broad daylight.

'I have a much better idea for right now …' I smile, and turn my face to his.

'Ruth, stop, stop. Later, okay. Right now we need to talk,' he says sharply.

An icy wind whispers down my spine on this lazy summer's afternoon. I am alert. I am on guard. What now?

'Tell me then,' I say, trying to keep the chill out of my voice.

'We need to talk … I need … I need to …' he falters.

José is nervous. Something is happening and I have no idea what it is.

'José, what is it?'

Suddenly he is rushing along, his accent thickening his words. 'I have not renewed my teaching contract for the next semester,' he says. The world is turning a little slower now.

'Oh,' I say.

'It's time for me to go home, to go back to Chile,' he says, more forcefully.

'Oh,' I say once more.

Now I know why today had felt so perfect, because it ends here.

'I have an opportunity to do something great,' he says.

'Great,' I say.

'It's exactly what I've been hoping for.'

I am yesterday's news.

He is gabbling away, but I can't hear him for the suddenly deafening noise of despair in my head. It is over, we are over. It is back to me alone once more. I should never have let him in. Now I am at risk of disintegrating into a crazed and chaotic mess at his feet. After all, this is a light affair that normal people conduct all of the time. How can I have been such a fool?

'It sounds good,' I say.

I am aiming for levity, and have no idea whether I have achieved it, seeing as I am not listening to him.

'Ruth, *maravilloso*. I'm so relieved to hear you say that. Is two weeks enough time?'

Enough time for what? Goodbye sex? A teary farewell? The slippery separating of our music and clothes and toothbrushes?

'How long do you think it should take?' I ask, hoping for balance.

'Well, I don't know. I never realised you would find this so easy, and yet of course, it is easy, it is so easy, *querida*. Thank you, my darling! You've been here for so long now I would have thought … well … Perhaps no thinking is best. After all, you've said yes when I didn't dare to dream … To think … to …'

He is crying now, and laughing.

What is going on? Is this how normal people say goodbye? He is acting as if … as if … It dawns on me that there is a part of the conversation that I have not heard.

José is holding me now, his lips on my mouth, my neck, my body. I pull away.

'José, stop!'

He stops.

'José, what have I just agreed to?'

He looks at me for a moment. He sees that I have not been able to hear him.

He gently takes my trembling hand in his two warm, reassuring, beloved hands. 'Ruth, you and me, we are going to Santiago, to Chile, to my home, in two weeks' time. We are going together. I have been invited to run La Solidaridad. It is a human-rights organisation I've been involved with since I was a boy, but always I had my studies and my work, so it was for only a few months every year. But now I have this chance, I can commit myself completely. Ruth, I really want to do this, and I really want you to come with me. First we will make a beautiful holiday and then we will work hard and make a beautiful life and there is so much interesting work for you to do there. It is such a dynamic time. We are on the edge of change, you will see. I have started making some investigations about funding for therapy groups for you to set up, to lead. You will see, it will be fantastic.' he says.

'Oh, you have thought of everything,' I say.

'Ruth, you can guide us, you can teach us, we can learn from you. Yes, I have thought of everything,' he agrees.

I feel my carapace being cracked open by his determination to get through to me. There I am, exposed and shivering in the ebbing sunlight.

'Ruth, it can be so beautiful. I can teach you things, many, many things about my people, my home. We will travel, we will enjoy my rich and beautiful country, our food, our music, and wine, the most delicious merlot you could ever taste. My mother is waiting to meet you, my aunties and uncles and cousins are waiting to meet you, my neighbourhood is even waiting to meet you. I am waiting to take you home. You have said yes. I will now not accept no, you cannot say no,' he says, some anxiety creeping into his voice.

He wants to take me home. Home.

'Oh my God, José!' I shriek, all composure gone. 'Oh my God. Oh my God.'

We fall off the bench into the long grass. Too bad it isn't dark. Too bad.

* * * * *

Some twenty-four hours later, however, I am unable to contain my anxiety. Chile: it's not that simple.

'How long?' I ask him. 'How long will we go for?'

'I don't know,' he says. 'I don't know how long we will go for. This is the time for us to learn all the things about what really happened to our people, things that it was not possible to know before. But Pinochet is finished, he is over, and we must find out the truth.'

'You mean about your father, and your brothers, and your sister?'

'Yes, but not just them – all of the missing, all of our missing are part of our family, Chile's missing family. Now is the time for us to use our strength to help our people to live their lives again. Since the people voted against Pinochet, eight months ago, we have become free once more.'

He is crying now. 'Ruth, you have no idea what it is like to be free from this heavy past.'

'No, I can't imagine,' I say fervently.

'And your skills will be so valuable. It will help the people to talk and to listen to each other. I have learned so much from the work you do, about how important it is for people to talk about their traumatic experiences so that they can learn to forgive in order to heal. You can help us. We don't have the skills, but you do. The people are ready.'

'Well, you can't be sure,' I say.

'Yes, I am sure. I know this must be true. You can show us. I know you will be brilliant at this Ruth. I can feel it.'

'Restorative justice, it begins by restoring the soul,' I say. 'Yes, that is true. What a good teacher you have had.'

'The best, the very best,' I assure him with a smile. 'But my Spanish, I don't think I'm fluent enough …'

'*Querida,* Ruth, your Spanish is coming along beautifully, although it has to fight with your impatience.'

'But it's not just the words, the language, it's more than that. It's also the culture – I don't … I can't …'

José falls silent. 'Do you not want to come with me, Ruth?' 'With you? José? Of course I want to be with you,' I answer.

I am suddenly elated to know I would go anywhere for him. I am relieved to have this simple, uncomplicated feeling.

'Then let us try, together. We will see what you can manage of our language and culture, and you will see what the work is going to be like. We will make it good, together.'

'Yes,' I say.

I am doubtful. I am anxious. It isn't that I am so entrenched in London, but it has given me generously for eleven years. This damp, overcrowded, irritable city has come to suit me well. My immense suffering and despair has matured into a more manageable sorrow. I have learned great British determination and courage. I am acutely aware of my begrudging willingness to embrace my British identity now that I feel I might lose it after all this time. How can I leave when I am still struggling to arrive?

José.

He is everything I have sworn against. He is my whole world. I hate myself for letting him in. I hate him for my vulnerabilities. I love him. It would be intolerable to be apart.

'We'll make it work,' I say.

He looks relieved. He breathes deeply and reaches for my hand. He clasps it in his two hands. This is good. This is very good. This is not good. This is very dangerous.

'How long will we go for?' I ask again.

He laughs, only partly registering my anxiety but thankfully none of my terror. If I surrender to my terror I will have to stay in London. I will be left abandoned by my own fear, and abandoned by José. But if I surrender to hope, if I go with him, I fear that I might be abandoning myself, my hard-won, renewed self. I feel my pleasure slipping through my hands. I am furious at José's freedom to laugh and to joke and even to enjoy the prospect of uncertainty, my uncertainty.

'I'm going running,' I say with authority. I like it when I have something to do. It fills up the space where terror might take up residence.

'Ruth, Ruth. What have I said? I don't understand. We are talking about Chile and you are now going for a run?' José suddenly seems less certain.

Good, I think. That is what uncertainty feels like, no laughing matter.

'Yes, I'm going running, now.' And I smile and stroke his curls. 'I'll see you in about an hour, *mi bello*. Don't stress, I'm just going for a run.'

I need to get out of here, away from him, before I unravel. I need to clear my head and pound the streets until I am sweating and breathless and hurting from my efforts to be controlled and calm. I need to change my clothes, but because of my habit of disbanding my clothes in small and chaotic piles I can only find yesterday's sweaty sports kit. I am rushed and anxious. But I need to get out of here, now. I throw on my soiled clothes. What difference does more sweat make over a layer of yesterday's sweat? I need my running shoes? Where are my running shoes?

'José? José have you seen my running shoes? Have you seen them?' I call as I tear around, looking in the cupboard, the bathroom, the kitchen. He doesn't answer me, he knows my untidiness is something I am wedded to.

'My shoes, my shoes, where the hell are my shoes?' I mutter, now scrambling around on my hands and knees by the foot of the bed. I am desperate to leave. The walls are closing in on me. I need to run through clean space. I have to get out. My hand finds my well-worn left running shoe under the bed. I sprawl out on my belly and reach further under the bed. I fish around for my other shoe. My hand brushes against a small box, and then my shoe. I pull my shoe out and put my hand back under the bed to pull out the box.

What on earth? I think.

The small, clear plastic Tupperware is filled with a brown clay-like substance. I shake the container and the contents lift and fall with ease. Cautiously I raise the lid and sniff. A pungent woody scent escapes from it, the smell of rich earth. I inhale again and my head is filled with fresh bark and early rain. What is this earth?

'José?' I call, and look up to see my beautiful Chilean looking down at me.

'Yes, Ruth?' he answers.

'José?' I ask again. 'What is this?'

'That is Chile,' he says, and crouches down next to me.

I look at him blankly.

'It is Chilean soil. I have carried it with me since I was sixteen, since I left my home. I fill up this box every time I go home. I know it sounds crazy, but … it makes me feel better, less homesad.' He corrects himself quickly: 'Less homesick.'

I feel tears now. I feel huge pain.

'Ruth, I don't know how long I will be gone for, how long we will be gone, and maybe this time I am returning forever, but now I have you also. We will try and live there, let us see what happens.'

My tears run and run. I have never thought about that before, about the comfort of lying above rich, red, African soil, land from my home. Home. Where is that? Is it land? Is it bricks? Is it people? Without it am I homeless?

I tighten my shoelaces.

'Ruth, are you running or staying?' he asks.

'I'm running, and I'm staying,' I say, 'but I'm going running now.'

I go running. Every step helps me to pound my fear into smaller, more digestible pieces.

Chile. José. Home. José.

I am filled with terror, that my meeting José's family, that my seeing where he is from, will be destructive for me. After all, it isn't as if I can reciprocate. If he were able to look into my eye and understand what he was looking at, he would have some inkling of where I was from. But it isn't his fault that he is unable to do this. After all, it's not really possible, even for me. There are still times when I look long and hard at myself in the mirror and I don't understand the woman looking back at me. I love José. It is more that I had hoped for, more than I had ever expected for myself, and now I have become soft and exposed. If I follow José, I will be even more unprotected, but by myself I will lose his love, which is holding and nurturing me. Why have I allowed him into my heart? I hate feeling dependent on and vulnerable with someone other than myself. I feel out of control, which I am. Our feelings for each other are creating choices I had not anticipated. I want to take only myself into account, and now I am discovering it is no longer only about me. I love, and I am loved. That changes everything.

* * * * *

It doesn't take me long to pack up my most personal belongings and rent out my home to a colleague of Neill's who is getting divorced. We agree on a six-month contract, to be renewed after the first four months, for a further six months after that, if I want. It is all so easy.

I hate the unsettled week of our leaving. I hate our packed-up, barren, abandoned homes. I walk around the empty spaces, touching the floors, the walls, anything solid. I cry when I am on my own. I am on the brink. I am filled with fear. Change is coming, change is coming. Why can't I embrace change? Is a small, safe life the best I can manage?

On our last night in London we have a farewell dinner with José's work colleagues, and he is presented with a white t-shirt emblazoned with the words *El Retorno*. José slips it on over his denim shirt, delighted with the gift. I understand the Spanish but not the significance of the words until he explains:

'For us Chileans, even when we think we are leaving forever, we continue to carry with us the idea that we will return one day, that it is inevitable that we will return to where we are from, to our home.'

He looks at me and whispers, 'Ruth, come now, it is just an idea, a beautiful ideal, which I am aspiring to, with you, but not instead of you.'

But he does not take the t-shirt off for the rest of the evening, and he insists on wearing it when we land in Santiago de Chile.

Janice and Neill are supportive of this new event in my life. My friends and colleagues are excited for us. I have no one I can share my trepidation with – it would feel like a public betrayal of José. I can't tell Shirley. It is time to grow up, to move on from her. I've had enough of being looked after and supported. I want to be normal. I want to forget and forgive my past. I don't want to look at myself. I don't want to look back at where I've come from, I don't want to look down at where I've clambered up from. Somewhere I've learnt that it is unhelpful to do this, to look back or down. The thought aggravates me, whirring round and round in my brain as if warning and alerting me to something that I can't remember, until I cycle past the public lido on my way to my last work meeting.

There he is, again. It is him, always him, his voice banging away inside my head.

'Don't look back, and don't look down, whatever you do. Just climb those stairs, my girl. Take the diving board with firm, steady strides and prepare yourself by looking out as far as you can before you dive. A high board, a low board – it's all the same, my girl. Just look out across the water. Whatever you do, don't look back, and definitely don't look down, I'm telling you, you won't like what you see.'

Yes, Daddy.

I remember now. I am ten. We are at the saltwater swimming pool pavilion in Sea Point, Cape Town. My father has taken us swimming, and he is teaching me to dive. My eyes are burning from the salty water, and I am shivering with cold. But Ivor is relentless in encouraging me to conquer my fears, any fear. It's not clear why I have to be able to dive off the high board. But it is important to him.

My father is my sordid secret that I carry with me, I can't seem to bury him.

Chapter 17

I am so far from home, wherever that might be. I have allowed myself to be set adrift in time and space.

* * * * *

I roll over in an unfamiliar and lumpy bed. José is lying next to me, exactly where I left him last night. He is my landmark.

'Are you tired? Do you need more sleep?' he asks me. 'I need a shower,' I say.

'You smell just beautiful, hot and sweaty,' he says as he pulls me close. 'Not now. I really need a shower, please.'

My words come out sharper than I had intended. 'I'm sorry, I'm just tired and grumpy and horrible. A lovely hot shower will sort me out.'

'It's at the end of the hallway,' he says sleepily. 'Hurry, I need you.' He laughs, and I remember I love him.

I don't like change.

I pull on my tracksuit and a pair of thick socks. I cautiously open the warped wooden door and tiptoe down the dark corridor. The bathroom light gives off a harsh and dingy yellow glow that emanates weakly from the single naked light bulb. The bathroom is a marshmallow pink. I can usually forgive tastes that are different to mine – but not this vile pink.

The tepid water trickles down my back and I will myself to accept the situation I have walked into. Luxury has the power to create only a false sense of security, but I like my false securities. I see them for what they are and enjoy their gifts. And right now I want a luxurious, overbearing, searing hot shower to calm my nerves. I want my power shower. Home – it feels so far away.

The water continues to drip lethargically down my back.

I am exhausted from travel and adventure. I have been in Santiago de Chile for nine hours. I feel like a child and want to ask over and over 'are we there yet?' in order to avoid the answer. I stagger through this first day.

The next morning I roll over in bed. I embrace my beloved. The most delicious aroma drifts through the bedroom. I am awake. I am ravenous.

'José, is that the smell of freshly baked bread?'

'Yes, of course *cariña*. *Pan amasado*. My mother, she makes the best *pan amasado*. This is why I come home, for her bread,' he laughs.

'It smells wonderful.'

'I will bring you some,' he says.

A flash of lithe, golden body, fluid and graceful, and he is out the bed. He returns with a small basket, two plates, coffee and a small terracotta bowl.

'What is this?'

'Breakfast in bed, my darling. You have not eaten properly for at least a week, and yesterday, with so many people visiting us, I think you hardly ate at all. Today we have breakfast in bed.'

He passes me a small, round bread. It is warm and fragrant. I bite in. There is a floury tang as it bursts on my tongue.

'Here,' he says and hands me the bowl. It is filled to the brim with guacamole. I poke a chunk of the bread into the avocado, and the fragrance of lime and cilantro floats up towards me. I eat with my eyes closed, savouring the piquant taste.

'You are starving.'

I say nothing, my mouth is too stuffed with food to answer him. I am trying to control myself from eating like an animal, but now that I am aware of my hunger I can't stop myself until I am full. I slurp down my dark coffee and savour its bitterness. Better, much better.

'Feeling satisfied?' he smiles at me.

'Not completely,' I say.

'More bread? More guacamole? Coffee?'

'No, *mi amore*, no more food. Not that …' I smile at him hopefully.

'Aah …' he says. 'Perhaps I can help.'

'Perhaps you can,' I smile as I slowly lick the last of the guacamole off my fingers. 'Perhaps you can …'

I have been in Santiago de Chile for thirty-three hours. I no longer feel the need to ask if I am there yet. I am in his arms. That is home.

Much too early the next morning I roll over in bed. José is asleep. I can't sleep. It is 4.00am. Just when I thought I was doing well, that I had surpassed myself, I discover that I am wide awake. There are some muffled sounds coming from down the corridor. I hear the whoosh of gas as it is ignited. I am not alone with my insomnia. There is a fellow traveller.

I get out of bed and dress from the puddle of clothes on the floor. I run a hand through my hair and open the door carefully. I can smell spices and herbs, and a warm oven. The light coming from the kitchen is soft and warm. As I get closer I can see that the light comes from the six candles along the work surface. I approach with caution.

I see a solitary figure hunched over the work surface, her shoulders and arms moving vigorously and rhythmically. I want to scurry back to my room, but I am uncertain whether the floorboards might creak. I stand still, willing myself to fade into the background. I tentatively lift one foot and place it behind me. I shift my weight backwards and wonder how long it will take me to reverse away from the kitchen.

'*Buenos dias,* Ruth,' José's mother, Gabriela-Juanita, says, without lifting her head from the concentrated task of kneading her bread. Her silver hair is loosely coiled in a bun that, when undone, surely reaches down to her waist. She is still in her long woollen nightdress. Her face is soft and serene in the candle light.

'*Buenos dias,*' I whisper.

Unlike me, she is unashamedly awake, and absorbed in her task. The dough looks soft and yielding in her strong brown hands. I want to touch it but I am anxious about intruding. I clear my throat and return to my warm bed. She does not acknowledge my leaving. But the following morning I am again awake at 4.00am, and after a few minutes of deliberation I pull on my clothes and tiptoe down the corridor to the kitchen. This time I stay for several minutes, transfixed by the rhythm of her hands, performing the ancient actions of making bread. Again I leave her and try to go back to sleep while thinking about the repetitive nature of the kneading movement, the symbolism of the candle light and the austerity of the early morning. Perhaps this ritual is more than making bread. The third morning I wake up at 3.45am. I rush into the kitchen, but it is dark and cold. I feel the sting of quick tears.

Just then a small soft figure pads into the kitchen. '*Buenos dias,* Ruth.'

'*Buenos dias*, Gabriela-Juanita.'

She hands me the matches and points out the candles. I struggle to light them because my hands are trembling. Gabriela-Juanita opens the cupboard and takes out two bowls. She tips out flour into both the bowls and adds sugar and salt, yeast, warm water and shortening. She pulls a bowl towards herself and begins to knead the dough with deft and supple movements.

'Ruth, *la bienvenida*, welcome, Ruth.'

'*Graçias*,' I whisper. She beckons to me and then gestures to the bowl that is waiting for me. She has been expecting me.

'I don't know how …' I say.

She ignores me. I take my place and attempt to copy her movements. I am clumsy and self-conscious but I plunge my hands in deep. The dough is sticky and resilient. There we stand, side by side, two insomniacs pounding away at the forgiving dough.

I continue to wake up at 4.00am. In silence, together, we spend an hour preparing bread, and then I tiptoe back to bed before the sun rises. If José knows about my secret rendezvous with his mother he does not say. Perhaps he doesn't know that she can't sleep in the early hours when the missing call to us the loudest. Perhaps he doesn't know that the reason the *pan amasado* tastes so fine is because it is so well pounded by the broken-hearted who need to displace their pain.

* * * * *

I am suffocated by the constant stream of cousins, friends and neighbours who are keen to see *El Retorno* and quick to mutter their traditional Catholic disapproval of our cohabitation in José's childhood bedroom. I long for a soothing cup of tea with Janice.

'José, Margaret Thatcher's professor,' they call him. 'Queen Elizabeth's teacher,' they tease. He shrugs them off with good humour and introduces me to each person with care and thought, as if I were a rare and precious orchid. He translates where I am unable to understand – it is surprisingly difficult for me to follow this rapid, sing-song Spanish that does not use consonants in the way that I am expecting. I had not appreciated that José talks to me in a slower, Mediterranean Spanish. When I reply to his family and friends in Spanish I notice most people prefer to answer me in English or to fire off a rapid stream of words at José, who digests their meaning for me. There is a lot of good-humoured laughter, which I join in with. But inwardly I am seething with my own impotence. I can't talk easily. I can't be understood. I feel as though my mouth is filled with a thick toffee that I can't swallow down or extract.

'It will come, it will come, you will see. It is the same Spanish, but we sing it with a different tune in Chile,' José reassures me.

'Okay,' I reply. 'A different tune, I can do that.'

I don't believe my own words but being there, by José's side, is all about being with José. How long can this last?

On the seventh day I ask José to show me where we will be working and to meet the staff so that I can start to think myself into my role. He is delighted. He interprets my anxiety for enthusiasm.

We travel by bus from Gabriela-Juanita's home into the city of Santiago de Chile. The worst of the pollution has lifted now that it is spring, and the fragrance of fresh peaches, watermelons and basil perfume the air around the plazas. Children run around with multi-coloured balloons and kites dance in the sky. Spring. The miracle season. It has been many years since I have celebrated spring in September.

José rushes me through the fluttering plaza and into the entrance of a dark and gloomy cathedral.

'We're about to begin our real Chilean adventure. Are you ready?' he asks, and reaches for my hand.

I smile and breathe in the pungent fragrance of the basil leaves that I am holding. Is this the smell of Chile? Is this the fragrance of a new kind of freedom?

'Yes, come on, show me, please,' I reply, squeezing his hand tightly.

We walk further into the dark, quiet sanctuary of the cathedral. Neill would approve of its dignified majesty and bearing. It is silent and solemn. At the entrance there is a table laid out with many candles in small glass jars. José lights one and then slides into a pew, crosses himself and kneels down. I stand alongside him, feeling shy. I have not seen him pray before. We have never discussed prayer. He closes his eyes and whispers silently to himself.

Uneasily I slide into the pew behind him and sit down on the dark wooden bench. I watch the sunbeams floating in through ancient stained glass. The contrast between the dense darkness and ethereal light is magical. The bench is warm and smooth beneath me. How many people have sat here with hands clasped in sweaty desperation, waiting for their prayers to be answered? How can an act so desperate as praying carry such an air of tranquillity? I rub my hands against the smooth grain. I sit back. It is very peaceful.

I stare at the light and shadows until my eye loses its focus. Is this where prayers get answered? I don't try it out. I've travelled far, very far, but I am a Jewess in a Catholic church. I am a visitor. I sit quietly until José touches me on the shoulder.

'I didn't know you prayed,' I say awkwardly.

'Yes. I have always prayed, every day For so many years my prayers came out of sadness, but now, for the last many months it is always to give thanks that I have you,' he says simply.

My throat thickens. It has never occurred to me to thank God, to be thankful for any of what is in my life. I am constantly struggling to maintain my normality. I am consumed with managing my anxieties around loss.

'I don't pray,' I say, in this house of worship. 'I don't ever pray. I haven't since I was a teenager. But it's lovely in here. Thank you for bringing me.'

He leads me down the central aisle and to the back of the altar, where there is a small door. He knocks on the door and opens it. An elderly man dressed in dark robes looks up from his work and smiles broadly at José. They embrace and talk a fast Spanish that I struggle to follow. José points to me and carries on talking.

'Ruth, this is Padre Salvatore. Padre, this is my Ruth.'

The old priest inclines his head to me. 'Welcome Ruth, we are very pleased you are here. We are very grateful to you.' And he shakes my uncertain hand in his dry and papery one.

'Follow, please follow,' he says and guides us out of a small door at the far side of the room, which even I have to stoop to pass through. We walk in single file through windowless corridors that take us further into the belly of the building until we reach a large, heavy door. The priest pulls out a huge bunch of keys from his robes and unlocks it, and then locks it once more when we are on the other side. We come out into a tiny courtyard that is filled with pot plants, and the unmistakeable fragrance of basil hits me once more. Padre Salvatore knocks on the only other door in the wall and it is opened by Gabriela-Juanita.

'*Buenos dias,*' she says to me for the second time that day.

I see a white washed room with six people to a desk, four desks in the room. There are people on the phone and on typewriters. There are cabinets spilling over with papers, and piles of documents and letters weighing down every possible surface. There is a sudden rush at José as women and men jump up to greet him. They hug and kiss him and laugh with pleasure. My José. He brings pleasure wherever he goes. And he is even more captivating now that I can see him in his Chilean landscape. He fits here, I can see it. He is lit from within. He is beautiful.

I blink as rapid introductions are made. I force myself to smile, to nod, to look each person in the eye. I always find the scrutiny of introductions difficult, until it becomes obvious to the other person which of my eyes they should talk to, until my non-seeing eye fades from conscious thought – theirs, but never mine.

'Ruth, this is Mariá, Francisco, Isabella, Viviana, Anita, Alfredo, Celéste. We have worked alongside each other, struggled alongside each other, since high school. Isabella, she was my first girlfriend, but she broke my heart when I caught her kissing my brother, Luis,' he laughs.

I am shocked by how lightly José refers to his brother, his murdered brother.

He doesn't know I also have murdered brothers. Even there, in the bowels of this Chilean church, what I can't say continues to feel overwhelming.

Isabella embraces me warmly. 'Ruth, you are very welcome. Thank you for helping us. We are very grateful to you,' she says.

'You're thanking me already? Oh no! What've I let myself in for?' I laugh. 'Yes, you may want to run,' Isabella smiles.

'Too late. I could never find my way out.'

Is it too late? Will I ever find my way out? Is this what I want? 'Come, Ruth, let's make a meeting now,' says Isabella.

'Let's make a meeting,' I answer in hesitant European Spanish. She laughs with delight at my efforts.

'Coffee?'

'*Sí*, of course,' I answer.

It is slow going, as I need to keep confirming that we understand each other, but we talk in a mixture of Spanish and English.

'As you know, we are providing spiritual and legal services, employment opportunities and health care. But we have not had any opportunity or skill to look after ourselves, our psychological health,' she explains.

'Tell me about the people who come to you for help. How do you think people have been affected? How have you been affected?' I ask her.

She is surprisingly candid. 'It is difficult, very difficult to know this. It is very difficult to be a Chilean and to talk. Our past is so painful. Some of us refuse to admit the past and some of us refuse to let it go.'

'Yes,' I say.

'It is memory that we struggle the most with. It makes us sick to remember and sick to forget. This sickness – it can destroy people; it can destroy families that are already broken by their sorrows.'

'Yes,' I nod. 'I have seen something like this before. I wonder if …'

She listens carefully and calls Viviana to join in, and Mariá too. We are having a coffee morning at the centre of the earth.

I am startled when José suddenly says, 'It's one-thirty. Let's go for lunch.'

I look at my watch. It is 5.00pm in London, a whole other life away. I am underground, literally and figuratively. I am clandestine. Is this what I've been waiting for?

'Lunch, let's all do lunch,' I say expansively.

'No, no this is not possible. Not all of us. Just you and me,' José says quickly.

'Oh, sorry, sorry,' I say. Now my British reserve kicks in. I want to disappear with embarrassment into the floorboards. What have I said?

'We can't Ruth. We can't be seen in public together. You and I of course, we can, and my mother, but not with anyone else in this room. We have all been watched for years, and we cannot afford to be seen together, ever. We must always arrive and leave separately. It must always be like this, it is dangerous.'

'But Pinochet, he is finished, what does it matter? You said you feel free. I don't understand.'

'He is gone, but not gone. He will be here until he is no longer alive. We are safe but not yet free from worry and anxiety that we are being watched, followed, written down in a file somewhere by someone.'

'I didn't know, I didn't think. I'm sorry.'

'Of course, you have only just arrived. How could you know?'

I've only just arrived and already I have planned to bring Santiago's troubled and damaged people into better mental health.

'Does Isabella understand what you need her to organise?'

'Yes, I need ten psychology students – top students, a mix of men and women. I'll need three weeks to train them up, and then we can start. It's not really long enough, but if they're bright and open-minded then it might be possible, but I think the sooner we start, the better. I'll supervise them in groups of four, twice a week for the duration of the project.'

'This is good, this is very good, Ruth,' he says. 'I know you will be able to show us what we need to do. I knew I could depend on you, *querida*.'

Depend on me? I still have days where I can't depend on myself to put one foot in front of the other. I am used to professional responsibility but personal responsibility is something else. How long has José been depending on me? Do I dare depend on him?

'Come, Ruth. Now you really look exhausted. Let's go get some food and I can show you my favourite places for taking girls like you. I'll call Padre Salvatore to come with the keys,' he says and picks up the phone.

I look around for Gabriela-Juanita but she is not there.

'Where's your mother?' I ask as the priest leads us back through the labyrinth.

'She left a while ago. She tried to say goodbye to you but you were too busy talking.'

'Oh, I hope she doesn't think I was rude,'

'No, she understands very well the intensity of this experience.'

'What does she do here?'

'A little bit of this and that. Her main work is outside of here. Now, enough of this work talk. A beautiful woman in a beautiful city, this is how is it should be. I am a very lucky man.'

I enjoy his Latino charm, which has intensified since we have been in Chile. I feel so British in his presence, which is confusing for me. I never feel British.

'I only just realised how exciting this is, being here, I'm really glad I'm here.'

'It makes me very happy to see you here, in my home.'

'I am happy,' I answer seriously.

I feel as light and effervescent as a summer breeze. 'I'm happy, happy, happy,' I shout, surprising us both as I start running for the pleasure of running and jumping and leaping. I pull him after me, both of us laughing and tripping along like six-year olds. This is what joy feels like.

I feel so alive in this abnormal, neurotic city. Perhaps I can fit in well, perhaps I can be completely normal, with my anxieties and paranoias blending well with everyone else's.

* * * * *

A week after we arrived in Chile it is the National Independence Day celebrations. We flock to Parque O'Higgins, Santiago's second-largest public park, to watch the great military parade and then walk over to the grass by the lake to lie on blankets, and picnic and barbeque, and drink and sleep, and celebrate Chile's independence from Spain. There is folk music and kite flying.

'Once, a long time ago, we were so many here. So many blankets, so much food,' Gabriela Juanita says. Sadness defines her face. 'We try to celebrate, to rejoice in our independence, but in truth there have been many times, many years when I don't feel free. I feel I am under the slavery of Pinochet.'

'Here, *Mamita*, have some *empanades*, have a glass of *chicha*,' José says, putting a protective arm around Gabriela-Juanita and gently steering her towards the food.

José has found a way to live with his losses, but I can see that his mother continues to struggle. Despite the passing of the years she is steeped in Chile's intense sorrows. José, however, can be a more carefree Chilean and he can also be British. He can refer to home and mean London, and also mean Santiago de Chile.

I look around me. There are many clusters of families and friends around us, but the overwhelming experience is female. The younger women are dressed in bright, bold, brief clothes that cling to their bodies. They cluck around their remaining men, serving the men with a deference I have not seen before.

'José, the men, there are so few.'

'Sure, *querida*, they are missing for sure. Missing, dead, gone. We are not as we once were.'

'Is that why the women rush to serve the men, the ones that are left?'

'I don't know about that. Our Chilean culture is very different from American and British. Women are different here. It is different in Latin America.'

I think back to my slovenly housekeeping and haphazard cooking. I eat better with José than I have done in years, because he does the shopping and cooking when we are together.

'Do you want that, José?' I ask.

Is this why he wanted me to come to Chile, to change me into a Chilean version of myself?

'You, my darling, you – you are untameable. You are none of these things that a typical Chilean girl is – you are a European woman. You are a bossy, independent, opinionated woman, and perfect for me. Do you not realise that yet?' he laughs.

What is the matter with me? Why do I take myself on this rollercoaster of self-doubt? José gives me every reassurance, both in private and in public, and yet I continue to try and find flaws to disprove love's hold over me.

We lie whispering quietly to one another, but our English and intimacy attracts attention from the other picnickers in our group. There is a torrent of Spanish, and José laughingly gets to his feet.

'I'm going to fly a kite now, but I'll be back. Don't eat all the food,' he calls over his shoulder as he lets himself be dragged away.

I lie back in the grass and look up at the clear, blue sky. A citrus sun bathes me in cool spring light. The last time the sky was so blue I was a teenager in Johannesburg. I close my eyes and allow myself to be caressed by the gentle heat. I fall further into the soft green grass while people talk and laugh around me. A cloud passes over the sun, and I open my eyes. I've no idea how long I've been asleep but it is darker now and there are fewer people around. I look around for a familiar face.

Gabriela-Juanita has vanished.

'Where is Gabriela-Juanita?' I ask Carmen, the woman I recognise as José's English-speaking aunt.

'She has gone. She always goes. She makes the food. She makes sure everybody is eating, and then she goes home,' she says.

'Why?' I ask.

'She needs to be at home on days like today. For some it is easier to be out of the house, away from the memories. Me, I like to be out, but for others it is better to be at home,' she says. 'I think it is difficult for you to understand this.'

'No, no. I think I understand. She is sad.'

'We are all sad, my dear, very sad. Our lives are crowded with our ghosts. Sometimes it is difficult to breathe the air because of the sadnesses that many of us are carrying. But we don't like to talk about it. We talk instead about jobs and mortgages and fridges and cars.'

I stare at this woman, who I have nothing and everything in common with.

'Auntie, what stories are you telling Ruth? Leave her alone, it is too soon for your fairy tales. She has only just arrived, stay away from her!' José says as he sits down.

His aunt smiles at him and turns away to break up an argument between her grandchildren.

'I'm sorry if I was too long, but the boys they wanted me for the kites,' he smiles apologetically.

'How long were you gone?' 'About an hour.'

'I fell asleep, I didn't realise I was tired. When I woke up Carmen was very sweet to me, she tried to talk to me.'

'I am sure she did, and of course she loves to practise her English. But she is heavy with her sadness. She shares it with everyone, and I don't think you need that. I've seen how other peoples' sadness affects you. Now it is time to celebrate Chile's independence from Spain, freedom from dictatorship. It is time to celebrate your being here with me.'

He brandishes two tickets under my nose.

'The great lady, the Latin American queen of folk music, the peoples' music, she is singing tonight. Would you like to see her?'

'Mercédes Sosa? She's here in Santiago? I would love to go. How fantastic. How did you get tickets?'

'Padre Salvatore had tickets for the concert. When I told him you love her music he insisted that we take his tickets as a welcome home present.'

'Wonderful, really so kind,' I say, the tears ever quick to surface.

It is on this night, at this magical concert, that I become Chilean. I will remember that evening for my whole life. Sosa is magnificent. She shares her *chacareras*, her tangos, her ballads with an audience desperate for her caress. I too am part of that audience – even though I understand so little, I feel so much. Her heart-breaking voice and the soaring music penetrate my South African, my British soul. On this night I become Latino.

* * * * *

It is my birthday. I am twenty-nine.

I can see what José will look like as an old man in his mother's weathered skin and thick silver hair, but it is not possible for me to see what I will look like when I am old. My grandparents are long forgotten, and I have no other vision of what or who I might look like after I am fifty. How will my skin sag and crease? Where will my hair thin and fade? How will I know if my aches and creaks are unique to me or typical to my family? I don't know. It is not possible for me to know. But this is a good birthday for me, my twenty-ninth birthday, in Santiago de Chile.

I book us overnight into the top hotel in the city. Gabriela-Juanita is lovely and kind, but I want twenty-four hours of undiluted José. I want to frolic and be carefree in this exotic city with my handsome Latino lover. I want to laze around in bed with him for uninterrupted hours, followed by a steamy hot shower in a chrome-and-white bathroom. Gabriela-Juanita is generous but I want to be indulged. I can indulge José and myself, for twenty-four hours. It is my birthday present to myself. José is amused and allows my every desire. I have given up everything for him. We both know this.

'You know, *querida*, I still can't believe you are here with me in Chile, that we are both here, together,' he says, as we lie head-to-toe in the foam-filled bath, eating oranges.

'I can't either. I didn't know I had it in me to be so adventurous,' I laugh, very pleased with myself.

'You, Ruth Newman, you are my home,' he says softly.

I shut him up with my lips. I want to play. I can't allow him to say out loud what I dare not imagine – a forever space. Not when I want it so desperately. It will give me a false sense of security that I can't allow. Even to have travelled this far, is far enough – too far really. I know this.

'Oh, *mi amore*, you know, now that I am a good, sweet, obedient Chilean girl, I would surely go with you to the ends of the earth,' I say sweetly.

'Would you, Ruth? You know, I think you might, I think you just might,' he smiles.

I smile too, relieved that we are joking around once more.

'What a very good idea I have just had. Yes! We must do it,' he exclaims suddenly and smacks his hand on the water, sending soapsuds all over the bathroom floor. 'We must organise, we must organise ourselves immediately.'

'What do you mean?' I ask drowsily. I want to lie back in this bath. I want to lie back and think of Chile, England, anywhere so long as I can lie back with José on top of me.

'We need to sort it out, immediately. A trip, a special trip.' 'Don't we need to start work?'

'Yes, of course, but I have so much of Chile to show you. First, we must go exploring, and then we will work. I will arrange for us to begin with La Solidaridad in ten days' time. That will give us enough time.'

'Time for what?'

'A very special journey, my darling. We will test out your words. I know you never speak lightly, and this time we can test it out.'

'What are you talking about?'

'We are talking about the ends of the earth, about you coming with me to the ends of the earth. Fantastic. Marvellous. Why didn't I think of that before?'

He jumps out of the bath. 'Get up, get dressed, we need to make some plans.'

I thought we were in the middle of our plans. I know exactly what I had planned for the immediate future, and it didn't involve getting dressed.

'José, please tell me what you are talking about? What have I said?

What needs planning?'

'To the ends of the earth, *querida*. That is where we are going. Patagonia, the Parque Nacional Torres del Paine.'

'Where?'

'Here,' he says. 'Look!' And throws me the hotel travel magazine that is displayed on the cabinet table. 'Look in the front of the magazine. There will be a map of Chile. At the southern tip where Chile touches Argentina – that, *querida*, is Patagonia, the end of the earth. That is where we must go.'

* * * * *

We leave Santiago two days later. It is a four-and-a-half-hour flight into Punto Arenas and then a five-hour drive into the park.

'My father came here when he was a boy. I remember him speaking about this place with such wonder and awe. I always wanted to see it for myself,' José says. His face is dreamy with memory.

I am spellbound by the vast expanse of land around me. I see huge plains and snow-capped mountains. It is silent, still.

'Glaciers, horse riding, kayaking – José, we can't possibly do all of this,' I say, looking at our itinerary.

'We can do whatever you like. You've made me so happy – I can't ask any more of you – the ends of the earth!' he chortles with pleasure.

Maybe it is possible to have it all.

Our first expedition is to the glacier. We are collected from our hotel at 7.00am and travel by boat through the iceberg channel to the southern side of the glacier. We disembark on an icy walkway and trudge gingerly for forty minutes until we arrive at a hut where we put on crampons and have a brief lesson in how to walk with claws on our feet. It requires huge physical effort to walk in the near-freezing winds, but we are rewarded by a dramatic, frozen landscape bathed in an eerie blue light that seeps from the ghostly glacier canyons and ice caves. We return to our hotel chilled to the bone, exhilarated.

The second day we kayak under a fiercely burning sun on a silent blue lake. The only sound is from our oars dipping in and out of the silken water. We picnic by the lake, surrounded by the calm beauty of the soaring mountain peaks. The contrast between this tranquil Garden of Eden and the frozen glacial world we left behind us yesterday is startling. We are at the end of the earth, a strange, impetuous and moody land of extreme weather and nature. It is absolutely magnificent.

We spend two days swimming in mountain streams, walking lazy nature trails and staring at thundering waterfalls. We walk through cool, dark forests on narrow, stony paths that open out onto expansive prairies. The sun shines down, embracing and nurturing me, us. I am free to be Ruth without restraint.

Our final day is a five-hour hike through meandering forests until we end up alongside the turquoise waters of Lago del Toro. We lie at right angles to each other in the soft, warm sand. I stare up into the brilliant blue sky. Every muscle is aching. I feel fantastic. This is the happiest I've ever been, this is the best I've ever known.

'You are doing very well, *cariña*. I think Chile is suiting you,' my beloved says.

'I am very happy. This is a very beautiful country. I am so glad to be here,' I say.

He beams at me.

'It also makes me happy to see you with your family. When you are with them it is like you have more of yourself together in one place,' I say.

'Yes, this is true. That is true for family, yes? Of course. We all need family. And you my darling, you look especially lovely with some colour in your face and body. Look, our skin is the same colour, the exact same.'

It is true. I am now stained several shades darker than my familiar pale. I stroke his hair, his arm, his face. He is the colour of nutmeg, and I am bathed in sunlight and love.

'When I was a girl I used to be so dark that people often mistook me for Asian – which is not ideal in a South African whites-only school, and a whites-only community hostile and suspicious of rumours about who might not have been what they said they were. You know – the threat of race. It was only when I came to live in London that I realised that without the sun I was paler. But not now. Now I am once more sun-kissed like you. How beautiful we are!'

I laugh with pleasure, delighted by our limbs. José rolls onto his side and examines my face.

'I would love to know about you – you as a girl. I bet you were gorgeous – I would have fought all the boys for you, even then.'

He wraps his fingers in my hair. He smiles his beautiful smile and draws me closer. I hold my breath, my eyes tightly closed to encase my salty pain. I force myself to keep smiling.

'Tell me about you, Ruth, how it was growing up, tell me what you were like. I want to know what my daughter will look like.'

His smile is broad, he is filled with pleasure. I am not. I need to focus. I need to find an exit route from my childhood.

'Daughter?' I whisper.

'Yes, daughter, son, some of each, of course. A big family. They will all be beautiful, just like you, and tall, just like me, and untidy like you, and bad at directions like me. Just like you and me.'

'Sons and daughters?'

'Yes. Sons and daughters. We will have to practise very hard, and very often to make that happen. You do realise that, *cariño*?'

'Oh. I didn't realise that,' I smile, my eyes still closed.

'Yes, it is very important, the practise,' he says, slowly tracing my face and down my neck with his delicate, beautiful fingers.

'Do you think that perhaps we should start straight away, practising?'

'Yes, I think so,' he says as we begin our embrace.

Slowly I fall back into the present moment, safe once more in our Garden of Eden.

* * * * *

We return to Santiago de Chile to discover from a neighbour that Gabriela-Juanita and her sister-in-law, Carmen have been summoned to the local police station in order to identify a body that might be Juan-Pedro, the youngest brother of Gabriela- Juanita, and Carmen's husband. José leaves to join them immediately, his face lined with anxiety.

Several hours later the three of them return from the police station, sad and defeated. The dental remains confirm that the dead man is Juan-Pedro, last seen alive when he was arrested at his home on 15th October 1973, at the start of Pinochet's Caravan of Death.

Juan-Pedro had openly identified as an Allende supporter. After the coup it had not occurred to him to run or hide. It had not occurred to him that he would be murdered by the state. For many weeks after his disappearance Carmen had gone every day to the local police station with pots of food and blankets and clean clothing, asking for information and begging the staff to pass the food and clothing on to him. She had endured denial, jeering and irritation but had continued to question the disappearance of her husband. How could she have known that Juan-Pedro had been shot dead in the same hour that she first reported him missing? She had waited sixteen years to learn that she was a widow.

'Juan-Pedro, he is never coming home,' she says sadly, 'He is dead, he is really dead.'

'Yes, he is really dead. We will never see him again. We now know this,' Gabriela-Juanita replies.

This discovery, along with others like this, becomes part of the fabric that makes up the new Chile. It is a Chile that is free of Pinochet, but in theory only, for Chile is a dark and dusty mausoleum, filled with ghosts and lurking shadows that continue to evoke a terror and anxiety in most of its citizens, dampening the desire for resistance and rage. Anxiety and fear create a social pressure, a collective attempt to forge an amnesia over the past sixteen years – there is so much that can't be thought about. But how can you heal if you can't remember? If you can't remember, you can't forgive, and if you can't forgive you can't heal, and you can't restore, which means there is no justice for the victims.

A period of quiet mourning and remembering sets in for José's family. I don't mind, I am not uncomfortable. I prefer the contemplative and sombre family atmosphere to the giddy euphoria that surrounded José's homecoming and had threatened to overwhelm me. It occurs to me that perhaps I've been lucky. At least I know enough about what happened to my missing, enough to know who to hate and who to blame and what to run away from.

We fall into sweet routine. José and I continue to live sinfully in Gabriela-Juanita's Catholic home. She gracefully continues to accept her son under any circumstances he offers her. She sees that I am part of the package and embraces me with open arms.

I have not yet tired of my peaceful, sacrosanct and shared time in her kitchen.

In the moments where my hands are deeply buried in the life-sustaining dough, I begin to think that I might do a little praying of my own, one day. Can it be only four months that we have been living so intimately, so intensely? It seems like forever.

José and me, me and José. I have him, and if I want it, I can also have his family and his community, his culture and traditions, until all that I ever was is obliterated by this altered state. If I want to I can apply a new layer of myself over the older layer.

* * * * *

Gabriela-Juanita and I sit on the porch and drink green tea. We chat about how my project is developing. My Spanish is more fluent and my ear more adjusted to the Chilean accent. London is so very far away. South Africa – when was that?

I shiver in the cool night air. 'I'll get you a shawl Ruth. Look how cold you are,' says Gabriela-Juanita, always quick to her feet.

'Thank you, thank you,' I say.

This lovely woman mothers me so effortlessly – she is not my mother, and she is not Janice, but she is a loving and good mother nonetheless. I watch her go into the house and see her open her bedroom door. From my chair I can see straight into her room and notice, for the first time, a huge tapestry on her wall. It is distinctive in the way it dominates the wall, and because she has no other art or craftwork in her home.

'Gabriela-Juanita, what is that – on your wall, the picture?' I ask.

'Come, Ruth, please come and have a look. You are welcome,' she says.

It is a huge wall hanging, unlike any I have ever seen. The tapestry looks like it has been constructed from leftover materials. The image is disturbing and arresting rather than aesthetic.

'Gabriela, what is this, please?' I ask again.

She shrugs, and points at herself and then looks down at her hands. This is not a language difficulty between us. This is about an inability to articulate an intense feeling of pain, which I immediately recognise. I look again at the tapestry. Its border is a thick yellow wool, the background cloth is a sky blue made out of rough denim cotton. The scene is dominated by a woman's face in three-quarter profile. She has dark hair, dark eyes, red lips. A single tear rests on her cheek, it is made out of a thick silver silk. She looks out across the sky at four distant balloons, floating in the furthest corner of the scene; navy-blue woollen, green heavy cotton, brown hemp and pink-satin balloons billow across the vacant sky. At the base of each balloon is a narrow rope in black cord and at the end of each rope is a tiny, human-shaped figure in light-brown felt. Three figures are probably male, the fourth figure, hanging below the pink balloon, has long dark hair and looks more feminine. The intense longing in the woman's gaze is unmistakeable. The woman is Gabriela- Juanita. She has woven herself into the tapestry. I am looking at the visual representation of her loss: her husband Héctor, her sons Luis and Patricio, and her daughter Adriana, suspended in flight somewhere between heaven and earth, with Gabriela-Juanita a helpless onlooker. It is unbearable. I look at her, but she continues to look down at her hands. I have no idea what to say.

She breaks the silence. 'Goodnight, Ruth. I am tired now. I hope you sleep very well,' she says quietly and kisses me quickly on the cheek.

I leave her and go to my bed to wait for José. I try to read through some work notes in order to distract myself from the distressing intensity the tapestry has evoked in me. A visual representation of the missing, all together in one collective piece is overwhelming.

I lie in the bed, unable to read, unable to sleep. I wait for José's return. I hear him open and close the front door. He walks softly through the silent house and tiptoes into the bedroom.

'Good evening my sweetheart. I am very pleased to see you. What a long day it has been, but with many hours of good work. I hear you were excellent today. Celéste was full of praises for you …'

He bends to kiss my head and talks away as he slips his shoes off, loosens his belt, tidies away his sweatshirt. It is several minutes before he notices that I am silent.

'Ruth, you are not talking back at me, you are not telling me of your day. What is the matter?' he says and sits down at the edge of the bed, watching my face with concern.

'The tapestry, José, tell me about it please.' He looks at me blankly. 'José, I saw tonight in Gabriela-Juanita's bedroom – a tapestry, please tell me about it.'

'Aah,' he says. 'Tell me, what happened?'

'Gabriela-Juanita, she showed it to me and then said she needed to go to bed. That was at about eight-thirty.'

'How did she seem?'

'She sort of disappeared inside herself, she withdrew.'

'Yes.'

'Please, tell me about the tapestry.'

'We call it an *arpillera*. In English I think you say burlap cloth.'

'José, she made it herself didn't she? The woman in it, it's her,' I say, rushing on without waiting for an answer. 'The balloons, with the little dangling figures, they're …they're …'

'Yes, this is true. It is of the family, you are correct.'

'It's so powerful. I've never seen anything like that.'

'This is part of her work. She is an *arpillerista*, a senior craftworker. She is also a trainer and teacher to new *arpilleristas*.'

'You mean like a cooperative of artists?'

'Yes and no. It is more than that. She is part of the *arpillerista* movement, it is a key voice of the Chilean resistance. The *arpillera* – it says what cannot be said.'

'I thought you said she was a teacher.'

'She used to work in a school where she taught craftwork, like stitching and modelling and perspective, as well as painting. But for many years now she has been a major part of the *arpillerista* movement. She was one of the early *arpilleristas*, part of the first group of women to make these angry and sad cloths. She helps the groups to interpret their experiences through this art work. Would you like to see more?'

'Yes, of course, please.'

'I will talk to her in the morning. Most of what is made is sold to sympathetic organisations in America and Europe. She helps to arrange this. Many of the women live off the proceeds. In the 1970s, when there was so much unemployment, the men all lost their jobs and it was the women who had to find creative ways of earning money for food to keep the family going. But this work, it is not just about money. It is a message of resistance. It is a permanent image of memory. The images capture loss and force us to be witness, to feel alongside the artist.'

'Yes, it has, I do,' I gulp.

'I should have thought to show you this. These women and their art is a unique phenomenon to the Chilean resistance, but we have been so busy, there is always so much to do, and I didn't think about it. I will talk to her tomorrow about you visiting.'

'Tell me about the *arpillera*.'

'Okay,' he says. 'What did you notice first?'

'I saw the woman, I saw your mother. At first I didn't stop to think it might be her or anyone, it was just a woman. And the balloons, they made me feel uneasy – they were childish and fun and yet so dominant in the picture. And then I noticed the little figures dangling below. And … and …' For some inexplicable reason I am now sobbing. 'And I looked back at the woman's face and I saw all the tears in one tear and the yellow sunny border and the bright-blue sky – they seemed mocking and surreal. I wanted to look away but I couldn't. I wanted to touch the balloon, especially the pink shiny one, it looked so pretty and smooth and … and …' I struggle to get my sentences out.

'The pink material is from Adriana's confirmation dress. My mother made it for her, it was white with a pink sash. I remember her dancing in her dress and laughing as it lifted up over her knees when she spun round. I also wanted a dress like that. I remember crying when I discovered that boys could never look pretty,' he smiles. 'Mama always uses a piece from the sash in her *arpillera*, she always weaves Adriana into her work as a flower petal, a kite, a pair of shoes.'

'All of it together, as one image, all that loss together, it is too terrible, too much.'

'It is too much,' he says quietly, and hangs his head. 'But this is who we are. This is what it means to be Chilean. Too much suffering, too much loss altogether.'

'How does your mother survive it?'

'She has survived for sixteen years. She brings her talents and skills to good use. She helps other women to find their creative voice to express their pain. And the women help her to find her voice. They help each other. Most of the *arpilleras* are sold, although sometimes the work might feel too personal to sell – like the *arpillera* you saw, on our wall here. But these women, they work together to complete what needs to be completed, and they sell what can be sold, and they survive their poverty and their loneliness and laugh through some of their suffering, where they can. They tell their stories through their art, forming part of the jigsaw in our dark history that we are piecing together, and that you are now helping us to piece together.'

I am reassured by his calm and measured tone. I notice how exhausted he looks. 'Have you had dinner yet?'

'I had some food, I think, at about six.'

'Are you hungry? Would you like something to eat?'

'Ruth, Are you going to cook for me? Seriously? What have I done to deserve that?'

I smile like a ten-year-old proudly showing off a new skill. 'I've made you a beef casserole, I believe it's a traditional Chilean meal that's usually served at lunch but I am serving it for dinner, if you'd like to try it.'

'Absolutely, yes, feed me now. I'm starving,' he says, rubbing a hand over his weary face.

I get up off the bed, smoothing down my t-shirt and reaching for my shorts. He watches me.

'What?' I say. 'Do I look a mess? Sorry.'

My hair is piled on my head with a pencil jamming the topknot. It's an old habit of mine which I copied from my … from someone, a long time ago. I quickly pull it loose, and my hair falls free around my shoulders. I smile at him. I know I should make more of an effort to look pretty when he comes in, but there is only one small, cracked mirror in the house, and I don't like looking at a fractured image of myself.

He stands up slowly. 'Oh, you …' he says with a sigh. 'Come, come to me.'

We tumble onto the floor. He strokes my hair, twirling his fingers in my curls. I look at his face, his beautiful face. He looks worn out.

'You're so tired, darling, don't you want to have dinner? I can make you something light,' I say.

'I can wait for food,' he mutters into my ear, enveloping me with his body, his beautiful body. José.

* * * * *

When I go into the kitchen for breakfast, José and Gabriela-Juanita are deep in conversation. They look up as I come in.

'Ruth, today you can come to the workshop if you are free, we will meet a few *arpelleristas,* they can tell you their stories, show you their work' she says.

'Thank you,' I say. 'I would like that very much.

This workshop is yet another gathering that is sheltered by the Catholic Church – both literally and figuratively. It is held in a small backroom in a clean but rudimentary church building that provides spiritual comfort to its local shantytown neighbourhood, a bus ride away from Gabriela-Juanita's house. She introduces me to each of the four women seated around a large square table. They nod and smile but don't break their concentrated focus on the cloth they share in front of them. The cloth is large, and each woman sits at a different corner, working around her task. I am anxious not to intrude, but Gabriela-Juanita beckons me further into the room.

'This is Inéz. Today is the anniversary of her husband's abduction. The police took him from his home and promised that he would return in half an hour. She is still waiting for him to come home. That was fourteen years ago. We have been working on this *arpillera* for many months. Today we are finishing it. We always want to complete an *arpillera* on the anniversary of a kidnapping, a murder, a forced exile. But it is always difficult to finish if it is your anniversary, so we all help each other to finish the work.'

I nod.

'Come, Ruth, please, you are welcome to look,' Inéz says to me.

The tapestry depicts two identical chairs, side by side. A woman stands behind the furthest chair, looking out at its partner, which looms large and empty on the canvas. At the base of the empty chair is a cup, slippers, a pipe and a book. On the wall behind the chairs is a large clock with clearly demarcated numbers, only the number 6 is where the 12 should be, and the 3 is where the 9 should be. The remaining ten digits float around the canvas. The slippers, pipe, cup and book are made out of a thick red wool. The chairs are made from a rough hessian with purple wool cushions. The numbers are made from a thick silver material that gives them a liquid instability. The woman is in pale-brown cloth with steel-grey wool for hair.

Inéz is part way through completing her embroidery of a note, turning it from ink into thread, which she then slips into a pocket on the back of the canvas. The note reads, *Until you return, time remains broken. But I will never stop waiting for you. Your tea is hot, my dear.*

I look at Inéz. Her face is deeply lined, her house dress straining to close around her spread of breast, waist and hips. Her lips are full and plump, almost girlish, and her eyes smile shyly at me. She must have once been pretty and young and voluptuous; now she is a shapeless, grieving, older woman.

'Thank you for showing me' I say. 'Thank you, Inéz.' I touch my heart and blink quickly to hold on to my tears.

'We are working to complete ten different *arpilleras*. They are to go to America. The church has arranged an exhibition and then the sale of them. This is very important work for us, for the money and for the stories that we are sharing. Please, come and look,' says Gabriela-Juanita and points to a heap of folded cloth on the floor.

Inéz helps her to open up each *arpillera*. Some are bleak in colour, others more dramatic. There are many images of fallen and uprooted trees, shattered houses, crushed flowers and female figures with open arms or clasped hands, or holding hands with other female figures. If there is a dominant figure it is female, usually with a tear falling down her cheek. There are empty places at tables. Each *arpillera* depicts a broken world, a fallen family, a life torn apart. Each artwork has a universal quality of suffering and endurance. I am shocked by the stark imagery that leaves nothing to the imagination.

'I am Valentina. Please, can I tell you about our materials that we are using,' says a matronly woman seated next to Inéz.

She picks up various materials from the table and explains her work. 'The brown, it is from my son's bed blanket. I like to use it when I am creating a male figure. The blue that is in the sky, we always use that material for sky. It is from the work trousers that our sons and brothers and husbands wear. It is the cloth of the worker. Even behind the clouds, somewhere it is blue over Chile, and that is where our *desaparecidos* are, waiting for us to find them. If we need a rich colour, like purple or pink or red, we use materials from our missing women, from their dresses, their hair ribbons, their nightwear. We are happy to share. This is how we are keeping them alive, in every *arpillera*.'

'Thank you,' I say again, touching my heart, again.

I remember someone once tearing their clothing at a funeral. I try to keep my focus on this room and these women. I don't want to remember my grandmother and Rabbi Levinson tearing her garment before my Papa Ziggy is buried, in keeping with the ancient Jewish mourning ritual.

With these Chilean women I am in the presence of collective mourning, collective memorial. My tears add to and mingle with the pool. The women are unperturbed. They fall silent now and continue their work. I sit and watch the needles fly in and out of the cloth, creating, assembling, completing, recreating. They work harmoniously and instinctively together.

'Can you sew, Ruth? Did your Mama teach you to sew?' Gabriela-Juanita asks me. It is a perfectly innocent and understandable question.

'No,' I say.

Mama, what did you teach me? Disappointment and envy? Laughter? Love? I know I never saw you sewing.

'No,' I say more forcefully. 'I could never sew, my eye, it is difficult for me.' I feel awkward with embarrassment. I never draw attention to my lack of sight.

'We need to sew the edges of these *arpilleras*. Gloria is ill today and we need an extra hand. I will show you how,' Gabriela-Juanita says, overlooking my explanation.

'I can't. I really can't even thread a needle let alone sew in a straight line.'

She busies in her bag and to my astonishment pulls out a magnifying glass. 'No one here has good eyes. We have all seen too much, but this glass, it helps you to see exactly what you need, and your fingers, I can teach your fingers. Come, give me your hand.'

I obey like a little girl at my grandmother's lap. I am unable to resist the pull of this collective resistance, this bond of solidarity with sorrow.

It is physically difficult for me, but Gabriela-Juanita is either very patient or simply determined and undeterred by time. My hands are sweaty and the needle slips and slides in my grip, but suddenly I manage to thread the cotton through the eye of the needle.

'Yes,' she says. 'This is a good beginning. Now I will show you the cross-stitch.'

The women gossip, drink coffee, and occasionally get up to stretch their legs. A break is decided upon, and the cloths are folded away while bread and jam, bread and tomato salad, bread and a sweet brown spread called *manjar*, and *empanades*, always *empanades*, are shared out.

'Ruth, I am going to visit another workshop in another town. Do you want to come with me or stay here?' Gabriela-Juanita asks.

I look at the pile of *arpilleras* at my feet, awaiting my amateur cross-stitch. 'I can stay if you think that's helpful.'

I really don't want to leave.

She pats my shoulder and hurries off.

I continue to sew, the magnifying glass next to me, helping me to see no more and no less than I need to.

The serene atmosphere belies the intense trauma behind this organised and empowering art. I have never before thought to create a monument, a memorial out of my grief. I have spent so many years preoccupied with trying to forget in order to live, and this has made living so very difficult for me. If I had been able to live with my memories instead of trying to obliterate them, then might I have had an easier time with myself? Would I be a more normal person?

I had not expected to find myself cross-stitching someone else's sorrows. I sew with red cotton, red the colour of blood, red the colour of the African sunset. I work until it is dark. I work until the other women remind me that it is time for us to go our separate ways, to go to our homes.

Valentina and Inéz insist on seeing me onto the bus, which is just as well, as I have lost track of who I am. I know I am not Chilean, I know I am not British. I can hardly call myself South African. It is enough effort to simply be Ruth.

José is waiting for me by the bus stop when I disembark. '*Querida*, hello my sweetheart,' he says.

That is who I am. I am his sweetheart.

'*Querida*, I was worried about you, it's so late. I can't believe you've been sewing all day. This is not good to be sewing so much sadness. Tomorrow night we must go dancing. I want to see you laugh and sway those sexy hips,' he says.

That is also who I am. I am his *querida*. But I feel my balance has shifted. I wake up several times during the night. I am restless and uneasy. José, securely cocooned in the soft world of our warm bodies and sleep, pulls me close. My dreams are a jumbled disturbance of near and far, of what is here and what is there. I hear childish laughter and the sound of my name being called over and over.

'Yes, I'm here, I'm over here,' I mutter, thick with sleep. 'I'm here.'

I open my eyes, and my brothers fade away from me. Of course they do: Jon- Jon and Mikey are somewhere over there, somewhere, dead, and I am here, alive, wrapped in José's embrace, stuck with my unspeakable, inexplicable, losses and memories.

'Sleep, darling, be still. Lie here with me. We will dream together,' he whispers.

I sigh. I lie still. If only sleep was as simple as closing my eyes. If only I could choose my dreams.

* * * * *

In the pale morning light I am exhausted and edgy. I am aware of José watching me.

'Ruth, *querida*, darling, do you have many meetings today? You should cancel them. I think perhaps you are beginning a flu? You don't look so well.'

'I feel very tired.'

'You have been working too hard. Do you have a bad throat? A headache?'

'No, nothing like that, I'm just tired.'

'You should stay here then, sleep, drink lots of water with ginger and lemon, and maybe have some of Mama's soup. I'll cancel your meetings for you.'

'Thank you. I don't think I'll be of any help to anyone today, but I'd like to go with Gabriela-Juanita this morning.'

'Today? To the Friday demonstration?'

'Yes, I would really like to go with her. I want to see the women, I want to see them dance. I can sleep later, when we get back. I have heard so much about La Cueca Sola but I haven't seen it. I need to. Know it is important to Gabriela-Juanita, to the women I meet and work with. I think it is time for me to watch, to see …' My voice tails off.

'Ruth, my darling, you are always so good at knowing what is the right thing for you to be doing. You should trust yourself,' he says.

José. José. I am my own worst advisor. I have no idea whether it is a good idea for me to be part of a group of women dancing in public with photographs of their missing, their dead. Their dead and mine are becoming intertwined. I feel compelled to go to the dance.

'Would it be okay if I came with you, to the plaza?' I ask Gabriela-Juanita at breakfast.

'To watch La Cueca Sola?'

'I … Would it be … Can I … Could I come with you, please?' I say again.

'You can come with me, yes,' she says. 'Of course you can.'

'Thank you. What should I wear? Do I need to wear a skirt? Are black jeans okay? Do I …'

'Ruth, do you want to dance with us? Is this what you are asking me?'

'I don't know,' I answer truthfully.

'Please. Come with me. Come and watch. Come and stand with us. Come and dance with us, if this is what you want.'

'Thank you, thank you,' I say.

I ready myself as quickly as I can, swallow my bitter coffee in one gulp and kiss José goodbye. He absent-mindedly strokes my hair.

Gabriela-Juanita's many years of this Friday-morning routine do not dilute her sombre mood. I'm sure it can't be easy to demonstrate the intimacy of loss in public, but perhaps the alternative – cowed submission – is even more intolerable.

When we arrive at the large plaza there is already a gathering of about twenty middle-aged women dressed in black skirts and white shirts. I feel self-conscious and out of place amongst these Chilean mothers, sisters, daughters and wives. I don't belong here. But Valentina and Inéz welcome me, and Gabriela-Juanita introduces me to her comrades. I nod and smile at them and slip in amongst their ranks. There is a whirr of activity as the women help each other to pin their photographs onto their shirts. I try my best to put safety pins to photographs, but my anxious hands won't do what I ask of them.

Now we stand three rows deep and we are silent, apart from my hammering heart. A single woman steps forward from the crowd and leads us by clapping her hands slowly and rhythmically. We stand in black and white, alone and yet together, our individual hands clapping to one beat.

The woman moves forwards, and begins to dance with dainty, demure steps. She holds her white handkerchief high in the air and moves rhythmically with our clapping, her steel-grey curls bouncing defiantly. I have never seen an elderly woman dance alone before.

Mommy loves to dance, and to dance with me. My chubby arms and sticky fingers clutch at her dark hair as it swings around and over me, our faces pressed to each other. Her spicy smell and her laughter spill out and over me as we sway and turn, her soft and welcoming body enveloping me in a world that is only for us two. She throws me high and spins me fast and never drops me, not once. I love dancing with my mother.

The silver-haired woman dances with concentrated determination. She calls out in a clear and slow voice: '*Luis, Luis, dónde está? Dónde está, Luis?*' There is no joy to her face. Her eyes are flat and sad as she dances this traditional courtship dance for two, by herself.

We continue to clap and now passers-by stop and join in the clapping. After several minutes a second woman takes up the dance, alongside but not with the first woman. She travels her own delicate journey, dancing with her photograph of her beloved missing. '*Augusto, Augusto, dónde está? Dónde está, Augusto?*' she says loudly.

A third woman is now dancing. It is Gabriela-Juanita dancing with José's father. Her eyes too are dulled, her face drawn in effort and tension as she dances her heavy steps on light feet. '*Héctor, Héctor, dónde está? Dónde está, Héctor?*' she calls out. How weary she sounds.

I am now thrust out behind her and it is my turn to dance, also with José's father pinned to my breast pocket. I am apprehensive with the responsibility of wearing this precious photo. I dare not falter or the woman behind me will trip and I will be responsible for holding up the proceedings. My steps are clumsy and hesitant. It is confusing to dance without joy, I don't know how to move without swaying my hips. I prefer to whirl around like a dervish and loose myself in pagan rhythm.

A deep pain washes over me, a grief that pushes through my well-armoured self until I think I might burst with longing and sorrow. What am I doing here? Why am I dancing among bereaved and grieving Chilean women? Now we have swelled to forty women dancing together, dancing alone.

Mommy loves to dance, and to dance with me. My chubby arms and sticky fingers clutch at her dark hair as it swings around and over me, our faces pressed to each other. Her spicy smell and her laughter spill out and over me as we sway and turn, her soft and welcoming body enveloping me in a world that is only for us two. She throws me high and spins me fast and never drops me, not once. I love dancing with my mother.

I'm really thirsty. I need to sit down. It is hot. It is cold. I can't see Gabriela-Juanita.

'Gabriela, Gabriela, Gabriela?' I call out.

I don't want to embarrass her or draw attention to myself and away from the demonstration. But I don't feel well. Perhaps the wind changes direction. I know that I do, without choice, without awareness.

My brother Mikey is round and plump.

I need to unpin this photo from my shirt. I need to get it away from me.

My brother Jon-Jon has brown tousled hair .

Everyone is busy with their photos and their dancing, and now there is the sound of people singing. I can't discard the photo, I can't abandon this poor, missing man to a second fate of being trampled on, ignored and overlooked. I'm really hot.

Mommy, so pretty and soft.

I tremble uncontrollably and my legs start to buckle. My blood pounds in my head.

My chest constricts.

'Dancing eyes,' Mommy says, 'You have your father's dancing eyes, my girl. Better make sure they don't land you in trouble like they did your father.'

I start to cry, silently at first. The women nod around me.

Dónde están? Dónde están?

The women are familiar with tears. But not these tears, not mine.

Mommy looks beautiful. She wraps African beads in her hair. She wears multi-coloured bracelets … dangling earrings … swirling skirt …

'Gabriela-Juanita,' I say. 'Gabriela, please … please help …. help me.'

My brother….Mikey… my brother.

I think people are staring at me. I wish they'd all stop staring.

'Leave me alone. Leave me, I want … I want to go home …'

Jon-Jon has brown … Jon-Jon has hair … Jon-Jon.

Who are these people? What am I doing here?

Who did this, Daddy?

Huge heaving sobs rush up out of my body and out through my mouth.

Mommy loves to dance, and to dance with me. My chubby arms and sticky fingers clutch at her dark hair as it swings around and over me, our faces pressed to each other. Her spicy smell and her laughter spill out and over me as we sway and turn, her soft and welcoming body enveloping me in a world that is only for us two. She throws me high and spins me fast and never drops me, not once. I love dancing with my mother. I love my mother. Mommy. I love my Mommy. Mom. Mama.

Something is happening to me. What is happening to me? Why can nobody understand what I am telling them? My mouth won't work properly. What is happening to me?

'Jon-Jon, Jon-Jon, Jon-Jon … Mikey, Mikey, Mikey …' I cry.

And then, finally, 'Mommy, Mommy, Mommy, Mommy, Mommy …'

There is the terrible sound of a woman screaming hysterically. She is screaming in English. She is whirring like a dervish, abandoning herself to her suffering. She sounds demented. Poor soul.

Gabriela-Juanita and Valentina get me home and into bed. There is a doctor who I don't understand and tranquilisers that I swallow without question. I sleep without dreaming.

When I wake up, a familiar silver-haired woman is sitting beside my bed. She strokes my hair and murmurs to me. She looks at me, not letting me out of her mother's watchful gaze. But she is only a kindly stranger who I don't know, and I am lost in a foreign land. How have I ended up here? And who is this man who is intent on holding me to his strong and hairy body? I have no idea what to do with this man. I have no idea what he wants from me. He smells so familiar but I can't say that

I know him, or at least that I know myself with him. I am completely undone and I can't do myself up again.

* * * * *

José flies me back to London and Janice meets us off the plane. She drives us immediately to London's foremost private mental-health clinic where a medical team are waiting. They diagnose extreme emotional exhaustion and acute post-traumatic stress disorder. My admittance is a blur that does not involve me. I turn my back on José and Janice, and follow the friendly nurse who leads me into my room. I am relieved to see the crisp white sheets on the bed. My nurse helps me undress. I lie down on my bed. I close my eyes.

'Let's count backwards from ten. Ruth, please do it with me now,' she says. How does she know my name? Why are we counting? Why am I agreeing? 'Ten, nine, eight, seven …'

I am slowly falling through the bed in a thickening fog of sleep. It must have been the cocktail of tranquilisers that someone somewhere … I don't remember anything other than sleeping.

I dream in red, a dark-brown red, a gushing fountain of treacle red that oozes and trickles and coagulates into a matted, scaling crust. Blood, I dream blood.

I refuse to see José, and my psychiatrist advises him to go back to Chile and return a few weeks later in the hope that I will be more able to tolerate him. José is distraught. He doesn't understand – how could he? I can't explain – how can I? Jon- Jon, Mikey, Mommy. *Dónde están? Dónde están?* I have no space for José. I see that now. It's different with Janice, Shirley, Neill. They are my comfortable, bland family. But I can't play happily ever after with José. I don't believe in happy endings.

CHAPTER 18

Blood, it's never as red as you think it might be, more a brackish brown. A smeary trail of the stuff oozes across the floor, signposting where the murderer is lurking, phone cradled in her lap. It is me. I am sitting, trembling in my father's pooling blood. I think I've killed him.

There's so much adrenaline coursing through my body I think I could take on the full fifteen kilometres of Victoria Drive and then straight up Kloof Nek Road without stopping once for a breath. Oh, what a fantastic run that would be, a once-in-a-lifetime achievement. I could do it with Liz, and then afterwards we could sit in the sand, drinking icy chardonnay and eating juicy peaches. Beautiful. Blissful. And I could leave him lying there in his own blood.

I need to talk to Liz. I phone her a second time. This time it's Nomusa at the front desk. Where's William? Is it shift change already? Why can't I think straight? 'Nomusa, This is Ruth. Ruth Newman. Please put me through to Liz van der Westhuizen.'

'Hi, Ruth, what time are you in?'

'Can you put me through to Liz, if she's in, if she's there?'

'It's complete chaos here today.'

'Yes, well … I think …'

'When are you coming in? What time can I tell people you are here?'

'….Well … I'm on leave for a few weeks now, a couple of weeks.'

'Really? A few weeks. You lucky bugger. Are you off to the beach or something? I wish it was me, man, I've been here for hours. I've had enough. I also want to go playing, *ja*, you lucky bugger. Hey, it'll be manic here by the time you get back.'

'Nomusa, please, put me through to Liz, I need her, I need to speak to her, now.'

'Okay, Okay. Keep your hair on, man. Jesus. Some people don't know how lucky they are. You're through. Enjoy.'

'You have reached Liz van der Westhuizen. I am afraid I am unable to take your call right now. Please leave me a message after the beep.'

'Liz, it's me again, it's Ruth,' I pause, my voice wobbling. 'Lizzie, I'm in a little bit of trouble. Actually a fuck of a lot of trouble,' I say, but she doesn't pick up the phone. She doesn't pick up the phone.

'Liz, Lizzie, please can you come and get me when you hear this message,' someone says in a breathless and panicky voice. I say, in my breathless, panicky voice. It's me. I'm beginning to panic.

'I'm at Ivor's house, my father's house. Ivor, he … Ivor, my father …' I struggle. 'His address is 98 Lillian Avenue, just past the fishery in Hout Bay. I'm with Ivor because … It's a long story, only now it's over, the story's over.'

I speed up, talking in a garbled rush to get the words out so that she will know where to go and what to do to fix this mess, to fix me. Liz, you always know what to do.

'If, when you get here, I'm not … well … I'm writing a letter. I'm writing a letter. It's not for you but you can read it, if you like. I'd like you to read it, really. I want you to. I think you should. I'm writing it now and if when you get here I'm asleep or something, the letter will be next to me, unsealed. I'm afraid that for one reason or another I'm not able to post it right now, so please, could you do it for me? I'm not quite myself right at this moment. I don't think I'll be up to that myself.

'Liz, there's so much blood. I didn't think there would be so much blood. I don't like it. I really don't like it. Please, come and get me. Liz. Something's happened. Something not good has happened. I really need you.'

I hang up. I want to call a third time, to listen to her once more, to let the familiarity of her voice wash over me in a soothing embrace. But I can't bear to hear her recorded voice. She's not there. I think I said something about blood in the message. That's probably not a good thing to do, but Liz will know what to do, she always knows what to do. Liz, please come and get me.

On the 29th October 1976 love was stolen from me. The most basic, the most taken-for-granted kind of love. And in my immediate, very first moments of searing pain and blinding terror, I was forced to confront what my family was and wasn't, who my father was, and wasn't. My body chose to cling on to life, but part of me died on the day that I learned I should not have taken love for granted, that I could never again take love, nor give it. But love came and took me. I wasn't expecting it, I wasn't looking for it. I didn't want it.

Darling, beloved José, whom I loved from the moment I met him. I entrust him to you, Liz, because I trust you with all that I am, more than I trust myself. So please Liz, send him this letter. This is what I need to tell you Liz. This is what I need you to do for me. Please.

Chapter 19

José

Querido, amado, mi amor.

Here I am.

I'm sitting at my father's dining-room table. And I am writing to you. I always seem to be writing to you – it is true that most of the letters are in my head and the rare few that make it to paper are quickly ripped up. But this letter is different because I am committing myself to every word that I am writing.

I am sitting at my father's dining-room table, in his home in my beloved Africa. And my father, yes he is here as well, although I am not sure for how much longer on account of the immense quantity of blood that has left his body.

José, I need to tell you a few things, only it's difficult to know where to begin.

Perhaps it is best to start with my surroundings.

I could describe the intensity of southern-hemisphere light as it pours in through the windows and the way in which it bathes everything in its wake with clarity and strength of purpose, even a nearly-dead person.

I could describe the charm of my father's whitewashed cottage with its green corrugated-iron roof, so typical of this middle-class suburb. I could detail how beautiful the bougainvillea look as they trail the outside walls with flaming oranges and hot pinks. It is these walls and this roof that separate the inside from the outside, the public from the private, the acceptable from the unspeakable.

And then I could distract both of us with poetic descriptions of the sparkling blue sea at the front, and describe to you how all this beauty falls under the only sky worthy of the name Heaven – the vast, bountiful and brutal sky that is Africa, nature in all her contradictions.

Even with the best of intentions I could not manage to cut myself off from the land of my birth, my home. Perhaps it is fitting that finally I am writing to you from here, for I so nearly found myself at home in your eyes, your arms, and your immense, enveloping, generous love.

José, I tried to be with you, with all that was available of my heart. I discovered that I was unable.

But let us not waste time on what was not possible, not when so much time has been already wasted. I know you will forgive me for being bold, but please could you stop everything else that you are doing in order to attend to this letter. Tell your beautiful wife you will be with her soon, tell your exquisite babies that you are hurrying as fast as you can and that soon you will be with them to read their favourite stories.

Is it presumptuous of me to assume a wife and children? Of course not – I know how loving you are and that love surrounds you, as you so deserve. But right now, for a very little while in such a long time, I need you and your attention. You see, I haven't got a photo to send you, and this communication would be so much easier if we were face to face, so please pick up your pencil, find your paper. I won't accept your protestations that it has been several years since you've drawn. I have not forgotten that your need to create accompanies you wherever you go, so mi amor, *for me, just for me, please create me. Let me form from the loving caress of your pencil on the paper. Let my image emerge from your mind's eye and spill out onto the page so you can look at me. I know it's been a while since we've done this, you and me. A quick note on technicalities – I don't think I can hold a pose for very long as I can't seem to stop shaking. But I will make it easy for you. I will describe myself in the greatest of detail and you need only draw whatever grabs your fancy.*

And so, in no particular order, this is what I look like:

My eye, perhaps now for the first time in nearly twenty years, my eye no longer looks haunted. I know what I am looking at, I do not fear any tales of the unexpected, for me there are no more unexpecteds.

My hair – it is the same long, dark curls, my darling. But, I'm not so sure you would want to wrap my hair around your fingers or bury you face into it, on account of it being tangled from – well I guess there is no delicate way of saying this – on account of it being tangled from the blood and gore that splatters from a stab wound. I think this is what happens when you pull the knife out of the body, something to do with a mixture of gas and air and a vacuum.

My lips – yes they are as full and ready for you as ever. I know this is possible only in my innermost thoughts, for even if you were here in front of me right now, I would not inflict my hunger and need on either of us. I love you too much to destroy you in this way. I know, I know, mi bello. *It is okay to cry – look, I'm doing it as well. I love you as much now as I ever did, and more, far more than I ever thought possible.*

I pray with all my heart that you are loved by someone, and that you have had the sons and daughters we were meant to have, even if it was with someone else. I truly hope so. You deserve to be happy. I have never stopped loving you.

We both know that we will never see each other again. But my journey is about making peace with my past, and there is so much that I owe you, that I can never repay. This letter is the most complete way in which I can offer myself to you so that you can put us to bed. Oh how lovely that would be if we could once more bed each other, but then once more would never be enough. I can even now feel the heat flickering up my thighs and my heart quickening. Forgive me if I embarrass you. Forgive me if I make your beautiful wife jealous of what we once had.

Jealousy. This is what made me so wretched. I was sick with a jealousy, consumed with a jealousy and envy that was unbearable for me. Not of you, my darling, not of you and another. I had too much, more than enough love and reassurance from you to ever doubt your single-minded commitment to me. But I was consumed with jealousy nonetheless, jealousy for how you mourned, for how you remembered. And it was not just a jealousy when I was with you, but also when I was with your mother, your aunties, your community, but especially when I was with the women.

And remember, querido, *if any of this is making you feel anxious then look deep into the face that you have drawn, look at me and remember how much you are loved.*

You see, José, what I am trying to tell you is that I too suffer from not knowing enough about what happened to the missing. Not your missing, not Chile's or Argentina's or Paraguay's, and before you get all political on me, this is not about South Africans either, at least not in the collective political sense, although it is about a South African family that went missing. It is about my missing. Some of us were buried under the ground and some of us, like me, were buried under the weight of grief. José, while I have tried desperately to live as freely as I can, I can never, have never, taken a single clean breath that is free of this weighty despair over those who are missing.

Your missing were revered and honoured, mourned and grieved over, both publicly and privately. I was so alone with my pain. There were days when my jealousy rose as choking bitter bile in my throat, threatening to prevent me from life itself. I was so jealous of your mothers-of-the-disappeared with their status and purpose, their identity and community. They had enemies and supporters. How I too longed to be recognised as an official mourner-of-the-disappeared in black dress and white scarf, with my free-flowing tears, with my photographs. How I longed to have the power of a cause behind me, instead of just myself. And, in my efforts to reinvent myself, I was utterly unable to tell you, or anyone else, of any of my anguish.

How could I have told you that I was suffering from a festering, illegitimate loss without a cause to substantiate it? I was trying so desperately to learn dignity from a community that had learned to suffer its missing. I was trying to learn how to be a legitimately mourning person for myself, when you thought that I was being compassionate and empathic for your losses. And for this cannibalistic voyeurism I am so deeply sorry.

I can feel your stunned silence filling my head like a thickening mist. I can sense how your mind is racing back to all that we were and all that we did to try and match what you thought you knew about me with what I am telling you of me now. I know, I know, there does not seem to be a fit. It's as if I am insane. I'm not, mi bella. *I am probably the sanest person you know, although the question of my sanity has come up in my own mind. But that of course is different. After all, don't we all question our sanity from time to time?*

José, José, José.
I love you.
José.

CHAPTER 20

Forget it.

Obviously I can't send this letter to him. It's too heavy, too intense. I think it needs to be more low-key.

Oh, what I would give right now to sit with Liz in her mother's kitchen, drinking milky, sweet coffee and stuffing my face full of crunchy rusks while we dissect every bit of the letter until we are done. Only this is not possible, of course. There is no dissecting to be done, and it is not possible to send this letter to anyone, especially José, and it is not possible to track him down. He is dead. He died in a motorcycle accident in Santiago de Chile, on 14th December 1993.

There were those who thought his death suspect on account of the circumstances of the deaths of his father, uncles, brothers, his sister, a brother-in-law, fifteen and twenty years before, on account of José's history as a human-rights activist, on account of his courage to speak out on what was so often unspeakable, and to keep searching for what was missing.

As for me, I didn't find his death suspect in the least. How could I when my experience has taught me that Death is a spiteful and malevolent enemy who freely takes whomever I love. The sentiment 'till death do us part' is a chilling reminder that relationships can only offer fleeting comfort and distraction, for death always parts, always comes between. I can't be doing with any thoughts of the after-life when there's too much struggling with the here-and-now life that needs to be lived. So if José had lived I would have found it suspicious. I would have continued to brace myself for the day when I would hear about his death, and force myself to bite back the words 'yes, of course he is'. Love always dies, mine does anyway. And that's not my anxiety speaking, that's my actual experience.

José is dead, and even though he has been dead – to me – for some time, the possibility of some other life, where he might track me down and force his way into my life, is my secret, cherished fantasy. José is dead. He died some time ago. José is dead. He died some time ago. José is dead. He died some time ago. Dead and died dead and died dead and died. If you say the words quickly enough they become devoid of meaning. I have, often. Still do.

José is dead. He died some time ago. This is often my waking thought. I will never stop regretting that he is no longer somewhere in the world with me. Mommy, Jon-Jon, Mikey, José. I carry them all in my heart, my overburdened heart.

CHAPTER 21

I remain in my exclusive, reclusive hospital for five months. José returns to London several times, but I continue to refuse to see him. I can't see him. I don't have the capacity.

Group therapy, individual therapy, drama therapy, this is how I fill my day. I learn how to live again. I want to work, I want to run, I want to drink tea with Janice and argue with Neill. Now I know my limitations.

José. He writes to me for a while, all love and good will, memories and longing. There is only one phone call. He cries. I remember what I don't say to him, what I can't and won't tell him. I mean, how do you ever talk about something like that? Is it worse to have a betraying father or a betraying fatherland? Both father and fatherland suggest enduring support and some kind of endless and ongoing identity. It's one thing to be obliterated by the state, but by your own father, now that's in a different league altogether.

José. My post-Chile hospital stay teaches me that he was my moment of sweet abandon, a beautiful escape from my reality. Fantasy.

On my release I reinvent myself once more. I choose now to live within the small and self-imposed confines of brief and fleeting relationships so that I can manage my life without any great expectations. I know I can do casual friendship and comradeship and have professional relationships with colleagues. One-night stands are fine with me, so long as I don't have to remember anyone's name or send a birthday card. I focus on my work with rape victims at the Holloway Road Clinic and also at the International Trauma Institute's clinic for refugees and asylum seekers. I discover that to be described as an 'even-keeled presence' is the kind of compliment I strive for. I work hard at it, being even-keeled. I learn to cook extremely well and to change the wheel on my car.

Three years pass.

My phone calls with Liz become more frequent. At first we talk about who is doing what with whom, which allows us our girlish currency. But there is not enough of what I know and who I remember, or feel safe to remember, that can maintain and sustain us in any real sense.

The weighty responsibility of rekindling this relationship seems to come with a more contemporary charge now. She's carried me for years – it is the least I can do. But it isn't easy. She knows me as I once was, which means that she knows the real me, the me that I would have been rather than the me that I have become. It is complicated, I was complicated, I am complicated. When I am not known my bones ache with a longing that only the past can remedy, and in my friendship with Liz, where I have shared history and belonging in my grasp, I am easily overwhelmed and become repulsed by any hint of an intimacy that might threaten to envelope me. I am complicated.

I work hard to entertain Liz with invented love affairs that inexplicably burn themselves out after a few months. It would break her heart to know that my one- night stands are more akin to an evacuation of the bowel than an opening of the heart. She couldn't possibly understand, and I won't account myself.

Liz is bursting with the majesty of the 'new South Africa' as it teeters on the brink of its own history. She is the lead social worker for a non-governmental organisation in Cape Town that focusses on supporting the transition between the old and the new political regimes. I am jealous of her easy identity and envious of her membership of this club. This 'new South Africa' is as tantalising as sticky sweet mangoes and succulent steak, the tastes of home. How have I ended up so dispossessed?

'Our department is going to be supporting the Truth and Reconciliation Commission, the TRC. Ruth, it's going to be an incredible opportunity for me, for all of us,' she says.

I allow her this, her vanity. But I recognise my quick pang of regret for the opportunity for truth and reconciliation that was not possible when I was in Chile, not back then when I stood so close to, so among, so part of, what it meant to be Chilean, and not now, when I am thousands of miles and an insurmountable heartbeat away.

'We're creating a proper place where victims can come to talk about how they've been affected by apartheid, a place where we can hear how they've suffered. It's just amazing,' she says. 'We're making history, Ruth.'

'Mmm,' I say, still remembering Santiago in order to soothe my envy.

'The worst thing about horrors is denial. The people, the victims, they can say what needs to be said, and this national pain that we've carried for so long, well, we can just let it go now. It's going to be beautiful.'

Something of what she has just said penetrates my Chilean daydream; something of what she has just said doesn't sit easily with me.

'Liz, hang on, can you repeat that please?' I say.

'It's going to be beautiful.'

'No not that, the other bit about talking and letting go.'

'*Ja*, that's right. Everyone just talking and listening and forgiving and moving forward, like beautiful flowers growing through the rubble, you know,'

'How Liz? How does that work? Do people just forget about their pain? I don't get it?'

'Come on, Ruth, you know what it means to be a white South African, even after all these years of living somewhere else. We're weighed down by our guilt, by our fears of what might happen because of what has happened, you know, revenge, retaliation. But now, right now, we have something more. We have hope, we have a chance for a really fresh start.'

'How? How do you have a fresh start?'

'Through talking, through the telling of stories. The victims will get to tell their stories, to say whatever it is that they need to say to an impartial hearing. They get to have their experiences recorded for posterity, and the perpetrators can request a hearing to give testimony in exchange for amnesty, to say whatever it is that they did, to face themselves, and we can learn what happened, *ja*, especially to the people who vanished without a trace.'

'The disappeared,' I say, unthinkingly.

'Well, *ja*, you could say that, the disappeared.'

'The disappeared,' I repeat.

I feel my stomach lurch. I have not heard that phrase 'the disappeared' for a very long time, at least a continent ago.

'Liz, do you really know what it is like to have a "disappeared" as part of your life?' I say.

'Well, we both know that I know something about the shock and suffering that comes with loss. You know that's how I feel, although I do accept that it's not the same as having someone disappear and not know what has happened to them, but—'

'Then you can't know what it will be like to have all of this … this … this stuff, this trauma raked up and left to dry in the air,' I interrupt her, unwilling to rescue her.

'What do you mean?'

'Well, think about it, if you had lost someone through some unknown but suspected atrocity, or if you knew that your person had been taken away by armed soldiers or police in the middle of the night, with a promise of a quick return, and then they had never returned, if you knew that they or whatever was left of them was lying somewhere, wouldn't you do anything to hear what had happened to them, to get them back, to get back a part of them to bury, to mourn over?'

'But what's wrong with that? Our focus in South Africa is healing through truth, healing through forgiveness. People are really positive about it here. Not everyone, obviously. There are some instances where people just aren't comfortable with the whole amnesty thing, but on the whole it's a brilliant idea, a great symbol of optimism for a new South Africa, a rebirth.'

'Well, if you're that desperate you'll probably agree to anything to find out something, you'll make a deal with the devil himself.'

'Yes, but—'

'What will happen after you learn about how your person was tortured and killed, and after you learn where their remains are lying, and after you are given permission to dig up and to bury what is only the few remaining bones of a foot. After all that, after you have tried to swallow down the horror, then what?'

'I don't understand.'

'The trauma, it has to go somewhere. Who's going to pick it up?'

'Ruth, come on, we're all keen to move on here. The alternatives aren't so great you know.'

'It's irresponsible to subject people to these horrors without having something in place to prepare them for what they might hear, what they might learn. We do that here at the Trauma Institute all the time. You need to help people prepare for what they might hear about their families, or what might happen to their families when they apply for asylum. We offer one-to-one therapy for before, during and after any legal procedure that triggers their trauma. That's what I do. That's my job. Fuck, don't you think that there is more at stake here than just sitting in a room and hearing someone say "I done it"?'

Sweat is pouring off me. I need to sit down to control the tremor in my legs. Why is it only me who has to do the thinking? Why can't people see that healing is a complex and complicated process that looks great on paper but in reality is often so intangible? Why does forgiveness always need to rear its sanctimonious head?

'Ruth, okay, I'm listening. Please, please calm down.'

'I'm calm, for fuck's sake.'

I feel my eye fill. Damn.

'Ruth, tell me, what will work? What do you think will work? What are you suggesting?'

'Give the victim sufficient counselling in order to prepare for the ordeal. Healing through dialogue, it's great as an idea but it needs huge back-up and an experienced team of clinicians, who will have some idea of what the victims are letting themselves in for. You can't afford to be naïve here, you only get one shot with each and every victim, and then it's over, damage done, and you can inflict further damage if you get it wrong. It's irresponsible to open up Pandora's box without allowing Hope to flutter out. Basic Greek mythology, or don't they teach that in the new South Africa?'

I am ugly and cutting. She is silent.

'Liz, I've said enough. I just don't hear anything about responsibility that's all. We're very focussed on personal responsibility in our clinics. It's my main objective, to be responsible in my practice, in any practice where there is significant work going on with vulnerable and abused people. Although we didn't have much funding, experience or time, in

Chile we were careful with our work. We were determined to put the victims, our clients, first, over and above "the truth". Truth must support the victim; the victim shouldn't have to support the truth. We planned to run the clinics like a therapy session, you know, don't open the client up if you have nowhere to go, and don't leave your client exposed. Keep your client at the centre of your attention at all times.'

Liz says nothing.

'Look, Lizzie, I've got to go …'

'Wait, Ruth, what's this about Chile? I didn't know you worked in Chile. I thought you went backpacking there. '

I hear my heart creak.

'It was a few years back, when you were in Namibia and we were out of contact for about eighteen months.'

'I thought you were in London all that time. How weird. I had no idea.'

'Yes, well, it was no big deal. Anyway it was meant to be a groundbreaking piece of work, but it didn't really take off, it was too early on in their process of change. I was there as an advisor … a consultant … a policy person. I speak some Spanish but because of my work with trauma and terror victims, well … my work was known by a leading activist … I was known, and I knew what needed to be done to facilitate an environment where people might feel able to start to talk about their experiences in order to facilitate a healing – both personal and collective. I think it ran for a while after I left, but I don't really know. I lost touch with the organisation. I got caught up in other projects in London. '

I stop. It occurs to me that I've had too much experience of too many things, and that I can only ever be truly known by myself alone. My relationships can only ever tolerate a fragmented me, even Liz can't ever know me.

'Please, Ruth, carry on,' Liz says.

I fight my desire to shut down. It isn't her fault that she has no idea what Chile is for me.

'I helped to establish a few trauma clinics on very limited funds. We thought about getting funding from a peace institute in the States – there are grants available for all kinds of social action that constitute peace initiatives. If you know how to present yourself, there's money. After the brutalising Pinochet era, well, America was still involved, deeply caught up in the outcome. But there were also peace-building initiatives that strongly disapproved of the American government's involvement and managing of Chilean politics. As you can imagine, these projects would have done anything to get in there, to make amends. They practically throw the money at you if you can prove your objective. Liz … I've got to go now, I have a client in about five minutes,'

'Wait, can you help with this? Can you help me? Please?'

'Me? No. Don't be ridiculous, you know me, I'm just spouting.'

'No you're not. I think you're right, you're absolutely right. Do you still have information or contacts I can talk to about funding?'

'Probably,' I say, turning to look at my ordered filing system. 'Probably have it lying about somewhere,' I continue as I reach for the file marked 'Chile' and start leafing through it. 'Why? What're you thinking of?'

'I'm thinking, you know, like you just said, we can't afford to be naïve here, we only get one shot with each and every victim, and then it's over, damage done, and we can inflict further damage if we get it wrong.'

It is my turn to be silent.

'Ruth?'

'*Ja?*'

'If I get the funding, will you set it up? With your experience and all? Just point me in the direction of the money and I'll do the rest. How long do you think it might take to set up?'

'Maybe three months,' I say, staring at the paperwork detailing the process of applying for funding, and a full list of names and phone numbers. This list holds the golden names of key people I had once spoken to about funding therapy clinics to work with victims of the disappeared in Chile. I was, once, only days away from sending off the application. Once, a very long time ago, in a faraway place where I was yet again someone else.

'How realistic is it, Ruth? What d'you think the chances are?'

'Not bad,' I say, already certain that it would be a coup for the International Trauma Institute to broker such an opportunity. I am due there for a meeting in two hours.

'I suppose I could make a few phone calls for you. I might know someone who knows someone who knows someone,' I say.

'And you, Ruth, what about you?'

'What about me?'

'If we get the money, will you come and run it, or set it up for us, start us off. You could live with us and work with us and be part of the new South Africa?' She is laughing euphorically now. 'Ruth, would you at least think about it? Rent out your home for a little while and come to Cape Town for long enough to make a difference?'

'You mean, like, for twelve months?'

'I mean like a whole year, damn it, yes. Until this TRC business is done,'

I am confused. South Africa. Home. After so many years. How is it that we've just had this conversation?

'Mmm, twelve months? Probably, I think, possibly, yes. I could think about thinking about it,' I say.

'Ruth?'

'Mmm?'

'I can't believe we're having this conversation.'

'Me too. I'll make some calls today.'

I am intent on injecting some even-keeled calm into this unnerving state of affairs.

'Okay,'

'Okay,'

'Bye,'

'Bye, Lizzie.'

Is it possible that I too can feast on sticky-sweet mangoes and succulent steak? Is it possible that I am finally going home?

* * * * *

The money comes through. Enough money to run several clinics for eighteen months, to pay salaries, to pay for findings and outcomes reports with a view to being published, with my name on the front cover of a lovely black-and-white academic journal. How has this happened? Is this what I had intended?

* * * * *

I think about love, a lot. I remember the falling-in-love phase of love, when there is no room for anything else. During my last few weeks in London, in my anxiety to prepare myself for going home, I become like a lovesick, self-absorbed teenager. I think about South Africa constantly. It is difficult to be in London now that I have thought myself back into South Africa, albeit an out-dated fantasy – a South Africa of my past. I need to stay hyper-vigilant for the disaster that will surely open up in front of me, but I can't seem to arm myself. I can only float, high on love's oxytocin.

I pack my bags – it doesn't take much time to sort through bikinis, shorts, sandals – and I am ready. I add a few sweatshirts and jeans, and then a few professional outfits – a silken scarf and soft, swirling skirt. Shit. I'll never be ready at this rate. Nearly forgot my trainers and perhaps one pair of boots. The black ones. The brown ones as well. What about … What if … Maybe I should repack. Maybe I should lock the bag and give someone else the key until it is time to board the plane. Maybe I am losing my mind.

I am disorganised and chaotic. My love affair oscillates between a heady, lustful love and an empty sense of foreboding that lurches in the pit of my stomach, and then rushes back again to full love once more. I fluctuate between euphoria at the idea of returning home, and an overwhelming fear that I will never have a home. Perhaps I am an exile who can never return home, as home exists only in my imagination.

I choose to take myself to Heathrow Airport. I fear that I am on the edge of something untameable, that I will not be the same on my return. I weep uncontrollably in the taxi.

'Hard trip, love?' says my driver I snuffle some reply.

'Your people going to meet you at the other end, are they?' he says.

'Yes.'

'Good girl, that's the ticket. I'll get you to the terminal in good time for a quick cuppa. That'll sort you,'

'Thank you,' I whisper.

Now I am the heroine with a tear-stained face, off to meet my people after a quick cup of tea.

I have no idea who I am. I have no idea what I am doing. I can't even go back home to my house, as it has strangers living in it for the next twelve months. I certainly can't go back to Janice and Neill. This awful thought snaps me out of my dark mood.

I can already taste that tannin on my lips, with a chocolate digestive to dunk.

'Hurry up, driver, I've got a plane to catch,'

'That's the spirit.'

I am now a sturdy 1950s heroine displaying the best of British gumption as I travel off to a brave new world full of adventure and adversity, armed with fortitude, determination and a cup of tea.

I travel on my British passport, although I have taken advantage of South Africa's policy of allowing dual nationality to renew my South African passport at regular intervals. I think my choosing British is something about wanting to slip into South Africa unnoticed – not that anyone is looking for me.

Chapter 22

Dear Mommy,
>Dear Jon-Jon,
>Dear Mikey,
>Love, Ruth.
>My heart is broken. I can't continue like this.
>Dear Mom,
>Dear Jon-Jon,
>Dear Mikey,
>Missing you,
>I am always lost. I have not been Ruthie for the longest time.
>Dear Mom,
>Dear Jon-Jon,
>Dear Mikey,

I loved you. I love you. I can't stand to be alone anymore. Where did you go? Do you miss me? Do you think of me? Do you remember me?
>Why not me?
>Dear Mom,
>Dear Jon-Jon,
>Dear Mikey,
>*Dónde están?*
>Where am I?

Part Three

Chapter 23

'Welcome to Cape Town. Are you here for business or pleasure?' 'Both.'
'Have you been here before?' 'Yes.'
'When was that?'
'Twenty years ago,' I answer, anxious not to seem defensive while I surreptitiously rub my sweating palms on my jeans. Defensive posturing at passport control is never a good move, but my hands are my business.
'Twenty years ago, that's a long, long time ago,' he says.
Twenty years ago this border patrol guard would have been a toddler, and I … I would have been someone else.
'Well, you're in for a really great surprise. It's changed so much, you won't believe it.'
'Thanks.'
'Enjoy your stay.'
'Thanks.'
'Ruth,' he says.
'Yes?' I answer, my anxiety now fully engaged.
'Ruth – it's one of my favourite names. It's my baby daughter's name. A good biblical name for a strong woman, *ja*?' he smiles.
'Yes, *ja*,' I stumble. 'Can I go?'
'Sure, have a great visit. And come back soon to see us again.'
What am I doing?
Somewhere outside this building is Table Mountain and the Indian Ocean and the Atlantic Ocean and the African sky. And Lizzie. I need to hurry, Lizzie is waiting for me.

Any minute now we will see each other. I've been to the toilet. I've checked my hair, my face, my overall outward appearance, better than my worst days, but not as good as I would like to look, whatever that is. Who hasn't wished to be thinner, taller, better groomed? My hair is squashed mawkishly around my head because of the pillow static on the plane. Maybe one day someone will invent a pillow that leaves you looking rested after a night's sleep in the sky.

'Close your eyes, Ruthie, lie back now. Feel that cuddly cloud ready to rock you to dream land,' I remember my father whispering to me.

When I was a little girl I loved to fall asleep imagining I was lying in a soft, white cloud that floated on a black sky twinkling with stars. It wasn't my dream from the outset, it was my father's dream that he used to let me borrow on the nights I couldn't sleep.

'It's dark, Daddy, I'm all alone,' I would mutter, reluctant to go to sleep. 'No, doll, I'm here with you, and you're glittering in the starlight. Ruthie, you look so beautiful, my girl, on your beautiful cloud. Sleep well, my darling girl.'

And I did, not realising that was yet another lie my father told me – I've never slept well on a plane, and now I was about to meet Liz, looking like a dishevelled hag, which is not how I'd ever pictured our reunion.

I stare at myself in the mirror. I could try lipstick. A quick swipe leaves me with a crimson gash across my mouth. I hastily scrub it off. I muss up my hair.

London grunge, edgy and cutting edge. Tired, very tired, and anxious. This is my look. I feel my heartbeat speeding up and again rub my wet palms on my jeans. It will have to do. I will have to do.

I push through the arrivals door and walk a few steps, and then stop. In the moment that I see Liz I forget about my hair. I can't see anything else but Liz. My hand jumps up to wave childishly. I want to control my reactions so I can be warm, loving and friendly, but sophisticated enough not to cry. Liz does not seem to know anything about this unspoken agreement about how we might behave in public. She rushes to me. She throws her arms around me. My veneer is shattered. We hug and hug, laughing at first, and then we are sobbing in each other's arms. It is so good to cry, in the arms of my oldest friend, my only friend. But I am afraid I will drain away like water down a plughole. I pull back and look at Liz's face. I see freckles, and I see where the sun and wind have lain on her face. I see the keeper of my secrets, the witness to my past.

'Ruth, you look fantastic. I never get off a flight looking like that. I love your hair. I look like a farmer next to you.'

'Hey, Lizzie, you look wonderful, so many freckles.'

We hug some more, this time my tears under wraps. We walk and talk, pushing the trolley, looking sideways at each other. I stand on the left. I need to see where I am going.

I have been gone a long time.

Stop, stop, I think. I need to step out of this scene and sit in the nook of an embracing corner with a comforting cup of tea for a few minutes. I want to tiptoe around Liz and myself, to weigh us up, to consider us in the cold light of day. Who are these two women who appear to mean so much to each other that they fall on one another in a huge public display of emotion? It is hard to walk and talk and think and feel, and to stay in the present.

'Hey you, did you hear any of what I just said?'

'I've no idea. Was it worth listening to?'

'You are hilarious. As smart-arsed as the day I met you.'

I am shaking and my teeth are chattering in my head, but Liz is oblivious to my shock and continues to smile and talk as she guides me through the airport. I need to get back on the plane and return to England, I need to go back home. No, not home, I have no home.

'It's good to be home,' I say.

'It's good to have you home,' she says.

'Where's Gorgeous Greg then?' I ask.

Liz laughs, her girlish glee still visible within her womanly exterior. 'He's sitting in the car with Jon-Jon.'

'Okay,' I say.

It is just a name, I tell myself, just a name, to honour a boy who died. I don't own the name. I have no control over what name Liz chooses to call her son, and while I clearly have first option on the names of my deceased family, it is meaningless, seeing as I have no intention of having children of my own. This is what I told Liz eighteen months ago when she asked for permission to name her long-awaited son after my dead brother, Jon-Jon. She and Greg had tried unsuccessfully, over many years, for a child. It was only when they had exhausted all medical interventions and started to think about adoption, that Liz had fallen pregnant. I wonder how she feels when she calls his name.

We push our way through the airport terminal, which buzzes with vibrant colour and fourteen official languages, and other unofficial foreign languages that come with the territory of the arrivals lounge. We step outside into a dazzling sunlight that rushes to greet me with a familiar caress. My foot catches the uneven pavement, and I lurch forwards under a wave of dizziness.

'Ruthie? What's the matter?'

'It's nothing, I'm fine, I'm okay.'

'Do you want some water? Do you want to sit down?'

'No. I'm sure it will pass.'

I hope it will pass.

'Okay. Oh, look, there's Greg and Jon-Jon. Hey, we're over here. I've got her. We're coming,' she shouts, and pushes me in the direction of a burly, bearded blond man standing in front of a battered white jeep.

'*Howzit, howzit*, Ruth,' he shouts back, his thick, beefy legs in rugby-tackle pose.

'Hello, hello,' I wave back, sounding like the queen.

We keep pushing against the other trolleys and travellers and greeters.

Brace, brace, I tell myself as I prepare to crash land. We are nearly at the car and I am about to meet Jon-Jon.

'Hey Ruthie, finally, *ja*. Finally we can go eyeball to eyeball after so many years,' Greg says, and carefully, politely, he kisses my cheek.

'Hello Greg. Yes, finally. It's very good to see you again,' I say.

I am cut-glass vowels and inflections that lend me a formality I don't want. I am awkward and stuffy. He turns to stroke Liz's face.

'Hey babe, are you happy now that you've finally got your Ruth, huh?'

Liz glows at him. Is this what an enduring love looks like? Too bad I will never know. Too bad.

So much bad.

'I thought we'd go out for breakfast, but I can see you're ready to pass out,' says Liz. 'Shame you're so exhausted. Let's take you home instead.'

Home – there is that impossible word again.

'No, breakfast sounds great. I'm starving. Where's the little man?' I ask.

'Here, come. Look, he's asleep, such an angel now he's passed out. *Ja*, but just wait till he wakes up, then you'll see what a bugger he is, *ja*.'

Now both Greg and Liz are glowing, and Liz draws me closer to the car, and through the open car window I see a pink-faced toddler with a shock of white hair, asleep in a car seat.

'Very cute,' I tell them.

I lean in and touch his cheek with the back of my forefinger. He is warm and plump.

'Hey guy,' I whisper into his sleeping ear. 'I'm Ruth, and I'm going to call you Bear.'

I straighten up.

'He's gorgeous. Breakfast now, please,' I say to Liz and Greg.

'The good thing about arriving on a Friday morning is that you now have all weekend to acclimatise,' said Liz. 'I'll take you to the clinic on Monday so that you can meet everyone, but you don't need to begin until the following week.'

'I thought there was a huge pressure to begin sessions immediately?'

'Well, there is a lot on, but I thought that you might want to get used to being here before you plunged in.'

'Thanks, not necessary. I'll be perfect with a weekend of good sleep.'

'I didn't mean sleep. I was thinking more about being back, being here, you know …' Her voice tails off.

'Monday works for me.'

'Oh, okay …'

She sounds hurt. I get that she needs to acclimatise to me. But I don't want space to think. I want to do what I do in order to hold on to myself, and only then, when I am in place, then I will be able think. That's how I function best. But Liz has needs too.

'Thanks Lizzie. I really appreciate you trying to ease me in, but honestly I know myself. I'll be raring to go on Monday, and I don't want to be treated with kid gloves. It's not necessary, you know.'

'Sorry. Didn't mean to impose my stuff on you.'

'No, you haven't, and it's so great to see you, it's great to be here,' I say. I reach for her hand and give it a squeeze. She clutches at mine and beams at me.

'Monday is perfect,' she says.

I should never have come back.

The drive from the airport bypasses the shantytowns and takes us to the suburbs of extreme privilege that glitter with all that money can buy.

Liz and Greg chat away at me and to each other, and I allow myself to drift off.

'Shame, she's really drained, both physically and emotionally, I'm sure,' I hear Liz whisper to Greg.

'I'm awake,' I mutter, now an eight-year-old desperate not to be left out.

'Okay, sleepy head, whatever you say,'

'Whatever ...' I close my eyes. I need to work out what to do with the useless refrain that keeps on repeating in my head: What am I doing here? If only I hadn't said yes, if only I hadn't set Liz up to ask me, if only ...

I wallow in the sunlight. It is lovely, especially now that my teeth have stopped chattering. I undo my buttons.

'Mmm, warm,' I sigh.

'Do you want the air-con on?' Liz asks, alert to my every need.

'No, no. Warm is good.'

If I am going to have regrets, it is better to do so in a golden haze. But I do regret. I regret returning to South Africa, and I've only been here a handful of seconds, minutes, barely an hour. I regret the feelings of rage and terror that threaten to expose my peaceful demeanour. My protective layer is undernourished, insufficient. There is not enough of me to provide adequate coverage. I hadn't realised it, until this moment. I rage inwardly at myself for what I hadn't known, for what was not possible to know until right now. How could I have known that it would feel so difficult to breathe in this sweet air that my brothers, that my mother, my family, had once breathed in.

England is now long ago and far away. With each of the eleven hours that I have travelled overnight I have lost bits of my composure, and of the safety of who I have become, of myself as a survivor. I'm now in my victim guise. I am trapped. I am back in Africa where my father can get to me. I am not safe, and I have brought this on myself. What am I doing here?

Liz fiddles with the radio and the sounds of a *kwela* beat fill the car. My heart leaps, and I remember how my body once loved to dance to this distinctive rhythm. I am a contradiction of pleasure and panic. Perhaps I could live off this African light and music. Maybe I will be destroyed by my dark, ugly feelings. Perhaps this paradox will drive me mad, but I want to give in and let the possibilities of an African heat seduce and penetrate my bony carapace so that I can thaw. I do not want to feel consumed with hatred and self-loathing. Thankfully my head is a sealed container for my overwhelming thoughts and feelings. I can hardly keep up with myself.

'Mmm, so warm,' I sigh again.

My foot taps to the music. I am flooded with pleasure. I am not sure why I am here.

* * * * *

I sleep for fourteen hours.
Bliss.

* * * * *

Wings.

Today is a day for wings, for soaring through the blue stratosphere. Or perhaps, today is a day for getting up and making coffee and smiling at myself in the soft Capetonian summer light. I am here, thank the gods. I am here and I know, if nothing else, that I am still, in spite of it all, alive. Hallelujah. *Nkosi sikelel iAfrika*. God bless Africa. And I too am blessed.

If only I could see this splendour with both eyes, would that do me? Would I be at peace then?

I have come to understand, yes, yes, from years and years of therapy, years – bloody boring they were as well – that my blind spot is my physical expression of my internal loss. I need to be blinded now. My pain is all I have. I need to feel blinded, it is who I am. I need to be back in Africa, it is where I belong.

Chapter 24

The first few nights of my return to South Africa Liz and I stay up talking until the early hours, but she is a mother now and needs her sleep, and I am grateful for her exhaustion. I know my limitations. As much as I long to be completely enveloped by Liz, I also recognise that I can't tolerate being alongside my past without reprieve, and with Liz there is no escape from the past.

The first few mornings of my return to South Africa I start from a deep sleep with my usual sense of dread, bracing myself for the familiar and wearisome damp, grey air. And then, still on the edge of my dreams, I slowly become aware of an exquisite clarity of light and a soft warm air embracing me as I remember what I have forgotten while I was asleep. I have forgotten that I have been breathing in the sea air that floats in from the tip of Africa and that I could, if I wanted to, if I willed it, I could breathe in the air that drifts down from all of the continent of Africa. I could fill my lungs with Africa, just for the pleasure of it. These are moments of joyous expectation and hope. Perhaps it is something to do with the intermingling of sun and air, the sea and mountains, but my broken heart soars with an unfamiliar optimism.

But one week, that is the most I can manage with Liz, Greg and Bear. I know my limitations.

I move into a small cottage a few streets away. Liz protests at the speed of my transition from guest to neighbour, but I have become good at transition through experience. I have a front door again. I can lock people out. I can close myself in. I can hear the sea. It is a beautiful thing. And I am here for work that needs me at my sharpest and most clinical. I cannot afford a sloppy descent with Liz.

We settle into an easy routine that includes and integrates me. Liz and her family give me the best of both worlds – my privacy when I need it, and the familiarity of family when I want it. She is determined to 'be.there.for.me.' She doesn't put a foot wrong, such a generous, wonderful, loving friend. I am anxious not to seem ungrateful.

We take to meeting at 6.30am on Saturdays and Sundays for the pleasure of walking barefoot on the beach. We revert to our childish need to be the first footsteps on the pristine, early-morning, gently warming, powder-fine sand. It is only the lingering pain of our bone-achingly cold feet and ankles caught in the Atlantic Ocean that serves as reminder as to where we have walked long after the sea has washed our footsteps away. Bluebottle jellyfish sprawl at the water's edge, just as numerous as I remember from my childhood.

'Do you remember the summer we all got stung?' Liz says as we stop to stare at a particularly remarkable blue creature, its tentacles an impressive twenty metres.

'No,' I say.

'Come on, of course you do. Don't you remember we kept poking at them with our ice cream sticks, trying to see if we could burst their bubbles?'

'No, I really don't remember that.'

'Oh my God, Ruth. I had nightmares about it for weeks afterwards. I remember its tail lashing out at all of us, we were all so badly stung …'

Her voice trails off. The idea of 'all of us' hangs in the air. It is far more lethal than any jellyfish sting. We have not yet negotiated how to talk about our memories.

We eat out a lot. I'd forgotten Cape Town was so beautiful, that steak could be so good, and beer so bad.

'Icy beer? You've got to be kidding, right?' I hear Neill's English voice splutter in my head. South Africa. England. My worlds are colliding.

'Icy beer? Seriously, Lizzie!' I splutter.

I have become a hybrid. Do any of my parts work in the right way in the right place at the right time? I embrace my mother tongue by way of my pronunciation as I hear my vowels flatten out and my accent take on the guttural South African clip of my first sixteen years of speech. There are moments when I allow myself to succumb to the joy of love and care. But I can't wallow there for long. It makes me nervous.

Greg is familiar in the way that all South African men are familiar to me. But where I have expected only rugby, red, bloody meat, and an indigenous chauvinism from him, he is vegetarian, changes nappies and is a keen cyclist. He too represents the new South Africa. He is calm and quiet, solid and well meaning. I am pleased for Liz. She has a gentle giant to look after her. But I am under pressure to be someone or something for her that no longer fits me. She offers an intensity that I can't match.

The toddler is sweet. Although I can't ever bring myself to call his name. I think that Bear suits him well enough. I laugh with him, read to him, try to captivate him. I think I can do some of this. I can fit in, I can belong.

Liz is a difficult but vital presence for me. Increasingly I have no idea what to do with her, or how to be. I want to pull and push at her. I can indulge in my agoraphobia and huddle down in her guard. She is the witness to my childhood, there is no other witness. It occurs to me, for the first time, that I am as important to her as she is to me, that I am a witness to her childhood, to the time when she was more than just an only child. I am the witness to her by-proxy family, my family. I am witness to her loss, my loss. I am claustrophobic under her suffocating vigilance.

We need time to re-establish and rebecome something new. It has to be something new. I know that, but does she? Sometimes I think that what she most wants is for us to remember how it once was, together, bit by broken bit. Looking backwards is a luxury for her. For me it is the enemy. I know I will never be able to play the game of 'do you remember when?' because of my ongoing effort to will myself to forget what I remember. It is not the same for Liz. She has Bear, and looking backwards is not part of the package of being a parent of a young, demanding toddler. She has replicated herself. She has exceeded herself. I have only myself.

She doesn't react when I withdraw from her, in the same way as she does not react when little Bear growls at her. Lately she has taken to calling him Bear too.

Perhaps it is dawning on her that growing up is hard enough in itself, and that perhaps it is altogether too heavy with the weighty memory of a dead boy whose name cannot be mentioned out loud in terms of himself. Jon-Jon already exists. There is no space for another.

* * * * *

Life moves so fast, sometimes, but seldom in a straight line, even with work. When I am part of a clinical team I feel intolerant of protocol and bureaucracy, and when I work alone I feel unappreciated and cut off. Wherever I am, I long for the other. I bristle at the idea of being accountable to anyone other than myself, but I quickly discover that here, in the new South Africa, I am free to follow myself.

I have no doubt that this is in part due to the hype that Liz has spread about me, my experience, my training, my skill in arranging the international funding for several therapy clinics to support people through the truth-and-reconciliation process. This is also due to the lingering colonial history, where all things British have that slight edge, and in this case it is my British therapeutic training. I do nothing to dispel the myth that I am slightly, somehow, better and more-than, while I model a version of myself who is gracious, understanding and appreciative of what Liz and her social work team can teach me.

Liz and I work in different teams but out of the same non-governmental organisation building. We overlap for the meetings and briefings that I run. I am glad of our separate spaces.

We are a twelve-person team, a mixture of social workers, counsellors and psychotherapists, plus a psychiatrist. There are several official languages between us, but English continues to be the dominant language in the new South Africa.

Truth and reconciliation – such a worthy ideal, such a clear headline. But do any of us know what we intend here? In my role as lead therapist I know what my remit is, I know what my end goal is for my client. I am here to help prepare a person to withstand the consequences of the Truth and Reconciliation Commission they have submitted themselves to. I am here to facilitate an internal tolerance and greater love that goes beyond an ordinary, everyday notion of what it means to be a person. Under the TRC we are all required to be more than ordinary, to do more than simply want answers for intolerable acts. We have a responsibility to facilitate a greater humanity around us, without a drop of blood being spilt. We are here to practise an amalgamation of all the great God-fearing practices under the wider concept of forgiveness. We must learn to tolerate the intolerable in order to forgive the unforgiveable. Our reward will be an internal peace that nurtures an external peace.

Perhaps.

I know I couldn't sit opposite a force of evil that had changed my life forever. I doubt I could accept what feels unacceptable. Still, there's work to be done, and there's learning to be had. I'll take it wherever I find it. It could be a life-changer.

Constance Mshlawawele, my 10.00am Monday morning client, now she is a life-changer, she is my life-changer.

Chapter 25

In the last week of June 1996

To my dear Patience

This month was the anniversary of my Moses being missing now some eight years. Haai, *but he is now so long gone. I have not spoken of this with you before now because we didn't know anything, and I have always been trying not to think of him being missing, but now it is feeling so difficult and I am feeling weak from my loneliness, and so it is time to be writing this to you, to tell you of my pain.*

These eight years have been so hard and dry for me. I have not known what to do in the business of how to find him, or how to ask for him. The police are no good in these matters. In the beginning they tell me they know nothing of any man called Moses Mshlawawele, and then also they tell me that I am a foolish woman and that probably this Moses had good reason to run away from me, and lastly they are telling me I should just leave this Moses in peace and quiet, and stop being a meddlesome old woman. I always am telling them about the night of the blood, but they tell me I am a stupid woman and know nothing of what I am talking about. I am telling them that Moses Mshlawawele has indeed lived a good and fruitful life with sons and daughters to prove he lived as a man, and that he has an employer who needs him but now grows tired of waiting for him to come back and grows tired of helping me with the money, and I am telling them that he has friends and family who need him, and I am telling them that he has me. I need him. And then I am not telling them anything anymore.

And now I am sent a letter from this office of our government to tell me that there is some talking to have about my husband, the man who has not existed for all of these eight years. On the day of the meeting I take the sons of Moses with me, Jeremiah and Nathaniel, to hear whatever there is to hear about their father.

I feel heavy and empty as we climb the grey stone stairs into the building of our government. I sit on a brown wooden chair with a red plastic seat. It has one leg shorter than all the others and it leaves me without my balance. Somebody is giving me a cup of water. My mouth is dry, my throat is thick. I cannot drink even a drop as my mouth would not know what to do with the liquid of life, for I know I am about to learn something about death.

I am glad for the company of Jeremiah and Nathaniel, I am glad for their support and comfort, even though I know that it should be me who is their support and their comfort. But I am no longer able to be strong. It is in this too-hot room with this uncomfortable chair and these uncomfortable government men that I become the weak and broken widow of Moses Mshlawawele. For it is on this day that I learn that I am truly a widow because my husband is no longer a living person, because this government tells me there was a day in the winter of 1988 on which Moses Mshlawawele died by the wrongdoing of politics, by the hands of one black person and two white persons. Our government tells me that there will be a time to learn more, but that for now they need me to be signing a form that says I have heard and I have understood that Moses Mshlawawele is deceased, because of the politics business. It is on this brown wooden chair with its red plastic seat and one short leg that I am turned from a wife into a widow.

I will not be crying in front of these people. They do not know me and I will not allow even one tear to escape from my body. Moses has been taken, and I will not let any more of me to be taken, no, not even a tear from my eye. My sons are silent.

They look at me to see how I am being. I look at them and beg them with my eyes to follow me in my silent ways. I stand. My sons stand.

It is truly as if the spirits of our long-gone mother and our long-gone father now take me by the hand and guide me out of this room and along the corridors and down the stairs in the first steps of my being a widow. I am as unable to walk and talk and think as when I first was born. I am now a dead wife, and I am now needing the strength to be reborn as a widow so that I can continue to be a mother and also a sister, and so that I can continue to be an honourable daughter to our long-gone parents, and so that I can now live my days as an honourable widow to Moses.

Your sister, the new widow Constance

In the first week of January 1997

Dear Patience

Thank you for the apricot jam. It is very good and a special treat in the morning. We are all enjoying of it very much.

As you are knowing, the whole country is now busy with our archbishop's Truth and Reconciliation Commission, and now I am finding that it is also the Truth and Reconciliation Commission for the family of Moses Mshlawawele. We, the family of our husband and father, Moses Mshlawawele, can be choosing to be sitting in the TRC hearing, in the same room as the persons who are saying that they broke his body. We can be hearing what they did and even why they did it. I can then be looking at these persons as they are talking their stories about their beatings and kickings, and other most awful acts. I will be looking at the faces of the murderers of Moses. I will be breathing the same air as the murderers. If they are telling their story of what they did to Moses then they can become free men. I will be a widow, and Moses will be dead and his children will be without a father and these men will be free. I do not know if this is good or this is bad. How can a person be knowing something when they have not been knowing yet what there is to know?

Haai. What am I going to hear? Patience, what did they do to him? How much was the suffering? He was a proud man. No matter what we will hear, we will always be honouring him.

After this business of listening to these persons I am hoping I will know where his body is lying so I can be able to go to that place and to gather up the body of Moses and take him back home to his final resting place alongside his mother and alongside his father and alongside his brothers and sisters and all of his other people. I am waiting to return him to the earth so that he can finally find his way towards our ancestors, and finally he can begin to watch over us.

Your sister, the widow Constance

Second week of June 1997

My dear Patience

I was just now teaching my youngest daughter Thembisa how to make umqombothi *the way that we used to make it when we were younger. In all of our tastings do you remember the headaches and how Mma would be shouting at us so much because of us laughing at everything that was not even funny because of tasting so much?* Haai! *It was a long-time-ago day, a good day, my sister, a simple day that cannot be brought back. But it is making me smile, and I am being careful so that Thembisa does not do so much tasting, as she is still so young and she is needing to have a good head to do her school work. I am wanting Thembisa to have a good life without the business of the drinking. But I want her to know the business of making the* umqombothi, *of course, for the men cannot love a girl who is too green of not knowing. But this Thembisa, she is my sunshine and I am looking after her as strongly as I can be doing.*

Dear Patience. Here is how I am. Some days pass, all of them without colour. My children, all of them are as strong as good trees. Each one finds a way to bend to me and to support me in my pain, while each of them too is struggling to understand that they are now truly fatherless.

One day not so long ago, Jeremiah brings me a big government letter. This letter is inviting me to meet with a woman who is not government and not comrade, for a reason that is to be between her and me, seeing as I am the wife and widow of Moses Mshlawawele. I do not understand this letter. I do not understand the reason of this woman, but this letter explains that she is some in-between person but does not say what she is in between or why I should be needing an in-between.

The letter is telling me I am to talk with her and that it will be good for me to talk. The letter is not telling me what I am to talk with her about. Maybe she is a spying person who thinks that she can catch me out with something that I say that is about Moses. This woman is writing to tell me that we are to be meeting next Monday at 11.30 for one hour that is not really an hour but only fifty minutes and that she will be waiting for me in the building next door to the building that I visited when I learned about my husband, the late Moses Mshlawawele. This letter tells me that I can come to the building with some person of my choosing but that it is best that I meet her by herself so that we can have privacy. I know that I am not liking the sound of this privacy with someone that I have never met and have not asked to meet with.

Talking is not for me. I know what is for me. It is not words that disappear into the air for no reason. You can't touch words, you can't hold words to your body, you can't bury your face in words. And you can't bury your face in a body that is no longer there.

I go to meet with this woman who I do not know, to meet with her for a reason that I do not know.

I feel myself shaking with fear as I allow Jeremiah to lead me towards this building of bad news. He is a good son. He leads me from the front. He holds my hand with the firm and steady grip of his father. He talks to the front-door people in his quiet, steady voice and tells them that we are here, that I am here to meet with the person who needs to meet with me. He tells me that he is not leaving me to be alone, and also, he says, he is also here, with me.

There is a woman on the front desk of the waiting area that we are waiting in. She tells us to take a seat. She tells me that I am expected and that Mrs Newman is coming in a quick minute. Jeremiah squeezes my hand. He is now truly in his father's shoes. While I would prefer for it to be his father in the shoes, I am grateful and relieved that Jeremiah is with me.

Before a very long time a white woman walks up to both of us and tells her name. She tells that she is very pleased to meet with us. She tells that Jeremiah is welcome to join us in our meeting that is for an hour but not really an hour. I see Jeremiah breathe more easily.

The woman takes us to a waiting room. My son and I sit down as one. We will not be separated. He will not leave me here.

'My name is Ruth Newman. I am very pleased to meet with both of you today,' says the woman.

We look at her, we do not say anything back. She knows our names, she knows where I live, she knows why I am here. I am waiting.

'Mrs Mshlawawele, perhaps you do not know why you are here,' she says.

'Yes, madam,' I hear myself answer. Jeremiah squeezes my hand hard. He is trying so hard to help me to lose these words of our oppression, but I have a lifetime of madam and baas, *like you, Patience, and I cannot see myself speaking as Jeremiah speaks.*

'Mrs Mshlawawele, would it be okay if you called me Ruth?' she asks me.

I want to answer 'Yes, madam,' but I know that it will anger Jeremiah. I do not want to shame him. I also know that I cannot shame our long-gone mother and our long-gone father, who would be fearful for me if I forgot to speak in this learned language of our oppression with madam and baas.

'I would like to be blunt,' the woman says. 'If you call me Ruth then

perhaps I can call you Constance.'

I am full of shock that she has decided to talk in a way that we are not agreeing, and I am ashamed and sad for my son that he has to see this. He is so keen for a new South Africa feeling, and so often he is telling me of it, and now, here we are with the truth of how the old South Africa and the new South Africa are not as far apart as is needed.

'I do not work for the government. My role here is to be in between,' she says.

That in-between word again.

'In between what, madam?' I say. Jeremiah stiffens. I feel myself being tired. I thought that I would be disappearing into myself without Jeremiah by my side. But now I am getting squashed by how he needs me to be for the new South Africa when I am full of the struggling with how to be here for myself as the new widow. What does it matter whether I use words of the old or of the new? Words are words, not like a body, which can be hurt and torn and brought to its knees.

I say to her why am I here?

And so she tells me, in too many words, the why-reason that I am here. Her voice is gentle and with softness. Her face is kind, her eyes look wet. And she is also very still, like an impala tensing for the lion. Where is the lion? Why is she so scared of me?

Jeremiah does not yet know that I do not need him. I have only at this moment known it myself. After some quiet and peaceful minutes of no words, I tell Jeremiah that it would be fine if he wanted to wait for me out in the front waiting area as I am choosing now to be here with myself. I tell him this in the language of his birth so that he does not have to be ashamed. I tell him like this so that we can have some privacy from this woman who is interested in my secrets. I am not a woman of secrets though, and perhaps she will be bored of me soon, when I do not have anything for her.

Jeremiah is anxious not to leave me, but he can hear from my words that I am truly preferring to be alone. And with Jeremiah now gone I can notice this woman. She smells of a heavy sadness, and I am thinking why have I been sent a sad woman? It seems to me that she needs some person for herself. And for a little while I am thinking about her sadness and I am thinking about how she is trying to be sitting with me to think about my sadness.

We sit together for an hour that is fifty minutes. I do not understand what I am doing in this room with this woman, and I do not know why I promise her that I will return next week, at the same time, on the same day. She is not paying me any money and I am not paying her any money for this service. We do not even drink tea together, we do not share some bread.

Ruth Newman is thinking that she told me who she is because she told me her name and she told me what her job was, but she did not tell me whose daughter she was or which children she had carried in her womb, or whose body she was loving alongside hers. She did not tell me anything of her father's family or her mother's family, except for her name. She did not explain how it was that she had come by such a name so I cannot know who she is. But I like her name, it is a good and strong name. Perhaps it fits her.

Now I am needing my tea. This letter to you, my sister, is taking so much more time than I was thinking. I am hoping that our father and mother named you well, sister Patience, for I have still more to tell you. Please be waiting for me one minute till the water is good and hot, and I'm going to put in three spoons of white sugar and some milk, as a good and sweet drink will help. Come let us drink tea together. I will wait in my storytelling until your tea is ready and I can hear you take your first sip. Yes, that is better. A good tea is very good, this is what our mother always told us, and this is indeed a true thing.

I want to be telling you of the room of the woman Ruth, the room that we are meeting in. It is square, a very good shape for a room. We are sitting on chairs that are the same. We are sitting with a small table between us. On this table is a box of tissues and a clock that I cannot see. It does not matter as I have my watch if I am needing to know the time. I like to hear the passing of time in this room. It sounds like a tick and a tock, like our father's clock from when we were small girls. It is very comforting to me. The walls are painted white and there is a large, square window to one side of the room with a view of some veldt and an old tree that once was struck by the lightning. I like looking through the window and at the tree. I like looking at the twisted branches of the tree that no longer grows any leaves. I like that this tree is left to be old and useless, offering shade to no one, bearing fruit for no one. Sometimes I have been thinking who was sitting in the shade of this tree and where do they now sit? I am thinking about the fruit that used to fall from this tree and how good it must be tasting. Perhaps some of the people now say 'come let us remember the sweet, sweet taste of those juicy fruits, haai, *you cannot find another tree like this in all of these veldts. Back then the fruit was good but now the fruit is not like it used to be. Now we are needing to go to the supermarket to buy the fruits and this is not so good.'*

The tree is reminding all of us that everything is for changing, nothing is for staying the same, no matter how I am crying or how I am laughing.

I like to confuse myself with these thoughts. It is better than the thoughts that I am trying not to be thinking. I am needing to be very careful also about the woman Ruth, because she is so wanting to know my thoughts, my thoughts, my thoughts. She does not understand that if my thoughts are my thoughts it means that they belong to me and that she cannot be sharing in them. But sometimes when I am with the woman Ruth, I am noticing that I am not feeling so strong in myself and then I am becoming desperate to tell of my thoughts so that they no longer belong to me, because then somehow she finds a way to take my thoughts and turn them into the thoughts that are between her and me.

I am tired now. I am thinking that you are tired also, and the light is now dark. I am posting this letter tonight and I will be thinking tomorrow of it travelling to you. I will write again soon.

Your loving sister, the widow Constance

Third week of September 1997

Dear Patience,

The house is quiet with the sounds of everybody sleeping, except I am not sleeping. Sometimes I am thinking that I will never be a sleeping person again. Moses would be laughing at me so much because of how he was always teasing me for the sleeping. 'You are a cat in the sun,' he always was telling me, and this is true for I have always been liking to stretch out in the sunlight and sleep a sweet sleep and be woken up by a good strong tea and a smiling face. But that can be no more, now that the smiling face of Moses will not be visiting me again, because I am his widow and I cannot be hoping for his return, because there is no returning, and the sun is feeling so cold, like she too has left me. Perhaps she is using all of her energy to warm up the spirit of Moses. Perhaps that is good. He can have her. I will wrap myself in blankets if I know he is warm, somewhere. But sleeping is not belonging to me anymore, not these days.

My dear sister, I am thinking of how to be telling you about the woman

Ruth and me. It is true that still I cannot tell you what the woman Ruth and I are doing together in this sadness room, but at the end of each meeting she is saying to me, 'I hope you will come back next week, Constance, and we can talk together some more,' and I am agreeing and I am not knowing why.

Each time I am thinking that I do not know what we will be talking about in the next week. She looks so full of the sadness that I cannot say no. I do not understand why I am caring about her – the Lord knows I have so many other things to be worried about and people to care for, and she is not one of mine. But every week she is telling me that we are meeting for me. And me, I am so too-busy and also so too-empty that this one-hour-that-is-not-an-hour meeting every week at the same time is some business for me that is a little bit filling me up.

And now, Patience, I am giving you a secret. It is very, very bad, so it is very, very heavy, and I do not want to have it for myself. But please, when you are reading these words now, please be thinking of our cooking with our mother and please be thinking of our laughing and our climbing trees and our whistling and our school-girl secrets and then you will remember and you will not forget that I am your true sister Constance.

For some of these passing weeks I have been knowing that in the middle of my strong, sad feelings there is becoming a new and bad taste. It is the too-bitter taste of wanting something evil that I have not felt in all of my life before. As the date for our listening gets closer and closer, so my needing to know all of what happened to Moses, all of how he was broken and destroyed, fills me like a wild, burning forest fire. I am needing this pain so that I can be knowing that I can take revenge, that I can make a very, very bad punishment back. My revenge feeling is making itself know to my body like a weed slowly destroying a tree with its greedy claws. At first I do not understand what poison I am tasting, but I am becoming filled up with a hard, killing feeling, and I am filled up with such a sour feeling that now I am a person without any free choice and I am wanting to destroy what has been destroying me. This is what I want. This is what I must do.

Yes, Patience, this is who I am now being, a bitter and very sad Christian woman, an African woman, a grieving woman with bad, murderous feelings that I have to try to not feel each time I think of the children of Moses. For if I am letting myself be filled with this need to destroy, and I take a knife and I strike out the stone for a heart that lies beneath the cowardly skin of the persons who destroyed Moses, then I will become Constance the destroyer, and this will destroy the children of Moses. And truthfully, it is fortunate that Moses is not here to see me like this for I would not be able to be his wife because he would no longer be knowing me – but then, if he was here I would not have to be feeling so filled with bad and bitter.

I am telling the woman Ruth, yes I am telling Ruth about this feeling and she is quiet for a long time. I do not care. Now she knows who I really am she will tell me that we cannot meet anymore and I will no longer have to wonder about what we are doing, or whether I am helping her sadness or not. I have enough of my sadness without having to think about her sadness, which has nothing to do with me or my family. Or Moses.

The sound of Ruth's voice is calling me back into the room with her, even though it seems like her voice is coming from beyond the now-dry rivers that lie next to our parents' burial ground.

'Constance, I hear that you feel you have no choice here, yet we both know that you are a free person,' she is telling me.

I say nothing. I am full of a trapped feeling, and she is busy with her words. 'You talk about your feelings as if they do not belong to you, as if you are being ruled by feelings that are not yours. Tell me about this Constance, tell me why you feel you have no choice but to take a heart for a heart?'

I want to throw myself at her and claw out her eye with my long fingers.

Maybe this is why she has only one eye, because she made somebody so angry that he was taking her eye out. I hear that she does not have any knowing or understanding of me, of what has happened to me, or what needs to be done. I turn my back on her, I spit three times to the left to curse her ancestors' spirits. I scrape my right foot on the stone floor to grind her to dust. She watches. She does not disappear. She stays.

'Constance,' she says again, 'I am interested to understand what you really feel. If you feel that you have no choice, then in here with me you are invited to think about choice. We all have choice, particularly in how we think and what we feel. I am wondering how it is that you feel you have no choice but to give in to the power of evil and become evil yourself?'

I stand up. I have to leave. I can no longer allow myself to be staying with myself in here. I am a disgrace to our mother and our father for my wicked thinking. I am shameful and I am evil. I cannot allow this woman to look at me and know me like this. It is too too much. I hear a sobbing and groaning sound. It most surely comes from the very bottom of a person's soul. It is a sound so terrible that I hope never to hear it again as long as I live. It does not seem to come from her but it is only the two of us in the room. I feel my legs weakening as I hear that the sound is coming from me.

'I am here Constance. I am here with you,' she tells me.

'I am ugly, I am dirty,' I say in my voice that is not my voice.

'I hear that you are feeling ugly and that you are feeling murderous and you are feeling desperate. These are your feelings, but these feelings are not who you are. You have a choice. Let's talk about this,' Ruth tells me. And I am staying.

And in ways that I do not know how to share with you, Patience, we, the woman Ruth, Ruth, and myself, we are talking about what we cannot be talking about. We are thinking about what we cannot be thinking about – which is not the same thing as making my wicked thinking an idea of something to do. A person has to know what is thinking and what is doing. Ruth is guiding me with these ideas, and I am knowing that without her I am crumpled and destroyed by myself, but with her words and her thinking, I am now becoming again a human, a little bit of a human, an African woman who is not proud of some of her feelings and thoughts, but who is learning to forgive herself for being only a human being, and not our archbishop, or like the Lord.

We are now getting closer and closer to the date for our listening time in front of the Amnesty Commission. Ruth is telling me that I am needing to be prepared to be hearing the story about Moses Mshlawawele and I am needing to be prepared to be feeling the story. Our archbishop is telling us that we are all the children of God, and for that reason we can never be giving up on any person, even any bad person, because God is not giving up on any one of his children. Our archbishop is telling us that God loves us and that we are being blessed with extraordinary willingness to forgive, and we are all of us having goodness. But in truth I am only a very ordinary woman who is not feeling the willingness to forgive. I am not wanting to do the healing for all the peoples of our beloved South Africa. I cannot do what our archbishop is telling.

I am feeling angry, mostly at our archbishop, and also at Madiba, our president, for giving me the too-big responsibility of bringing peace in place of blood, for the new South Africa. It is the same kind of angry feeling that

I have with my beloved Jeremiah when he is wanting to change my English words.

I do not care for words. What business is it of anyone else what words I am choosing, so long as they are good enough for understanding? I received a Standard 7 pass in English, so I am knowing that this is being acceptable even if I didn't go up to Standard 10, but not even Stanley Lobise with his glasses did the studying of the Standard 10, so I know that my English words are being correct.

I am very, very angry that the peace of the new South Africa is my responsibility when the war of the old South Africa was not. I am wanting one thing and one thing only, to know where I can find the body of Moses so that I can bury him deep in the earth. I think that Ruth has forgotten about this. But I have not, just as I never have been forgetting him for even one day when we did not know where he was.

In truth-telling, I am not being interested in the new or the old South Africa. I am being interested only in the time of when Moses and I were being the two of us with our four children, and our sometimes not enough money and our often laughing and some of crying and trying and yes even fighting, but always of loving of each other and of our family. I think that Ruth cannot understand that. But I do not want to be thinking of her.

It is daylight now. It is time for some good tea and warm porridge, with the last of the apricot jam.

I am always thinking of you my sister. Constance

Second week of October 1997

Dear Patience

Thank you for the new Bible. I am not sure that God will be helping me any better with a new Bible than my old one, and I am not these days so interested in God, because he has left me all alone, but I am enjoying the smell of the new book and I know the words are kind and of love. It is always good to open up a parcel tied with string for it is a sending of love and surprise.

My dear Patience. I want to be telling you about the first day of our listening.

The night before, I am imagining these people who are the destroyers of my life. I already am knowing that I will be listening to the story of what happened, from some three people who are two white men and one black man.

It is taking me so long a time to get ready for this day, and now the morning is here with a clear and cool breeze and a full sun. I am fussing inside myself and outside myself. I am not knowing what to be wearing. I keep losing my watch, and then my purse with my money, and then my keys. Finally Thandi, your oldest niece, is sitting me down with some nice sweet tea and making me eat some of the porridge with sour milk that she has prepared for me. Jeremiah is ready, Nathaniel is ready, Thembisa is ready, every one of the children of Moses is ready. We will go, we will hear, we will be strong.

It is not easy for me to be writing all of this to you, because I am having to think about what I am feeling before I write it down so that I can choose each word so carefully. Ruth is teaching me this careful thinking about how I am feeling. I always was thinking that I did know who I was, but I am less knowing now as I become more knowing of how I feel. Here, with Ruth, I am learning to think only about how I feel, and I am knowing I have never done this before, and my head feels empty and clear, and my heart feels so so so heavy and crushed. Ruth is always pleased to hear how I am feeling. She seems always pleased to hear that I am feeling for myself and not for any of the other people who belong to me. Maybe she knows what she is talking about. But if she is so keen that I am thinking only about myself then I do not understand this too-big responsibility to be part of forgiving for the new South Africa. So maybe Ruth, she does not know everything, even if she knows my secrets.

I always was thinking that I was a knowing person of what was right and what was wrong, and who was good and who was evil. I did not know of mixing it all up inside one person so that when I am walking into the Amnesty hearing I am going to be knowing of my own evil and that I will then have to also be thinking that murderers also have their own good, for I am also a murderer if I choose it. I did not know this about myself, or about any other persons before now. Sometimes knowing this makes it another reason that it is very difficult for me to sleep at night. When the morning light arrives my children are being worried about my not sleeping, and my struggles, which are on my face. I see that they are talking many times about me when they are thinking that I am not noticing. I feel troubled that I am worrying them, but what can I do? Perhaps it is time to think about some sleeping muti *from the* sangoma.

Poor Jeremiah, he is struggling and suspicious. He is wanting the new South Africa to be all good, and he too is finding the losing of his father too too much, and now we are going to the listening to hear how it is that Moses is come to be lost.

Although Ruth and I have talked about how this day is going to be, I cannot be knowing of it until it happens. And it happens like this. There are so many people, some of our people and some of their people. And there are television cameras and television people, and newspaper people and policemen, and police dogs and lots and lots of the other policemen who think they do not look like policemen because of their not wearing the policeman uniforms. And exactly like in the old South Africa days, there are two different entrances into the building. Instead of separate entrances for black and white persons, here there are separate entrances for family of victim/family of perpetrators. At first it seems like it is the same thing, that our colour makes for our deeds. But as I am starting to be spending so much of my time here, I am coming to learn that evil comes in every colour, which leaves victims of every colour. Who would have known that? Such a lot of things I now know that I did not know before.

Family of victim has a front-row seat. When the room is filled, our archbishop walks in, dressed in his beautiful purple robes and gold threads. He is a splendid peacock, and for a few moments I am forgetting why I am here and enjoying being in the front row to see such a spectacle that I have only been hearing about but never before been seeing. There are some other men and women who are sitting with him. I do not wonder about who they are. My eyes are only on him.

Our archbishop begins to talk, and we are silent. He tells all of the people that we are all sharing in the history of South Africa and part of the future of South Africa and that the outcome of these special truth hearings will have a huge meaning for all of us, and even the rest of the world. He tells us that we have the responsibility to get it right. I am listening carefully to him. I want to get it right.

I like his voice. It is deep and musical, and it sounds even stronger in this room than it does on the radio or tv. Now he pauses to take a breath and says to us that we are all brothers and sisters in here, and let us pray for strength to be able to listen to what we have to say and what we have to hear in here together. He tells us to close our eyes and to hold each other's hands and that together we can pray to our Lord. I reach for Thembisa's hand, and it is sweating and trembling. I reach for Nathaniel's hand, it is cold and trembling. I close my eyes and let my mind grab at every word of the prayer that our archbishop is giving to us. Perhaps I will feel God looking after me now. Maybe God will let me see him once more. Our bishop uses words like 'strength' and 'forgiveness' and 'humility'. I am holding on tight to my children. Our bishop is then silent. We all breathe together like one person. He says, 'Come, children, let us open our eyes and begin now.'

He then directs his gaze to the front row of family of victim and he looks at the mother of the children of Moses Mshlawawele.

'Mma, welcome to you and to your family and to your friends, we are welcoming you here today. We want to learn about the truth of the death of what happened to Mr Mos …'

His mouth is moving and there are some sounds but it seems as if they are coming from very far away. There is only a thick sound in the air between the archbishop's mouth and my ears. I cannot hear any sounds that I can turn into words. My blood is so noisy in my head, in the space between my ears. Thandi, she is noticing that there is something troubling me, and she quickly is finding the medicine to wave under my nose, and the drops to put on my tongue. I am not sure how many moments have gone by since I am enjoying the archbishop's gold-and-purple robes but the hearing has come to a stop. Jeremiah is on his feet, waving his arms and saying some words which I cannot hear. I am now wondering how it is that I do not recognise the sound of my firstborn's voice. I am not feeling in my body, which makes it difficult to move myself when I am helped out of the room, followed by Thandi. I am taken by a helper to a cool, dark room, and suddenly Ruth is with us. We sit in silence and after some time I am now starting to hear my own breathing, and I am noticing that my blood in my head is not making such a noise. I am tired, but I am feeling in myself once more. Ruth asks me if I want a drink, and I say that I would please like to have some sweet tea, and that I would please like my daughter to make it for me. Ruth tells Thandi where to find a kitchen and then it is only me and Ruth and her voice and her sad eye. We sit together. Thandi is back now with the tea, and I drink some of the sweet taste of home and close my eyes. I am remembering all the times I have been drinking this tea with Moses, during cold winter nights, and also fresh summer mornings. I am remembering the first teas he made for me after each of our children took their first breaths and we were their mother and their father. And now my children have no father, and now we have to learn what happened to their father. It is their right. It is needed for honouring Moses, and it is needed in order for us to be able to bury Moses. I am feeling that I am now ready to hear what happened to Moses.

Your loving sister, the sad, sad widow Constance

Second week of November 1997

My dear Patience

Soon it will be Christmas. I am thinking how good it would be if we are being together this one time after such a long time of being apart. Suddenly the idea came to me as I was braiding your niece Thandi's hair. This is our quiet time when she loves me to tell her stories of how it used to be with me when I was a young, young teenage girl like she is now, and always my stories are full of you and me, and all of our mischief and all of our fun, and she said to me Mma, I wish that I could be meeting with your sister, my auntie, and this has made me think about how we can be meeting. Patience, I am thinking that even if it is not a Christmas meeting at a Christmas time, we can still be having a meeting of being together. I am thinking that I would like something sweet to be looking forward to. This TRC hearing, it is so dark, it is of death, and I am feeling fearful of what is at the end of this all for me and for my children. I am still waiting to understand if this is a good or a bad thing that we are doing, being part of this hearing. Sometimes I am thinking that it is taking so long, that it is taking over all of my life, and that it is not good, and sometimes I am thinking that it is good that it is taking over all of my life because I do not have any other life, and sometimes I am thinking that I am very tired.

My neighbours Mmbotle Mphawetsi and Mary-Rose Magunya have long ago finished their business with the TRC, and only last month Mmbotle had a big funeral with lots of flowers and gun shots for her husband, Simeon. She told us that she was happy now because she had buried Simeon deep in the earth, and that this TRC business was over. But she does not look so good. She is not good in the face, and she spends her money drinking any cheap spirits she can be finding. I tell her to come and drink in my house, that I will brew umqombothi *for her, that mine will be good and that I will keep her safe because I will watch over her and know when she must stop. But I am fearing that she does not want to be stopped, that one, that she wants to be drinking until she drowns. And then I am full of the fear of what will happen to me when all of this TRC is over. And I am thinking that it would be good to see you again, my sister. I am needing to be seeing someone who knows me from when I was a fresh girl. And I would like God to come back to me. But I have heard such things in these past weeks that makes it difficult for me to be a believing person.*

Patience, I cannot tell you all of what I heard, because once I heard it I needed to start to forget it, which I will never be able to do, but I must keep on trying to forget it so long as I am alive. But to tell you some of it, I can say that Moses was hurt over and over until he had no last breath to take, until he was destroyed, as much as possible. But it was not possible to destroy all of him, and there are some pieces of his body that are for us to have, to bury. There are some reasons why Moses was taken that night, some of which I did not know, and some of which I did know, and some of which I knew but did not to ask him about, because he did not tell me. That was the way that we loved each other and lived with each other. We did not tell what we did not need to tell.

I am not telling you of the persons who took Moses's life. They are not deserving of my filling them up. I am understanding our archbishop and his needing me to think about forgiveness, because when I do not forgive them I continue to make these persons big and strong, and I'm always remembering of them, when instead I need to make them like the dust with my forgetting. I am finishing this letter now because it is too too much.

Your loving sister Constance

Fourth week of November 1997

My dear Patience

I am very happy that you are making the plans to meet with me. You are thinking well when you are telling that we should come to your house so that we can be away from where we are. It will be a proper holiday. I cannot remember the last time of a proper holiday. It is good to plan. I am hoping it can be when the summer is dying. We will be finished with the TRC at this time, and I can do some cooking of our favourite food and we can be getting ready. I have told the children, and they are all very happy to be doing a holiday. I will make sure that the hospital is knowing my plans so someone else can be on duty in my place, and you can make sure that you are doing the same thing. Do you think South Africa will manage to look after its sick on the days that we two sisters are not being nurses? Ha! This is a good joke.

And now, Patience, I am ready to be telling you how I am feeling about what happened that night, the last time I saw Moses, eight years ago. Haai, *but it sounds long ago, even though I can remember it like last night. I remember his face and his too-frightened eyes when they came for him, those men. I did not know then that when they took Moses that they also took me, for I have not been the same since some eight years ago.*

My life is not the same since he is taken. I want my life to be like it was with Moses, even on the many days that we did not see each other because of working in the jobs at different times. Maybe if there had not been so much blood that night when the men came for him, maybe if I had not seen how frightened he looked, deep in his eyes, maybe if I had not seen that he knew something bad was happening, then I could tell myself, I could pretend, that somewhere on this land he was still breathing as I am, then I could sleep some sleep. But he is not and I cannot.

I am thinking of our Lord, who I have not spent time thinking about in these hard days. I am thinking about his teachings on forgiving, and I am thinking that perhaps this is the difference between me being an ordinary woman and him being a man who was more than a man, and I am thinking about this forgiving business.

Perhaps this is why our archbishop is the archbishop and I am an ordinary woman. Our archbishop, he is loving forgiveness. I think that he will forgive any person who is saying they are sorry. And I am feeling angry at our archbishop for giving me the feelings that I am being mistaken in my not being forgiving. I am feeling strongly angry. Yes, I will tell you this is how I am FEELING, now that I know how am I feeling. It is too, too much for an ordinary woman. I am trying to be good and I am trying to hear, and also I am trying to listen to the words of the others, and hear the words of myself. But I cannot because I do not want to. I am not managing this forgiving or understanding or listening. It is hard to be thinking of anyone else, and impossible to help the people of the new South Africa, who are needing my forgiveness so that we can all be in the peace. I know only that I am a widow and that Moses is murdered.

It is hard to remember the days when I was only sad and worried about where Moses might be. Then came the time of the knowing of Moses being dead, and that was filling me, and that felt like all the feelings in the world were squashed inside of me. But now, in the times that I have been looking at the faces of the murderers of Moses I am feeling a hot and a cold sickness in my body. I am dreaming of Moses's left leg bones, which are lying on the perpetrator's farm. The rest of his body is gone in ways that I cannot tell of. But his leg bones are all that remains. And they follow me in my dreams, such terrible dreams. I am waking and screaming and crying and shaking, like the tokolosh *have taken over my spirits. I tell Thandi that it is the* tokolosh, *they have come for me, and she soothes me and gives me the* muti *to appease the struggling spirits inside my mind. But the* muti *cannot help, for it is true. The* tokolosh *have come, they have taken my soul. The* tokolosh *do not look like those dried-up, toothless witches of my childish nightmares that I could melt under my opening eyes and the good morning sunlight. No, these* tokolosh *are of flesh and blood, hair and sweat, and bones and teeth, of a stinking of evil that I cannot get out of my nostrils. I am telling Ruth this, and she is liking my words. She is bringing me a big box of tissues, and I clean my nostrils and pull out all the mucus, but still it is stinking. Ruth is waiting. She is slow and with lots of time for me. She brings me a dustbin and she counts for me the number of times I am putting the tissues into the bin. She is asking me about the smell, and I tell her it is like pigs' trotters that have been left for days in the heat and are busy with crawling maggots, and this is bringing yesterday's food rushing up my throat and burning and sickening into my mouth with the smell. Ruth says she understands that I am feeling sick to my stomach, and she looks proud and pleased with herself. I am thinking that this woman is surely simple. I am telling her how it is stinking and she is telling me back how I am feeling, which I already am knowing. I do not want to be rude but I am feeling rude. I say nothing more.*

Your sister and widow Constance

Second week of December 1997

Dear Patience

Thank you for the very good Christmas cards and also for the decorations. My house is beautiful from their shining colours. I am very sorry that the meat that I have been sending to you was not good. I thought to give some to you because Jeremiah came home with too much meat last week. He did not say where he had got it from, and I did not ask him. I was thinking that if I am liking it then you will also be liking it, and that I am wanting to send it to you so that you can also eat this good meat, but I did not know that it would catch worms before it got to you. Mary-Rose promised me that her brother had a cold bag with lots of ice in his car and that it would last for many days. I am sorry also that she was wrong about this meat.

In these days I am feeling wrong about lots of things, and I am also not knowing when it is time to feel right. I often am telling Ruth this. Ruth is bringing me paper and coloured pencils and mud. We are drawing together. I draw and she watches and then we talk about what I am drawing. The first papers are no good. I am pressing so hard down on the paper that it tears and the pencils lie broken. But we continue, each visit, and we are talking some of the time, and the TRC is going on some of the time, and I am listening and hearing some of the time, and hating and hating and angry and hot. Some of my days I am hating our archbishop and want to tear his clothes off his body to see if he does have a heart that beats beneath his clothes, like me. I am thinking it cannot be possible. Can he not hear the words of the perpetrators, the murderers, in the way that I am hearing the words? He is loving and I am hating. He is kind and I am filled with cruelty. He is brave and I am filled with terror. He is filled with forgiveness and I am filled with blood. I am an ordinary woman, he is the archbishop, nurtured by the goodness of our Lord. I am not.

I can be describing the faces of the murderers to you but I will not. I cannot see any human beings underneath their skins. I am hearing their words, aimed at me, at my kind forgiveness and understanding, but I hear the words as if they are coming from far, far away, and my brain is working hard to understand these sounds so I can learn about everything of the death of Moses.

If it were not for Ruth I would be so alone that I would no longer be a person, except for in my letters to you, Patience. And it is only because I do not have to look you in the eyes that I am able to tell you what I am being. Ruth, she is doing what she said she would do when we were first meeting and I was not yet understanding any of what I am now understanding. She is staying and staying with me, no matter what I am telling her I am feeling or thinking about. She loves my dreamings and listens to my thinkings.

She never tells me it is enough, although she is always telling me that we have now finished for today. At first I did not like this rudeness – when a person is telling you their thoughts it is very rude to be telling them that there is no more time left to listen, especially when it is something like morning time and there is a whole day left in front of you. But she sits with my ugliness, even when I am thinking that today is the day when she is going to run out of the room to fetch the police to lock up me and my wicked thoughts.

I am becoming tired of thinking about the hating and the killing and the destroying feelings, because it is destroying me. I am becoming tired of thinking about anyone but the children and myself.

Your sister Constance

Third week of January 1998

My dear Patience

I am writing to you with blessings and many thanks for all the ways that you have been thinking of me in this past too-difficult year. I have been so weak for so many days of the old year, and now it is the new year, and we must be hoping for better times.

In these few weeks of this new year I have not been having so many words to share except with the children. I am feeling quiet in myself. When I have no more words with Ruth she brings again the papers and the coloured pencils and the mud. And I am noticing in these times that I am not so often remembering about hating, and I am more times forgetting a little bit about killing, and some of the times I am forgetting a lot about ugly thinking and ugly feeling. And I am drawing and I am making mud objects, like a child at his mother's knee, and I am just sitting with Ruth, and suddenly it is many weeks past and my tokolosh *drawings are complete. And it is on this day that Ruth brings the matches and we walk out of the meeting building and we walk along the hot street, and we walk into the veldt that lies behind the school, and I strike the match and I set fire to my* tokolosh *papers. I watch as my too-strong and suffocating wicked thoughts go up, up, up in red-*

hot flames and fly away. I grind the mud objects under my foot until it is a powder of dust returned to the earth.

My dear Patience.
I am hoping to see you very soon. Your sister
Constance

CHAPTER 26

Recently I have been waking up to a slow, uneasy churning in the pit of my stomach that I take at first for hunger. I force myself to eat more, but the churning continues and I can't ignore the bile that lodges in my throat. I drink herbal teas that I don't believe in, I spend time staring at the copper bracelets in the pharmacy.

'Excellent for morning sickness, really just the ticket,' says the elderly pharmacist who is growing tired of my loitering.

'I don't have morning sickness,' I say.

'Sure, whatever, sweetheart, whatever,' he agrees.

I buy the bracelet, avoiding his eye. He takes my money, avoiding my eye.

All day long I wear the bracelet, well hidden beneath a long-sleeved shirt. I press the cool, smooth metal into my pressure points on my wrists. I resist the urge to retch up my breakfast. On my way home from work I pass the pharmacy and dump the copper voodoo into the bin outside the shop front.

I continue to feed myself with nuts, hot water and lemon, fat, white kingklip fresh from the sea, alfalfa sprouts and sweet potato, but to no avail. I don't have morning sickness. It is an all-day sickness that is becoming increasingly difficult to ignore.

'You are not looking so good to me,' Constance says.

I know I should be wondering what it is like for her to have me not look so good, after all her sessions are about her not me.

'Mmm,' I manage.

'You are feeling green to me,' Constance says.

'It's time,' I tell her, indicating that our session has now ended.

I cancel my other sessions and go home to bed. I fall into a restless and disturbed sleep, and in my dream I discover that I am looking down into a doll's house with an interior of one large, square room. The floor is laid with a plush, dark-red carpet, as are the walls, which gives the room a claustrophobic, bordello ambiance. I don't like it. There is no ceiling, only me above the room. I don't like that. I feel myself fall into the room through the open ceiling. I recognise that the room is laid out for a therapy session. There are two chairs diagonally opposite each other, and a small table with a clock and a box of tissues on it. There are now two women in the room, each on a chair. I am one of the women and the other woman is Constance, only when I look at her I see my face atop her body, bathed in an unearthly green light. When I talk it is her voice coming out of my mouth.

'Where am I?' I call out.

'I am here,' I answer, my voice coming from a long way off.

'Ruth, where is Ruth?' I try again.

'Here I am,' some of Ruth answers.

Part of me is crying, some other part of me is consoling.

'Yes, but which one am I?' I ask, struggling to pacify my panic.

An explosive release, a rising, insistent tide of waste rushes up my oesophagus and spews out of my mouth. I continue to gag and instinctively cup my hands to catch the parts of myself that I cannot swallow down any longer. A thick, gelatinous blood gushes out of my mouth, with hair and skin, limbs and innards all afloat on this red tidal wave. I am both dispassionate and also gasping for breath. I am the energised blood and guts and gore, and I am also myself drowning in this vile fluid. I am choking now. There is something stuck in my throat, threatening to block off my windpipe. I gag and gasp, desperate for breath, but the slimy lump sits lodged in my gullet. I draw in as much air as I can, desperate to fill my emptying lungs.

'I am dying, I am dying,' I gasp.

Perhaps this is true, but not today, as just in time, in dream time, I manage to dislodge the blockage with a violent cough. Up the suffocating mass rolls, up through my windpipe, smooth and slow. It comes to a stop, round, warm and full on the middle of my tongue. It seems I have laid an egg in my own mouth.

'Aaaargh,' I splutter.

From out of my mouth falls my own perfect, all-seeing, chocolate-brown eye.

It is my lost eye. I watch in frozen horror as my eye continues to roll like a marble across the dried-blood-red floor that lies between me and my Constance self.

My eye continues on its lonely trajectory.

'Constance, Constance, do something. My eye, my eye,' I cry.

She slowly reaches for my eye, which is rolling towards her. She bends down and picks it up.

'Beautiful dancing eye, exactly like your father's. Chocolate brown,' she says, and pops it in her mouth.

I wake up choking for breath. I am drenched in sweat, bathed in the green glow of jealousy, sick to my core.

I am jealous of Constance. I am jealous of her ability to face her demons and voice her ugliness. I am jealous of her capacity to heal herself by letting go of her hatred. I am jealous of her ability to embrace these opportunities for healing, for forgiveness. She is absorbing her grief and her trauma through honesty and openness, through truth and reconciliation. I too want my shot at redemption, a healing, a second life. I also want a Truth and Reconciliation Commission. I am nothing if I can't be unflinching when it comes to the truth. I am nothing if I can't be committed when it comes to reconciliation. So here we have it – either I am nothing or I am unflinching and committed. There is no halfway house, not now.

CHAPTER 27

My work with Constance comes to an end.

'*Hamba kahle, sala kahle*,' Go well, stay well, we tell each other.

I book myself out of the office for a week and take my favourite route home along the spectacular coastal road. Usually I stop at a lookout point to watch for dolphins and hope for a whale. There is dark ocean as far as the eye can see, attached seamlessly to a steadfast blue horizon. The sky is enormous, it usually brings me welcome relief from my agitated thoughts. But today I am too engrossed in thinking about my father to achieve an inner peace from a vast horizon. My tyres screech as I careen around the hairpin bends and into the path of an oncoming car, which swerves out of my way with curses and gestures. Shaken and contrite I continue the rest of my journey with caution. Ivor – he is lodged in my brain.

I have always known that the day would come when I would see Ivor again, one day, when I was ready. It has never occurred to me that readiness steals up on you in the guise of something else.

I make myself a strong black coffee and sit down at my desk with my recently acquired dossier on Ivor. The private investigator I hired in my first week back in South Africa has been happy to take my money in exchange for information that no one else has wanted. My having the information has helped me feel safer, despite not having been able to read it until this moment.

I read:

Subject: Ivor Louis Newman
Age: 67
Family status: widower.
Wife: Maureen Sadie Newman née Glass, deceased 1976.
Children: a son, Jonathan Manfred, deceased 1976; a son, Michael Leon, deceased 1976; a daughter, Ruth Naomi.

My eye struggles to focus on the black print and white paper. Letters form words, and words form sentences that describe how we had once been, and how some of us have been buried, one of us has emigrated and then repatriated, and how the others have been incarcerated and then liberated. The information that I have always avoided is now in my hand. All I need do is unscramble the code of the indigestible and I will know something more about Ivor.

I learn that my mother was having an affair with a junior lecturer in the Industrial Sociology department of her university. He had a beard, a home in New York, and a young son by a former lover. I discover that my father was in huge debt to a local Swazi mafioso who helped to finance his porn imports long after my grandfather's money was used up. I know, because I was there, that on 29th October 1976, Ivor Newman, my father, pulled the trigger of his gun four times. He killed my mother and my two brothers. He tried to kill me too, but somehow I survived. He blinded me in one eye.

A faded police report from 1976 details that their first sightings of my father showed him lost in his own thoughts as he slowly raised a bloodied gun to his temple. He hadn't heard the police squad car screech to a halt outside our home or the rush of policemen smashing their way through our front door. He had not heard the kitchen door open and had not expected the rugby tackle that brought him smashing to his knees, his gun spinning and skidding over the kitchen floor, out of his reach. His arrest prevented him from blowing his brains out and left him instead to the mercy, the expense and responsibility of the state.

These facts, they don't help me to understand what happened, on that day, to us, to him. I lost myself that day, and I have searched ever since for something to help me understand how Ivor came to the moment in his life that changed mine forever. None of this information helps me, but I can't stop myself from trying to piece this jigsaw together. I can't find relief if I don't know what happened between my parents in the moments that led to my father shooting my mother, my brothers, and then me.

I can understand anger, I've felt it many times myself, but how do you go from ordinary rage to murder of the most absolute? How do you go from being beloved Daddy to embodiment of the most unimaginable nightmare? The truth feels unknowable. Once I had a father, his name was Ivor Newman. But when he murdered our family he stopped being my father. I died the day my father pointed a gun at me and pulled the trigger. I am dead despite my outward appearance.

I gulp down my bitter caffeine and force myself to keep reading: on his arrest the magistrate's court sent Ivor Newman for a thirty-day observation period to Valkenberg Psychiatric Hospital, a large psychiatric facility in Cape Town, renowned for its assessment of temporary insanity. On being found to have been of diminished responsibility at the time of the shooting, Ivor had been released back to the court to stand trial. These extenuating circumstances – his temporary insanity – led to him being found guilty on three counts of manslaughter. His sentence was therefore much less than it would have been for murder. He was given three concurrent sentences, each of fourteen years. The further count of attempted manslaughter gave him an additional two years. He served out his prison sentence with a brief period in hospital for electro-convulsive shock treatment for morbid depression, and continues to be supported by a variety of psychotropic drugs for depression and anxiety.

The report makes for a depressing and anxious read – I could do with a little psychotropic soothing myself. To acknowledge that he had been of diminished responsibility is an unacceptable outcome for me – what he did to us might have seemed certifiable if you hadn't known him. But I had known him. I had known Ivor Newman. He had been my father, and he had never been insane – insanely jealous of my mother, perhaps, and insanely optimistic about his own abilities, certainly, which I had believed in, for a very long time. But for me to believe that Ivor was insane and deserving of special treatment would require my empathy and sympathy. To condone a sentence that has left him with his liberty during my lifetime is insane.

I continue to read: on his release four years ago, due to fragile mental health, Ivor was appointed a care worker, Barney Thule, who acts as his ongoing advocate. Why is the new South Africa babysitting this old bastard?

I am not in search of bodies to bury. I am not waiting to hear how our bodies were defiled. I know what happened to us. But I don't believe in his madness. This leaves me no choice; I have to confront my father. It is time for the truth and probably an unlikely reconciliation. Unlike the process of the TRC, I won't sign away my right to prosecute in exchange for information. I will be judge, jury and prosecutor. I need Ivor to help me heal myself so that I can live. I need his truth so that I can reconcile myself to the reality of my life.

I put the dossier down.

'Daddy,' I try it out. It sits brokenly on my tongue. 'Dad, Father,' I croak. It too sounds hollow and empty.

'Ivor,' I say.

For the longest time I've banished Daddy to a faraway happy time, where my brothers are digging on the beach and I am at the edge of the sea, hunting for shells. I can hear Jon-Jon's fat laugh and Mikey's singing. Mommy and Daddy are setting out our picnic. If I squint a little I can see them all, slightly hazy in the late afternoon.

That's where my Daddy is, that's where my family is.

But Ivor, that is a different matter. Daddy is the man who gave me life and a sense of myself as loveable. Ivor is the man who forced upon me my life as I have known it for the past nineteen years.

'Why did you do it?'

Just like that I can ask him.

'Tell me Ivor, tell me what happened on that fateful day in October, October the 29th, 1976, to be precise. What happened to you, and to your family on that day? What do you know? What can you remember?'

And then I can sit back and wait for whatever happens to happen, as it should, with truth in order to facilitate a reconciliation, and finally a healing, so that we can all go back to bed for a good night's sleep.

If only it would work like that.

I don't often sit in on the TRC hearings as I am usually in the outer chamber in a supportive role in case anyone needs me. But I know there is some pomp and ceremony. Then there is a general reading out by the clerk of what had happened to whom, as much as it is possible to know at that moment, and that the defendant is noted and states their name for the record.

I marvel at the thought of how the purple-clad priest believes he can help the victim and the defendant to see one another. This is fantasy really. My clients mostly do not experience it like this, as they are traumatised and overwhelmed, both by seeing the defendant and by the formal legalities of the hearing. I won't have any of that, but I need to think of some way to help Ivor acknowledge the importance of what we might achieve.

I am loath to wear a costume, but I am drawn to the symbolism of supporting myself with something from the TRC, and the purple cape is the obvious choice, such is its majesty and drama. I remember a beaded lilac scarf that José bought for me in our first few weeks in Santiago. It is soft, luxurious and comforting, and it is reminiscent of lost love, another lost love. I can enter my father's house wrapped in José's embrace.

I need to embrace my loss as part of my preparation for meeting Ivor, and for running this TRC for both of us. Perhaps now I am ready …

* * * * *

I grab my keys and leave the house without looking back. I'll be looking back more than I can possibly bear, once I see him. I am only ten minutes into the journey when with great urgency and poor timing, I feel the need to empty my bowels. I try to talk myself out of it by acknowledging that it is a psychological urge to empty myself of my shitty feelings rather than an actual need to shit. It doesn't work. I have an actual need to shit. Fortunately this stretch of coastline is dotted with hotels. I drive into the car park of the magnificent Cape Sunset and rush to make good use of their five-star facilities. I splash cold water on my face and do not recognise the pallid and exhausted woman looking back at me in the mirror. I tug at my hair and reapply my lipstick, which leaves a plum stain somewhere below my nose and above my chin.

To hell with it then, he'll recognise me, I am his flesh and blood. He'll damn well recognise me. I recognise that I am truly terrified.

The final stretch of long road winding down to his house takes a lifetime. But there is no going back now. It isn't as if I can keep driving, or turn around and go back to my everyday. I am in the middle of something that can only be seen through to the end, and only by me, with or without Ivor.

I arrive outside Ivor's house.

It takes me several nervous attempts to park the car, and then I sit, sweating my anxiety onto the red leather seats until I think I am composed enough to slide out of my safe haven. But I am light-headed and dizzy. I trip on my unsteady legs and stumble into a rusty metal post box, which tears at my arm in a long, deep gash. I am too shocked to cry out, but mange to rummage for tissues in my bag to mop at my arm, willing the blood to clot. I run my shaking hands through my hair. I don't have a good feeling about this. I should go home.

Dear Liz.

Here I am. Please come and get me out of here. Love Ruth.

I don't have a postcard.

If I did it would be have been one of those Table Mountain scenes where the overfamiliar image sits perfectly at odds with the urgency of the message. I am daydreaming. I am postponing. I am delaying. These tactics are not working.

I am here, ready or not.

The exterior of the cottage is picture-postcard perfect against the inky-blue ocean backdrop. The cottage walls are ablaze with crimson and fuchsia foliage, contrasting dramatically with the green corrugated-iron roof.

All that lies between Ivor and me now is this path of crazy paving, which will take me from the road to his wooden front door. My legs are leaden and my feet are as unyielding as two planks of wood. I imagine this is what it must be like to walk in callipers, with no best foot to put forwards. Each step is an achievement of determination over disabling terror. Finally, after so long, a lifetime really, I have managed to arrive at Ivor's front door.

I lift the front door knocker and let it crash down onto its brass plate. I hope that one knock will be sufficient. I can't possibly manage it again.

CHAPTER 28

Tea was always at 3.00pm. Good, strong tea with a healthy dollop of milk, no sugar, and one digestive, for dunking. The kettle's hearty whistle cheered him up immensely. There was nothing as satisfying as a boiled kettle; if Ivor had learned anything in life, it was this.

Alcohol was futile as it made him maudlin. Food was simply a means to an end. He ate the same food at the same time every day: cornflakes for breakfast at 8.00am, eggs, baked beans, carrots and cucumber with three pieces of white bread for lunch at 12.30pm, a snack of cheese and crackers at 5.00pm, and a medium rare steak and mashed potato, followed by a crisp, green apple for dinner at 8.30pm. And a good cup of tea.

He dressed for comfort in blue t-shirts, blue shirts, jeans, or navy-blue slacks. Today he was wearing jeans and a faded blue t-shirt, black socks, no shoes. Slung over a chair lay his worn, navy-blue pullover with ragged cuffs.

On account of the tremor in his right hand, a significant amount of concentration was required to pour the milk into the tea. Some days were more successful than other days. He had learned to accept that. As he hovered with the milk, mid-air, there was a resounding crash on the front door, making him jump in surprise.

'*Ag*, who can that be?' he muttered

He scowled at the milk spilt across the Formica work surface and watched dispassionately as it trickled onto the tiled floor below. He looked at his watch. He was not expecting anyone. He paused for a moment, tempted to leave the front door to itself, but curiosity got the better of him, heightened by the fact that he had not had an unexpected visitor for some time.

With a sigh he turned away from his tea making and walked towards the door.

'*Ja?* Coming, coming,' he called. 'One sec.'

He always did that, these days. He didn't trust himself to move in time to his expectation. His feet were slow and befuddled, as if he had suffered a stroke, rather than just suffered. He peered through the peep hole but saw nothing that matched his impression of danger.

Several locks had to be undone and chains unbolted. It hardly seemed worth the effort of unlocking and unbolting for what was probably a woman collecting money for the homeless. He paused, released the locks, and flung the door wide open.

Time, so much of it gone on ravaged years, nearly all spent. It could break your heart – if it wasn't already broken.

Ruth.

At his front door.

Long ago and faraway had delivered itself to his front door. It was Ruth.

Chapter 29

I never knew that silence could be so intense. If only I had two seeing eyes right now perhaps I would be more able to absorb the annihilating presence of my father, Ivor Newman.

I am here, stuck on this precipice of past and present.

What have I done?

My feet seem fixed to the path, my brain feels as though it has shut down, leaving me with no possibility for thinking. I am unravelling faster than Alice could fall down, down, down the rabbit hole, and I haven't even got through the front door. This is a devastating outcome. Even my most fanciful imaginings did not include my disintegration in front of my father, not in 1976, and not now.

I try to speak, but only a hollow rasping sound escapes my lips.

'Oh, oh my God,' he whispers. 'It can't be ... it can't be you ... It can't, it can't, can it?'

I blink helplessly, blindly.

'Oh my God ... oh my God ... oh ... oh ... oh, for shit's sake,' Ivor splurts.

My catatonia ends as the sudden putrid smell of human waste hits my nostrils, serving as smelling salts to my shock. My father, it appears, has crapped in his pants, such is his shock at facing me.

My legs are released from my paralysis, and I step up and over the threshold into Ivor's house.

Ivor hastily backs away from me, shuffling and stumbling in his fouled trousers and dampening socks.

'Come in, come in, come in, please, please. It's you know, the shock, the surprise. Well, the shock of this, of you, of seeing you ... Look, wait, wait. Don't go, please don't go, wait, okay, I'll be quick, a few minutes to sort out, to ... you know... sort this out. Come, come, please, come in,' he pleads.

'Yes,' I reply.

'Just going to clean up. Clean up and be back. Coffee, tea? Do you want some Diet Coke?'

I am panicked that he might try and make it into the kitchen, with shit dripping down his legs.

'Go clean up,' I say.

He wades off. I breathe through the bile that lies restlessly at the top of my sternum.

'Shit,' I mutter to myself.

I stand blinking in the entrance hallway for several moments as my eye adjusts to the light. Off this entrance hall are three rooms. I peer into the nearest doorway and see an unfurnished room with some bookshelves at the far end. I edge towards the second doorway and see a dining area dominated by a yellowwood dining table and a side dresser running parallel to the table. The dresser is bare except for a blackening banana. There are a few paintings on the walls, some of fruit and two of the mountain, a ubiquitous scene in most Cape homes – as if to continue the external vista into the internal surround. The dining room tails off into a small kitchenette. Ivor has headed off towards the third room, which I can safely assume is his bedroom.

'Are you there? Are you still there?' he calls out.

'Yes,' I answer 'I'm here.'

'Good, good, that's really good. I'll be quick as a wink, fresh as a daisy, out in a few minutes,' he says.

'Okay,' I call back.

I hear my voice as flat and even. This chatting between rooms feels unpleasantly intimate.

I hear the flush of a water pump and realise that he is taking a shower. I have two choices now: I can find somewhere to sit passively and wait for Ivor to reappear freshly laundered, or I can choose to acquaint myself with where I am. I am not good at being passive. Perhaps a drink is not a bad idea.

I walk through the dining room and into the kitchenette.

'Aargh,' I gasp as my feet lurch me across the smooth floor. It seems there has been an explosion of milk in the kitchen. First shit and now milk. This quick descent into infancy is most unexpected, and unnerving.

I grab a hand towel near the sink and start to wipe up the milk from the floor. I put the kettle on and search for a mug and coffee. I make a small black coffee for myself, and I refresh the waiting cup of hot tea, remembering to add a splash of milk for my father. I open the small fridge and find apples, carrots and cucumber, cheddar cheese and bread. Perhaps I should be hungry. I can't remember when I last ate. I open cupboards and find mismatching plates. I open drawers and find a rusty vegetable peeler, a sharp steak knife, and bone-handled cutlery. With shaking hands I carry what I need to the dining-room table.

This home is spotless, in stark contrast to every home of my own making, and not something that I think to associate with Ivor. Obviously I have had little association with Ivor, and whatever might have come to mind about him over the years, I have done my best to forget. But I know that I do not have a childhood memory that hints at the fastidiousness around me now. I'm in the home of a stranger, of a man I do not know.

I gingerly place the hot drinks directly onto the mellowed yellowwood table, setting them on either side. But this makes me uncomfortable as it is too close for comfort, and yet to sit at either end of the table would be ridiculous. I settle on us sitting diagonally opposite one another, which creates a greater sense of space between us. I am working on the psychological set-up for a clinical session, where the deliberately placed diagonally opposed chairs offer the opportunity for both intimacy and space. I am reassured by my professional countenance. I try out the seat, feeling like Goldilocks. It's surprisingly comfortable. My back is well supported and my feet touch the floor. I open my backpack and put it on the seat next to me. I take out a candle and small saucer and place them at the head of the table. I take out matches and strike one to melt the bottom of the candle so that it will set on its heated base to the saucer. I take out my lilac scarf and with deliberation drape it over my shoulders, the beads clattering softly as they catch the back of the chair. I find paper and pens in Ivor's sideboard. I might want to take some notes. I am now waiting for Ivor.

Chapter 30

He stood in a bewildered daze as the hot water beat down on him. He let the water play across his shoulders, down his back and bounce off his buttocks. He wanted to stay here under the shower, where it was safe, where hot water was hot water and soap was soap. But he knew that he was not entitled to that simple pleasure, because his daughter was waiting for him. With reluctance and trepidation he turned the shower off and climbed out of the stall. He dried himself with a concentrated deliberation and then dressed quickly.

He did not like the unexpected, and the appearance of his daughter was unexpected. He had not expected to see her again, ever. He had no idea what to do with her, but perhaps she knew why she was there and she would tell him. That would be some comfort. He wanted to take control of the situation; she was a guest in his home so she would be expecting something from him. He wondered if it was a good idea to offer food, but it might seem presumptuous of him to think that she wanted to stay and eat with him. He had nothing else that she might want or need, apart from a small amount of cash. Perhaps he could call for help. Barney was big on talking so perhaps he could tell him what to do with an unexpected visitor. He imagined their conversation:

'*Howzit*, Barney. My daughter's turned up. Should I give her some food? Can you buy us some more steak?'

He didn't even know if she was vegetarian, but judging from her shoes she probably was. He allowed himself to think through what Barney might say.

'What's troubling you, man?' Barney would say.

'Barney, I'm feeling all confused, my head is like spaghetti.'

'*Ja*, spaghetti man, that's a bummer, I know,' Barney would say.

'What can I do, Barney, it's giving me a headache, it's giving me grief.'

'Don't stress, man, say it as it is – hey I'm feeling confused.'

'What? Just like that – hey I'm feeling confused?'

'*Ja.*'

'But I can't, man, I feel ridiculous.'

'*Ja*, you can, just say I'm feeling confused, I'm feeling ridiculous,'

'I'm feeling ridiculous, I'm feeling confused, and now I'm pissed off as well.'

'Well done, man, really well done, Ivor. Don't you feel better now?'

'I dunno. I'm feeling confused. I'm going to lie down.'

'Poor Ivor. I can hear you are really feeling confused. Take it easy bro'. Speak tomorrow, okay, buddy?' Barney would say.

'Yeah, tomorrow,' Ivor would say.

'Fuck you, Barney,' Ivor muttered under his breath. 'Fuck you, I'll damn well offer her food if I want to. It's my food and she's my daughter.' At that, he hesitated. After all he was not exactly an expert on daughters, not anymore.

He walked cautiously out of his bedroom. Where was she? He followed the smell of coffee.

'Hey, here I am,' he said. '*Howzit, howzit,*'

He smiled at the tea and coffee laid out, waiting for him. This was looking good. Perhaps she'd stay for dinner after all.

'Do you like steak?' he asked.

Chapter 31

Just when I thought this encounter could not become any more bizarre, I am proven wrong yet again with Ivor's offer of meat. I need to take control here before I lose myself.

'Perhaps you are wondering why I am here?' I say.

I let my words dangle in mid-air between us, a useful technique that helps people to open up while at the same time allowing me to guide them to where I want them to be.

'I'm confused. I guess you could say I'm really confused and feeling a little ridiculous,' Ivor says.

I think he means the poo thing and I certainly don't want to get into that. 'Yes, it is confusing for us to see each other again, isn't it?' I say.

I am attempting to appeal to his adult self, so he can join me as an equal at this table. He has something that I want, and I will not let anything stand in my way now, not even him.

'Yes, yes, but I think it's good. I think it's really good that you're here. But confusing, yes, I'm really confused,' he says again.

Wow, I didn't imagine we would get this far. I am silent.

'You look a lot like her, like my wife, you know.'

I'm here. I'm at the point of no return.

'Do you know we once nearly went to live in Swaziland. Rolling green hills. You'd have loved it.'

'When was that?'

'1976.'

'I … Do you … do you really remember me?' I ask him.

'Yes, doll, how could I forget you? I taught you to run, to swim, to ride a bike, to play tennis. I taught you to be great.'

Damn it. Tears, not now, please. I don't want to remember what I can't forget.

'Yes, Ivor, you taught me all those things.'

'I sure did. We were a great team.'

'Yes. I remember. We were a great team.'

'Do you still run? I bet you do marathons. You look great. What's your time? My fastest was well under four hours. I bet you could do under four hours. You were really fantastic, like me. I taught you everything I knew. No one learned it as well as you.'

'No, I don't run competitively anymore, I haven't for years.'

'Oh, why not? Little bit lazy? Can't have that, my girl. Leads to middle-age spread. Hey, hey, let's go running, you and me. I haven't been running for ages either. It will be sweet, so sweet, man. Just you and me, hey, doll? How about it? How long are you visiting for?'

'I don't like to run with anyone.'

'Why? Why not? Will do you the world of good. Come on, don't play hard to get here. Please, please, make an old guy happy. Get out a bit, join the human race, you know ... C'mon! Let's go running together, for old time's sake.'

His eyes are alight with pleasure. I did not come here to cause him pleasure. I swallow.

'It's hard for me to balance, with only one eye.'

'Oh, yeah, I heard something about that once, about how it affects the balance. Only one eye, *ja*. Cancer or something?'

'You could say that, a cancer or something.' Do I love him or hate him? 'Ivor?'

'Mmm?'

'Ivor, what happened?'

'When, doll?'

'What happened to the family? What happened to everyone?'

'Family' is a word from a long time ago, it is people who no longer exist. He no longer exists. I no longer exist.

'Do you know, that's a damn good question. What the hell happened to the family?'

I am startled by his response.

'Why? Why is it a damn good question?'

'Because I also wonder what happened to the family, but it makes me cry and get too sad, and Barney tells me not to think about it, so I try not to. But, sometimes, I really do wonder where my babies are, what it would be like to hold them all again ...' His voice tails off.

I look away. No way. Not this act of cute, helpless love. No. Fuck.
'We had some good times, hey doll.'

I am silent.

'Do you remember swimming in the river? Boy, it was freezing. But not as icy as your mother afterwards.' He giggles.

I am confused. Is he knowing or unknowing? Is he responsible or devoid of responsibility? Can I forget him or forgive him? I have no idea what to do with him.

'Tell me about yourself,' he says.

My father is diverting me away from my collision trajectory. 'Well, okay. I guess I can do that. I'll tell you about myself and how come I'm sitting here.'

'Sure, sure, whatever,' Ivor says.

'I'm a psychotherapist and a counsellor. I specialise in trauma, and in particular with victims of violence – domestic, criminal and political. I am a therapist for a non-governmental organisation that works with and for victims, and the families of victims, who are offering themselves as witnesses to the Truth and Reconciliation Commission,' I say.

'Uh huh, uh huh,' he nods. 'Very good. Very good work. You must make lots of people proud of you.'

'Well, yes. Maybe. Have you been listening to the trials on the radio?'

'*Ja*, *ja*.'

I suspect this might not be true.

'Look, do you know anything about the Truth and Reconciliation Commission, the TRC?' I ask, trying to keep irritation out of my voice.

'Yes, some. A little, perhaps,' he says.

I stare at him. How can he not know what is going on in his back garden? Has something happened to his brain? He seems to function well enough from what I can see.

'Well, good, I'm really glad you understand it all, that you get the TRC because of course that is why I am here.'

'Yes?'

'Yes, I need help. I need your help. I can't do this by myself anymore.' I wave a weary hand over my eye.

'*Ja*, sure, I can help. Sure thing. Happy to help. What do you need? I've some money, and probably enough steak for two if we both don't eat too much.'

I look at him carefully. Is it possible that he hasn't understood? 'Ivor,' I say.

'Dad,' he says, 'Please don't call me Ivor. I'd really like it if you could call me Dad.'

I feel an intense surge of energy crackle through me. I plunge on.

'Ivor, you see this candle, I'm going to light it now, and we're going to pray together,' I tell him.

He looks uncertain.

'Okay, if you really want to. Kind of like Friday night Sabbath candles. *Ja*, okay,' he says. 'Haven't done that for years, since, since …' He tails off.

I close my eyes and focus like I have seen the purple priest do before the beginning of a trial.

I wait. I wait until I feel ready to look upon this man, this beast, this murderer, my father. I open my eyes. Ivor is sitting, looking at me, with the unknowing expression of a child.

There is a tense silence.

'So, uh, do you want some more coffee or something. It's not yet steak time,' he tells me.

'Ivor, why am I here?'

'Uh, you're here to talk about the TRC, to pray together and to just be quietly here I think. Hey, my girl, don't stress so much. It's okay if you don't know why you are here. None of us really knows why we are here,' he says.

I feel the hair on the back of my neck standing on end. I am not his girl. That girl has been dead and buried for a very long time.

'Ivor, Ivor, it is now time for you to account for your actions, your actions on October the 29th, 1976 at 72 Primrose Lane, Parktown North. I'll tell you of my suffering and you tell me all you know. If you manage to give me sufficient information then this will help me to finally free myself. I am not in the position to grant you amnesty, seeing as we are not sitting in a court of law, but I am in a position to give myself the possibility of a decent night's sleep, the possibility of a fuller and more complete life. Do you understand what I am saying?' I ask him.

'I don't know. Do I need my lawyer?' Ivor says.

'No, you do not need your fucking lawyer,' I hear myself say in a cold and furious voice. 'You have me here. I am your lawyer. I am your judge. I am your daughter,' I spit out. His attitude is really getting to me, getting at me, getting under my skin.

'Okay, Ruthie,' he says. 'Okay.'

I stop. It is the first time he has addressed me by name. It seems like an eternity since I last heard my father speak my name.

'I'm not sure ... I mean I don't ... I don't really know what you want from me, but I can try my best to help you' he says.

'I need to fucking forgive you, Ivor. I'm worn out with every other emotion I have felt about you and need to forgive you so that I can move on. For so long I've avoided thinking about you, but now I can't get you out of my head. And I'm sick of looking at myself in the mirror and hating what I look like, that I look like you.'

'*Ja*, okay. So you don't want to look like me. But I'm your father – that can't be helped. I can see that's hard for you. But I don't know what you want from me, really I don't.'

'The truth, Ivor. The fucking truth, not that bull that you've defended yourself with for all these years. I want to know what happened. I want to know why. I want to know what you were thinking as you squeezed the trigger, as you looked at him, at Jon-Jon, at Mikey.' I suddenly sob. 'What were you thinking when you shot Mommy dead? What were you thinking?'

'Thinking? Ruth, I ... I don't know, I don't remember ...'

'And me? What were you thinking when you looked me in the eye, when you pointed your gun at me and shot me, shot at me, at my face, at me. Oh my God, oh my God!' I am crying hysterically.

Ivor, my father, looks right at me. 'I'm sorry,' he says quietly.

'What?' I say.

'I'm sorry,' he says. 'I'm sorry.'

'What? Sorry? Sorry? That's it? That's the best you can come up with – sorry?'

I am overcome with weeping. I am losing control.

'Ruth,' he says. 'Ruth, please ...'

I can't answer.

'Look, Ruth, it wasn't a good day for any of us,' he shouts suddenly.
'What?' I whisper.
'Ruth, we're still here. That's the main thing.'
I lift my head and wipe my face on my sleeves.
'C'mon, Ruthie. Stop the crying now,' he says in the commanding voice of my childhood.

I close my eyes. I could fall backwards if I wanted to. I could become Daddy's girl if I willed it. Peace is just a heartbeat away. I want to forgive him. I want to forget him. I want to live. While we are sitting opposite each other there is choice, there is chance, there is possibility for change. There must be or my life's work is a lie, which would make my years of work with rape victims and refugees a lie and Constance a lie and Archbishop Tutu a lie and the new South Africa a lie. I must find a way to forgive him. I feel myself slowing down. Time is congealing around me.

'Are you married, Ruthie? Are you a mom? Hey, that would make me a grandpa. *Ag*, that would be the best, that would be just perfect, man,' he says.

'No.' I say
'No? No marriage?'
'No'
'No children?'
'No'

'Really? I can't believe that. You'll regret it, you know. You'll be all alone in your old age with no one to care for you. That's not good for a person.'

Now I am on my feet, restlessly pacing the floor. 'Tell me what happened. Please. What happened on that day? Why? What? Just tell me,' I say.

'Seriously, Ruth, are we back on that subject again? I just want to know about you, doll. It's been so long. We've got so much catching up to do. Don't feel bitter if you haven't met the right person yet. I'm sure he's out there, waiting for you. Hey, you're not gay are you?'

'No, I'm not gay.'

'You're not into chicks and stuff? It's not that, is it? I really don't care for that.'

'I'm not into chicks and stuff.'

'Didn't think so. Nobody in my family's like that, you know. So don't worry about it. It'll happen in good time. There's definitely some lucky bugger just waiting for you, doll, you'll see.'

'Tell me what happened. Please. What happened on that day?' I say. 'Tell me what happened. Please.'

He stares at me. Does he finally understand that there is nowhere for him to go but where he is, right here in this moment of truth in the new South Africa?

'Ruth, Ruthie, look doll, we all got hurt. We nearly got completely destroyed. I was not in my right mind. I was sick, really sick, but I've had treatments and been punished and we've survived, you and me.'

I recognise his need for me to collude with his version of the events, where we all got hurt but that the two of us survived. I feel intense pressure below my sternum and an uneasy ache across my shoulders. It is becoming difficult for me to hold on to the words that are passing between us.

'Go on,' I say.

My legs stop their futile marching – there is nowhere for me to go. We are with each other. We are face to face.

'Well, look at you now. You have a great job from the sounds of it. You're really important and all that stuff. And the truth is it's all turned out for the best, in a funny kind of way.'

'The best?' I say.

'Sure. I think it's best to forget about that old stuff. What's the point? I say it's always better to look forwards rather than back. We're survivors, you and I. Two of a kind. I always knew you took after my side of the family. You were always like me, from when you were a tiny girl.'

'Yes,' I say after a few moments. I am slow to this reality but now I understand what I have never managed before. 'I guess I am like you.'

He smiles up at me. 'We're two of a kind, you and me.' I watch him.

'Hey, can I ask you something? You've studied, which means you can still read. You've got here by yourself, so you're independent. You look pretty good to me. So, my girl, what's it like with only one eye? It can't be that bad, hey?'

'No I guess not. It's not that bad,' I agree. 'What do you think?'

My arm shoots up and then straight down into his uplifted face. The silver blade glints at the end of my hand for only the briefest of seconds before it plunges deep into a mass of fleshy eyelid and iris and bony, hard matter that resides behind the eye.

I had no idea the steak knife was there, in my hand. I had no sense of how sharp it was or that I could bury a knife into a person's eye with every ounce of my being.

Chapter 32

All schoolgirls tend to look the same – each is a poignant mix of girlishness and emerging woman with fronds of sweaty hair framing a round, plumped-out face and the typical smatterings of yellow and red pustules on the forehead and the chin.

There was nothing remarkable then about the girl who pounded the leafy streets on a warm, lazy afternoon. She ran steadily but without urgency or alarm. It must have been hard for her to run the full distance in school shoes, especially scuffed, leather-soled shoes that did nothing to support or cushion the foot each time it struck the ground. She ran with a sense of purpose that encouraged stragglers to move out of her way. Her skirt lifted and fell in rhythm with her pace, her schoolgirl legs flashing with coltish exuberance. Her canvas school bag bounced up and down on her back.

If personality can be discerned from physical behaviour then it would be a fair guess to presume her to have an impatient disposition, tempered by a reluctant caution. She did not attempt to dodge cars on the crossings, but paused to let them pass while muttering to herself and looking at her watch. She stopped in front of a red-roofed family house and took her bag off her back. She rummaged around for a few minutes until she found her key. She slung her bag over her left shoulder, ran up the path and quickly opened the brown front door, dragging her feet across the welcome mat.

'Hi, I'm home,' *she called.*

She dumped her bag on the floor and rushed to the toilet and then up the wooden staircase. At the top of the stairs was a well-proportioned corridor with six rooms. She ran into the second bedroom, collapsed onto the single bed adorned with a pink floral bedspread and closed her eyes for a few minutes. She sat up again and quickly slid her school shoes off and pushed them under the bed, and pulled out her tennis shoes. She pushed them on, did up the laces and grabbed her tennis racket, which was propped up behind the bedroom door. She clattered down the stairs once more.

'Hey Mom? Jon-Jon? Mikey? Where are you?'

Her voice seemed to disappear into the emptiness of the house.

She pushed at the heavy, white swinging door that led into the cool white-and-blue kitchen, and walked over to the fridge. She opened the door and rummaged around for something to eat. She was suddenly aware of her father's presence.

'Dad! Howzit? What time did you get in? I thought you were in Swaziland until next week,' she said, her head still in the fridge.

The girl noticed the echo of her voice as it darted around the kitchen, en route for a recipient.

'I'm playing tennis with Liz. Just popped home to get my racket. Do you know where Mom is? I'd love a lift back to school.'

She closed the fridge door and looked uneasily at her father. He was sitting slumped on a brown kitchen chair in the middle of the kitchen. Her discomfort intensified. He sat bowed over, the loose folds of his white shirt hung off his rounded shoulders; he looked like a large, abandoned, white egg.

An unbearable tension rushed through her body, making her legs tremble.

She wanted to look around the room, to try and understand what was missing, but for some reason she couldn't take her eyes off her father, or the dark-grey metal gun that lay across his lap. She stood as still as an impala and looked at what she could not understand. They might have stayed like this for all eternity if he had not raised his head. She saw red swollen eyes, an ashen face and a dark-brown stain growing on his white shirt.

'Who? Who did this?' she whispered.

'I did,' he said, and raised his arm, steadied his gun-holding hand and slowly, deliberately, pulled the trigger.

The force of the bullet took her by surprise. She did not register any pain, but felt a sticky warm liquid gushing out of her face. She felt herself spin round and down like a leaf blown out of a tree.

* * * * *

I'm still spinning, round and down, never landing, forever falling. I can't land if there's no one left to catch me.

CHAPTER 33

He lay bleeding on the bedroom floor, where she had dragged him. It was a winning combination of strength, perseverance and focus that enabled him to reach up for the phone on the bedside table. It was his greatest achievement. He was exhausted from his efforts, but slowly and carefully he managed to pull the phone near enough to punch in 999.

His call was answered immediately. After all this was South Africa, where crime knew no boundaries.

'Emergency Services,' said the terse voice at the end of the phone, all precision and high alert.

'Ambulance, ambulance, please come now,' he managed 'Name sir, name and address please,'

'Come. 98 Lillian Avenue, Hout Bay.'

'Who am I speaking to please?' 'Newman, Ivor Newman.'

'Thank you sir, Mr Newman, can you keep talking to me please. Cars are on their way. Please, can you tell me what's happened? Don't hang up, Mr Newman, keep talking to me, please.'

'My eye, my eye … I've just … My eye … blood.'

'Mr Newman, the emergency vehicles will be with you in under four minutes. Just stay as calm as you can, Mr Newman. Are you alone?'

'No. My daughter, my daughter, she's here with me.'

'Can she help you? Can you put her on the phone? Can I talk to her?'

'No, no … We need help … please, come before it's too late …'

'Mr Newman, Mr Newman, keep talking to me please, Mr Newman. Are you there? Don't hang up, Mr Newman. We're on our way. We're coming to get you right now. Mr Newman, can you hear me? Ivor? Ivor?'

CHAPTER 34

⌒⁀⌒

My rust-torn skin is a sticky, throbbing mess. I'm going to have a nasty scar from elbow to wrist. I touch it lightly and it hurts. I touch it again, letting the pain sharpen my mind. It reminds me that the metal post box will still be outside. I can use my stamp and Ivor's paper.

Dear Liz
Please, deliver this letter for me. It's for Archbishop Tutu, for Desmond. Thank you. Love, Ruth
PS: No more letters after this, I promise.

Dear Mr Tutu
Your Grace, firstly I would like to say that you have been one of the greatest influences on my life. I have tried, with all of my heart, and all of my soul to stay true to your words, and I believe that to the best of my ability I have prepared my clients with dignity and sanctity to enter your court, to be as ready as is possible, to embrace the unembraceable. But you see, Mr Tutu, what I wanted to write to you about, what I wanted to tell you, is that sometimes, just sometimes there are certain circumstances, certain extenuating circumstances where it is not possible to forgive.

While the groundwork was being laid down for the Soweto Riots and the senseless shootings that took place on 16th June 1976, so too the groundwork was being laid down for the rioting and senseless shooting that took place within one upwardly aspiring home of a middle-class Jewish family on 29th October 1976. What developed out of the desperate politics of the terrible apartheid years was ultimately to end with greater freedom for all the people of South Africa – to make each and every person a free man, free woman, free child. The uprising that took place at the Newman residence, No. 72, Primrose Lane, Parktown North, had nothing to do with freeing man, woman or child. If anything it encapsulated a particular kind of middle-class labour that was driven by how things ought to be, where the reality never delivered the promised dream. In its grey wake lay a deathly self-hatred and despair that sucked out light, hope, the future.

I have spent my whole adult life running away from myself, and in particular running away from the parts of myself that are most like my father, the man I have struggled to forgive for murdering my brothers, for murdering my mother, for destroying my vision, and for the death of our family as we once were. I have only recently discovered that I have been running in the wrong direction – instead of running away from him I should have been running towards him. It has given me huge relief to learn this.

Mr Tutu, extenuating circumstances call for extenuating measures. I still believe passionately in all that you are doing for our country, for all our people. Your work is about helping all of us in South Africa to live together. That is wonderful and noble. I love what you tell us South Africans about finding a way to live together. It's such a beautiful idea. I have discovered another beautiful idea, however, which I have long suspected to be true, which is that I needed to become like my father in order to feel free of him.

With gratitude, and also love,
Ruth Newman
Lead Trauma Psychotherapist
Psychological Services for Victims of Torture and Terror

PS: It's been an honour and a privilege to work with you.

* * * * *

Fuck me, I can't stop fucking crying. What's the matter with me? Cracking headache like my head is cleaved in two, my whole body is aching. Oh, my … oh … I think I've just killed my father.

I look around the room, desperate to find something pleasant to focus on. I see bookshelves and my mother's favourite *Ndebele* vase, with its vibrant shades of blue, rust, yellow, black and white. These colours of sky, earth, sun and people are the colours of my South African childhood. There it is then, the vase, a mocking monument to how it should have been.

An intense longing to feel its reassuring weight washes over me. As I get closer I see my mother's elongated vase forms an unlikely coupling with a stout, square, silver photo frame that is balanced against it. Clammy sweat trickles down the nape of my neck and irritates the length of my spine with its dampness.

Oh … please … no … not this sweet photo. I close my eyes but my hand grabs for the photo, knocking the vase to the floor.

I don't care. I always hated that vase, but I have the silver photo frame and quickly press it to my beating heart. I hunch over my prize, sobbing with exhaustion, I can't bear any more carnage. Slowly, as if I too might disintegrate, I sit down on the yellowwood chair with the frame pressed into my chest. I sit for a long time, until my muscles cramp.

The cold silver metal is slick in my sweaty hands.

Hope and despair seep out of my every pore, making it difficult for my shaking hands to hold on. This photo – it is imprinted on my mind's eye. I want to look and not look. It is like scratching the scab off a mosquito bite and watching the sticky blood seep out, a simultaneously satisfying and painful experience. But this is not some annoying mosquito bite.

I turn the photo frame over. I stare, in order to cram in what I can see, to capture this scene for all time: it is me with my family in faded Kodak colour. Mommy and Jon-Jon and Mikey and Daddy and me.

I am no longer sure whether I am in or out of my mind right now. Out of my mind. For perhaps the first time that phrase now makes sense to me, for of course I would have to be out of my mind to have killed a person, and I think I've just killed my father.

I feel as though I am moving in slow motion through space and time, like everything, or something, is slipping through my hands. And there's this really horrible noise in my head right now, a desperate cry of suffering and anguish. It feels like it is coming from very far away and yet I can hear it as if it were next door.

'Jon-Jon, Mikey, Maureen, Maureen …'

'Jon- Jon, Mikey, Mommy,' I say out loud, to drown out the voice in my head.

But the voice is not in my head, it sounds as if it is coming from next door. Oh my God, it's Ivor. He's calling to them. He's calling to my brothers and my mother.

'What? What? What are you doing? Who are you talking to? You can't talk to them. You killed them, remember?' I scream and stumble into the bedroom.

'Maureen, my sweetie, my love, beautiful …'

Hot, painful tears blind me. I kneel down to hear him better.

'Jon-Jon, my boy, my boy,' he whispers.

'Jon-Jon,' I whisper back. Oh my God, he can see them. He can see them. 'Ivor? Ivor? Damn you Ivor, what are you saying? Stop saying that. Stop talking. Stop saying his name.'

Oh. The pain, like a knife in my heart.

'Mikey, Mikey, I'm coming, I'm coming. And Ruthie, she's coming, we're coming …'

'Mikey? Mikey, my Mikey?' I am sobbing, on my knees.

'Mikey …' someone whispers.

'Stop Ivor, stop, I'm begging you.'

'I'm coming my boy …' He splutters blood. 'Stop, please. Leave them alone.'

'Love you, yeah, yeah …' His voice trails off.

'Stop, stop, stop saying his name. Stop it,' I scream.

'Love you, love you, Ruthie, my girl, yeah, yeah …'

'Ivor, Dad, Daddy, Daddy,' I am sobbing.

There is silence.

I touch him. He is soft and familiar. He is my earliest memory of love. He is Daddy. I straddle my father and bury my face in his neck. I caress my father's face. I can become Daddy's girl. I can will it. Peace is just a heartbeat away.

I love my father.

I am not without choice, and I see mine now, it is a knife glazed with gore, slim and slimy by his side.

Chapter 35

As promised, it took less than four minutes for the squad car and ambulance to pull up outside the bungalow. The air was light and inviting, with no hint of mal-intent. But the emergency services were not seduced by the serenity of the afternoon. This was the face of everyday South Africa. The drill was straightforward: police must enter first, followed by ambulance crew after the all-clear is given.

'Hey, guys, this is the place. The caller, he didn't sound so hot. Let's take it easy, okay.'

'Sure. We're ready. What did you say the name was?' 'Newman, Ivor Newman.'

'*Ja*, you know who he is.' 'Na, never heard of him.'

'Sure you have. I'm pretty sure he's the guy who went ape-shit years ago, in Joburg. Killed his wife and sons.'

'What a bastard!'

'*Ja*. My cousin Liz was best mates with his daughter. We were really worried about Liz for a while. She came close to losing it a couple of times, but she's good now, married with a kid of her own. She's a great girl. I think she got some bad politics going on, you know from *varsity* and stuff, mixing with the wrong crowd, but she's a sweet girl and a great cook. Makes the best *melk* tart ever.'

'What about the girl?'

'What girl?'

'Jeez, is it really that hollow between your ears? The chick you were telling us about man, the chick who was friends with your cousin?'

'Oh, her, *ja*. Karen or Lauren or something like that her name was. She survived. Blind as a bat but alive, and him. The two of them survived.'

'Poor bitch. She'd have been better off dead than alive with a father like that.' '*Ja*, no kidding.'

'Look, there's a window. Can you see what's going on? Don't want to scare him or anything. Who knows what he's still capable of?'

'*Ja*. I'll take a look. Cover me,'

'*Ja, ja*, your fat arse, it's hard to miss.'

'*Ja*, do it okay.'

'Okay, okay.'

'*Na*, looks all clear. Hang on, hang on. I think there's a body. Too much sunlight, can't see properly. I need to get closer. Cover me. Seriously, cover me, man. Oh Jesus, Jesus, stop, stop …'

CHAPTER 36

White, ghostly shapes float around me. Ghoulish sounds surround me. I breathe in the smell of hospital.

What have I done?

When I close my eyes his face swarms in front of me, his voice rings in my ears.

'Dad,' I whisper to myself. 'Oh God, oh God, oh God, what have I done ...?' In my dreams we float silently above the windy mountainous pass. Our Mustard Motor Machine is as light and hollow as a paper bag. There seems to be no need for words between us. I don't think we have anything left to say to each other.

I can't get you out of my mind.

My descent – it was so quick. It happened in a breath.

I took the knife, I lifted my arm, I plunged it down. I couldn't look at you.

I didn't mean for you to die, I didn't mean for you ... I wish, if only ... You didn't have to shoot us, Dad.

I can't stop thinking about you.

I didn't really want to kill you, not all of you, not actually dead. But I had to stop you. I had to shut you up. I didn't mean to ... I didn't plan to ... It just happened. As if the knife and my hand didn't belong to me, as if my thoughts and intent weren't driven by my own mind.

If only ...

Chapter 37

He was good at pretending. He'd had a lifetime of practice and it sometimes paid off. He snored softly, taking care to let his chest rise and fall evenly. He could hear the nurses bustling around him, talking. It was the blonde and the brunette. He knew they'd be talking about him now that he was asleep. After ten minutes his vigilance and patience paid off.

'She's a real fighter, that girl.'

'*Ja*, like father, like daughter. These two – tough as old meat.'

'*Ja*, really tough cookies. I can't believe she survived, and him. Like a cat with nine lives. Do you remember that woman last year? You know, the one with the really good-looking husband …'

I should be there when she opens her eyes, he thought. I'm her father. I have the right to be with her. I have rights. She's my daughter.

The nurses clattered with their trays, tidying up the medicines, checking the support machines and refilling the water jugs. '*Ja*, so anyway, he then said to me she'll be asleep for hours. How about you and me …'

Slowly he stretched and moved around in his bed, no longer snoring. He'd heard what he needed to. Cautiously he opened one eye, but the nurses weren't looking at him. He cleared his throat tentatively. He needed to see Ruth.

'Nurse. Excuse me, nurse,' he said.

His voice startled the nurses, who had hoped for a longer break.

'*Ja*, Mr Newman, how can I help you? You've only had such a little sleep. I thought that you'd be gone for hours. You were out like a light, but so quick, hey,' the blonde said resentfully.

'Please, nurse, can you take me to see my daughter, Ruth Newman.'

'Your daughter? I don't …'

'Please, nurse, please. Can you take me to see my daughter.'

'You shouldn't be out of bed, sir. You need your rest.'

'I need to see my daughter, please.'

'I'm really not sure that's a good idea.'

'Please, I need to see my daughter, Ruth.'

'I understand that's how you feel, but I really don't think that's a good idea.'

'Look, I just ... want ... to see ... my daughter, please.'

'Calm down, Mr Newman, Calm down, please or I'll have to get security. Calm down, I said ... Jennifer, send for security now, immediately. It's Mr Newman. He needs a little ... Mr Newman. Calm down ... Jennifer, get Clive now, he needs restraining. Now. Mr Newman, please, don't touch those tubes. Don't ... no ... leave your eye. Mr Newman ... Mr Newman. Oh, for goodness sake. Thanks, Clive. What took you so long? How much have you given him? Really? He'll be out for hours ...'

* * * * *

It was his desperate thirst that woke him. His tongue was thick and his eyes felt swollen; his body was covered in multiple bruises that made him wince every time he moved. He groaned softly.

'Ruth, Ruth,' he muttered.

'What's this Ruth business? Have you met a chick in here, Ivor? I can't leave you for two minutes and you're all over the women like a bad rash, man. Hey Ivor, *howzit*, man.'

'Barney, Barney, where've you been? I really need you, Barney.'

'Sorry, man. Your bossy nurses wouldn't let me see you until now. Said it was family only.'

'You're joking, man. They won't let me see my family either.'

'What d'ja mean?'

'Ruth, she's in here. My daughter. I want to see her. I keep asking to see her, but they won't let me. Doped me up so that I could hardly speak. Barney, you've got to fix that for me. I need to see her.'

'How are you, Ivor? Nice set of bandages.'

'*Ja, ja*, I'm fine. I'll be just fine. My daughter's back. Ruth, she's back. She came to find me. She came for tea a few days ago, I think it was, or maybe the day before that. It was very nice, very, very nice.'

'Ivor, your daughter, I think she's the one that took your eye, man. She took your eye out.'

'*Ag*, Barney. You weren't there. It wasn't like that. She's very sweet, and beautiful, looks just exactly like her mom. I have to see her, Barney. She's in here, somewhere. I want to check on her, see how she's doing. She came for tea a few days ago.'

'I don't think so, Ivor. I don't think that's right. You've been here for nearly three weeks. You were like totally out of it until about two days ago. You nearly bled to death, gave me the fright of my life. You should be dancing with the angels, man.'

'No way.'

'Yes, really. Three weeks ago.'

'I can't believe it. She's been all alone for three weeks, Barney. I need to see her. Someone needs to see her. She's not married, not got kids or anything. I'm all she has.'

'Okay. I'll check it out, but you probably won't get near her, or more likely she won't be allowed anywhere near you. She tried to kill you, man.'

'Kill me? Don't be ridiculous. What are you talking about? Who said that?'

'The newspapers, the TV, it's everywhere, about how she broke into your house and attacked you, and then tried to kill herself.'

'No way. That's not how it happened.'

'Please, Ivor, tell me, tell me what happened.'

'Barney, I need to see Ruth. Please can you take me to see her?'

'You won't be allowed to see her. It's to protect you.'

'I don't need protecting. There're police all over this hospital. Best damn security I've ever seen.'

'Yes, Ivor, it's for you. The TV cameras are for you. The police and security are for you.'

'Oh.'

'*Ja*, Ivor. Now you get it.'

'Barney?'

'*Ja*.'

'Barney, just, would you please take me to see her, goddamnit? It's not like you say. That's not what happened. She came to see me, to get my opinion on some stuff, on praying and things. I'm her father. She wanted to hear my thoughts. She's really smart, and beautiful, just like her mom was.'

'Ivor, can you tell me what happened to your eye?'

'My eye. *Ja, ja*, well, it's gone. It's gone now. I don't have it anymore – just some bad headaches and a hole in my head. But I can see with one eye just fine.'

'But do you remember what happened to it? What happened to your eye?'

'I lost it.'

'*Ja*, you've lost your eye. How d'ja do that?'

'It was an accident. It was my fault, all my fault.'

'You dug out your own eye?'

'No. No. Why would I do that?'

'You're confusing me man, telling me it was your fault.'

'It was. Really Barney, it was my fault. I said some stuff I shouldn't have said. You know I can get like that sometimes.'

'*Ja*, I do. I know that.'

'*Ja*, well, I just said some stuff while she was sitting looking at me, pretty as anything. Man, she's nearly as pretty as her mom was. Nearly as good-looking as my wife.'

'Ivor, what shouldn't you have said?'

'*Ag*, Barney, listen to me. Why won't anybody listen to me? It was my fault. I deserved it. Really, it was my fault. She can take my other eye if it makes her feel any better. I deserve it. Barney, I deserve it.'

'Ivor, Ivor. Hey buddy, are you crying? Don't, man. Look, don't cry, okay. It can't be good for your eye … The bandages … Don't cry. Please stop. Stop crying. I'll get a nurse, okay, just, please, stop crying.'

'Hey, Barney, I'm sorry, okay. I'm sorry. I'll stop. I'll stop, I promise. What's the time now? I don't know the time in here. I don't know if it's day or night. I think I lost my watch.'

'I'll check for you. They might have taken it away from you.'

'Why? Who?'

'You know, security measures.'

'Is nowhere safe in this *blerrie* country? Can't a man even wear a watch in his own hospital bed without being mugged? I tell you, Barney, this is ridiculous. And have you seen the security here? It's like Fort Knox. Is it always like this or is it for the movie star?'

'What are you talking about, Ivor?'

'You know, there's a movie star here for some face-lift or something. Someone really famous is here. TV cameras, photographers, all outside. You can't miss them. Even I can't, with one eye.'

'Oh, *ja*, all that. I saw it.'

'Who's it for? See if you can find out who it is, and we'll go spy on them. That'll be a laugh. Did you bring me a blue t-shirt?'

'*Ja*, here. I knew you'd ask me that. This is one of your favourites. It's a really great t-shirt Ivor, good choice. But, you need to stop babbling about a movie star. It's nothing like that.'

'Of course it is. Have you seen how many of them there are? Who else would it be for?'

'It's for you, man. It's for you, Ivor.'

'Huh?'

'It's for you. They're all waiting for you to leave so they can interview you. They want to hear what you think about forgiveness. You know – can you forgive your daughter? Look what happens when you don't forgive. Clearly she hasn't forgiven you, man. It's a lesson for us all. It's biblical, fucking biblical. Jeez, Ivor, you're a media star, a damn celebrity. Everyone wants to hear what you think. You and your daughter are symbols of learning for our rainbow nation – the people want to know how much blindness we can take. What can we not face seeing? What can't be seen? You know, stuff like that. Makes great news headlines. You're hot news right now.'

'You're messing with my head, Barney.'

'No, no I'm not. Sit down, Ivor. We really need to talk about the incident.'

'The incident, the fucking incident, that was years ago, you know that. I've said everything. I've said what happened. I've done my time. I can't say it all again. I'm not saying any more. It's done, it's done. You know it's done, Barney. Don't make me talk about it again. I swear I'll crack up if I have to say anything else about the fucking incident.'

'Ivor, please, let's breathe nice and easy, nice and slow, together. Let yourself be calm. Can you hear me? Can you hear me, Ivor?'

'I've lost my fucking eye, not my ears, Barney. Who's the social worker here? You or me?'

'Me, Ivor. I'm the social worker. You're Ivor, and we're going to sort this all out. You and me, we need to talk about what happened between you and Ruth, three weeks ago – the incident where you lost your eye. There are people, important people, who want to know what happened between you and Ruth. I think there's going to be a big court case. She could go to jail.'

'Ruth ... why? What's she done? It's all my fault. She did nothing. I've told you, it's me. I did it, I did it.'

'Ivor, you didn't do this, you didn't do anything. You can't take the blame for her. There is evidence that she stabbed you. She gouged out your eye. Her fingerprints were all over the knife. Then she tried to kill herself. Cut through her own spleen, like she was trying to do hara-kiri. Made a horrible mess, but she survived. You Newmans are made of hide skins, man, I tell you. She's going down, Ivor, she's really going down.'

'No! No! I won't let them. They'll have to take me instead of her.'

* * * * *

Visiting Ruth hadn't been that difficult to fix, not when a person was as well connected as Barney. They made for an unnoticeable couple, adrift on the antiseptic hospital corridor: a plump, middle-aged, congenial-looking man in a white short- sleeved shirt, navy slacks and dark aviator sunglasses, pushing a shrivelled, elderly man in hat, dark glasses and a thick blanket that tucked neatly under his chin. The older man was a little over-dressed for such a warm day, but then elderly people did feel the cold more.

'C'mon, Barney, you're pushing my wheelchair so slowly I swear I could crawl faster. I'm about to pass out from the *blerrie* heat under these blankets, man.'

'Be quiet, Ivor, look around you. Look at the cameras everywhere.'

Ivor took a cautious look around. Despite his protests, he knew the disguise was necessary. There was a bank of photographers and TV cameras all jostling for space for the first sightings of the notorious Newmans.

'What's the matter with these people? Haven't they got lives of their own?' Ivor hissed.

But Barney didn't answer. He was busy negotiating the wheelchair through the large staff-only swing doors and along the back corridors of the hospital towards the staff-only lift. Barney pushed the heavy chair along the empty corridor until they came to the nurses' station with its panel of flashing lights and nurses in starchy white uniforms.

'You know, Barney, I always have confused feelings around nurses. I like them and feel scared of them. You never know when they're going to come at you with a needle, or try and tie you down with one of those crazy jackets with straps.'

'*Ja*, Ivor, I understand that. I really do,' Barney agreed.

He left Ivor for a moment to have a brief conversation with the nearest nurse. He pointed to Ivor and then to himself and smiled. The nurse nodded and pointed out the room with two guards outside. She walked over to the wheelchair.

'Mr Newman,' she said, 'you can have ten minutes in here. There's a panic button on the wall. It's red. You can't miss it. If you need it, press once and half the country's security force will be with you in five seconds.'

'I want to see my daughter,' Ivor said. 'I want to see her by myself.'

'You have ten minutes,' she said.

'Thanks, doll, ' Ivor said.

CHAPTER 38
BABY

She was the first baby he'd ever held, the first baby he'd ever known. He remembered being so scared he would crush her, anxious she would snap in half or fall apart in his hands. She seemed too good for him. She was pink and perfect, and he was huge and clumsy, with dirt under his nails and germs on his skin and bad smells rising out of his body. How could he have contributed to making anyone as beautiful as this tiny, dark-haired creature, his daughter?

'I'm your daddy,' he said to her. 'I'll always be your daddy.'

She looked at him with huge, solemn eyes. She yawned. Was she already bored by him? She wasn't even a day old. He carefully kissed her plump little cheek. He wasn't expecting such soft skin. He kissed her cheek again and stroked her hands. Her fingers wrapped around his.

'Let's call her Ruth, after my *bubbe*. I'd really like that,' his wife said.

He looked at his daughter. She blinked her eyes at him.

'I think Ruth likes that,' he said. 'Let's call her Ruth Naomi, after my *bubbe*,' he said.

'Ruth Naomi, a big name,' his wife said. 'A big, beautiful name.' 'Yes,' he said. 'Ruth Naomi Newman, a name to be proud of.' 'Ivor, please pass Ruth to me, I need to feed her,' his wife said.

He looked down at his daughter. He didn't want to let her go. She continued to stare at him. Perhaps she thought he had the answers, but he didn't even know what the questions were.

Carefully he passed Ruth Naomi to his wife.

Chapter 39

His daughter lay asleep on the hospital bed surrounded by tubes, bandages and medical equipment. He stepped out of the wheelchair, abandoning the hat, glasses and blanket to a small pile on the floor. He walked up to the edge of the bed. She looked so tiny under the blankets. He wanted to kiss her cheek.

'Don't wake her. She's sleeping, quiet, shhh,' he whispered to himself.

Her fingers were long and her nails small, neat ovals. Her hands reminded him of someone else's hands. His wife, she had hands just like that. He carefully touched Ruth's hands with the edges of his fingertips. He didn't want to wake her. He wanted to look at her, to be next to her when she woke up.

'I can never make it better. I can never make us better,' he whispered. 'I'm sorry, I'm sorry, I'm sorry. I'm sorry, sorry for it all.'

He couldn't stop himself. His crying just kept coming like waves on the beach.

He should have been watching her face instead of her hands. When he looked up he saw she had her eyes open, that she was looking at him.

'You're not dead,' she whispered.

'Ruthie, my girl, glad to see you, so glad to see you.'

'Your eye …'

'*Ja*, my eye. You got it well and good.'

Tears ran down her face. Tears kept running down his face. He gently touched a tear with his finger and brought it to his lips.

'Salt,' he said.

'Dad,' his daughter said. 'I'm sorry. I'm very sorry.'

'An eye for an eye,' he told her.

They both cried.

'Does it hurt?' she asked.

'Did yours?'

'I don't know,' she said.

'I don't care about my eye,' he said.

There was a knock at the door, and Barney stuck his head into the room. 'Excuse me, Ivor, I'm afraid you're out of time, man, time to leave now.'

'Okay, okay. I'm coming. Give me two more minutes please, I'm just finishing off here with my daughter,'

'Two minutes, that's it then. Let's not push this, Ivor.'

'Okay, okay. Keep your hair on, jeez!' he said.

He turned back to Ruth.

'Listen, doll, don't blame yourself. We both know it's not your fault, all this eye stuff. We're going to find a way to get through this together. I'm calling this guy I know. He's my lawyer. He's really clever. He'll be able to get you out of this. I won't let them get you, Ruthie. I won't let them touch you, okay? Okay?'

'Dad,' she said. 'Don't cry, Dad. Please don't cry.'

Chapter 40

17,531.6 hours. He was counting down each and every one of them until he could bring her home.

* * * * *

The first visit was the worst visit. And the second visit was terrible. The third time he saw her he was no good at all, just sitting and crying like a baby until the warden suggested that he should leave if he couldn't shut the fuck up. He tried really hard. But it wasn't easy, she was his daughter.

She was strong, she was stronger than him. She gave him tissues. She held his hand. She told him that he didn't have to come if it didn't make him feel good. He tried to explain to her that visiting her was the only thing that made him feel good.

She had a heart of gold, pure gold. Even in her orange-and-black prison uniform she looked stylish and elegant. Dignified, that was the word for her.

He had once believed he had so much to teach her, and that they had all the time in the world. He had been wrong about that. And now she was teaching him. Life was full of surprises.

He was free and she was not. That had been a *blerrie* shock, not just a surprise.

He had tried, he had really tried his best to keep her out of prison, but nobody had listened to him, what with his history and all that. His words had been worth nothing. But those other people who had spoken up for her, at least they had been listened to: Liz, that little blonde chick, and the *pommie* who had come all the way from London, and three of Desmond Tutu's Africans. These were Ruth's people – they all had said so many wonderful things about her, about his daughter Ruth. He was proud to be her father. She was a really important person. She made a difference to so many people's lives, they all said that. She made a difference to his life.

Two years, with immediate visitation rights due to exceptional circumstances.

He could visit her forty-eight times a year. It could have been worse.

730 days.
It was a long time to be locked up.

Barney was great at helping him get ready. Usually he was all thumbs and some extra fingers before the visiting time. He changed from one blue shirt to another, sometimes because it was not the right blue, and sometimes because he'd sweated through the shirt before they'd even left the house. He couldn't visit her if he smelled bad. He liked to bring her flowers even if she had to leave them with him when they said goodbye. He always chose flowers he thought she'd like so that when he took them back home with him he could think of her when he looked at them. But no matter how hard he prepared and practised with Barney, when he was with Ruth it always felt like someone had something to say and wasn't saying it. Sometimes he thought it was him, and he wondered what he was not saying, and sometimes he thought it was her and he got scared about what she wasn't saying. Now that he had stopped crying when he visited her, he saw that she was quiet. She was waiting for him to know what to talk about. And he was waiting for her to show him what to do. He had no idea what they were supposed to talk about. What did fathers talk about with their daughters?

550 days left.

She was very quiet some days. He was happy just to sit and look at her. Maybe she needed him to say something, but he had no idea what it might be. Between visits he counted the hours until he could see her, but when he was with her he felt sad and uncomfortable in his seat, desperate to be away from her look that he couldn't understand. He was scared of what she might say to him.

'Bastard, murderer, betraying piece of garbage' is what he'd have said to himself. But she didn't. She let him be with her, she let him sit with her.

Sometimes he thought about cutting out his eye so that he wouldn't have to see her looking at him when he didn't know what she was thinking, and he got very scared. But when she smiled at him when he walked into the room, and when she looked at him before she hugged him goodbye, with tears in her eye, just for him, then it made him feel as though he belonged to someone again, like he was a person.

He was Ruth's father

365 days to go.

'Do you still have the photo, the one with the Valiant? I saw the photo when I was in your house,' she asked him.

'What photo, doll? Which one do you mean?'

'From when we were all kids. The photo where we're all standing in front of your mustard-coloured Valiant. You had it in a silver frame,' she said. 'If you still have it, please can you bring it in, I'd like to see it again.'

'*Ja*, of course, I'll have a really big hunt for it, definitely,' he said.

When he got home he went straight into his bedroom. He lay down on the bed for a few minutes and then turned to look at his bedside table with the silver-framed photo of him and his wife, and his children. Ruth wanted to see this photo. He knew he would have to give it to her. What else would she ask of him? He didn't have any more answers.

On his next visit he handed it to her. 'Here it is,' he said.

'Thanks, Dad,' she said and put the photo face down on the table between them. She didn't want to look at it with him. She wanted to be private with it. He understood that.

'We were driving to Cape Town,' he said. 'Yes, I remember.'

'Hey, you three used to fight so much in that back seat. And your mom, boy was she scared of the Karoo.'

'I remember.' He said nothing.

'I loved the Karoo,' she said. 'It always made me sad that we had to rush through it so quickly. I always thought I would go back one day so that I could drive through very slowly, maybe even stop,' she said.

'*Ja*, all those stars twinkling like diamonds,' he said.

'Just like diamonds,' she said.

'It was really beautiful.'

'*Ja*, really beautiful. I also haven't been back.'

They sat in silence for a few moments.

'Your mom, jeez she was scared of that heat,' he laughed. But he could feel that he had gone too far, that there could be no joking about some people.

'Can I keep the photo for a little while? Would you mind?'

'No, no, of course not. Keep it as long as you need. It's for you,' he said with a breaking heart.

'Do you have other photos?' she asked him. 'No. It's the only one. No other photos.'

'Oh. You better keep it then. Anything could happen to it in here,' she said.

'Well, I mean, I could look for more photos. There are probably lots more, I've just not looked for them. You know, this is the only one that I could stand to look at.'

'How come just this photo?'

'It's so long ago, I can hardly remember the people in it. It's like it's someone else or something. But it makes me happy to look at it. Does that sound weird?'

'No,' she said, staring at him. 'That's why I like it too.'

She looked down. It was too hard for them to look at each other during those moments. He hung his head. His shame crept up his back and over his chest. But he couldn't cry or he wouldn't be allowed to visit her, and that would be even worse than how he felt at that moment. A big tear landed down onto the table though. He quickly wiped it with his sleeve and felt Ruth's hand on his hand. He looked at her. Her eye was also full of tears. Maybe it was her tear on the table and not his. They held hands and sat in their silence, together.

Twenty-one days left.

504 hours.

Ruth was coming home.

He was going to get her hair done. Barney knew some place that all the ladies liked to go to. Barney's wife liked to go there. Grey hair was not what a father wanted to see on his daughter. It could have been worse, like fifteen years, but still two years was two years. 730 days.

He liked the clock, it told you where you were in your day. It told you if you were late for your thirty-minute visit, and when your visit was over. He was never late. Not once in two years and ninety visits. The clock meant they didn't have to worry what to talk about. Even when they didn't have any words, then they sat together, as the clock ticked away. Knowing when it was time to go was as important as knowing when to arrive. He liked that a lot. It made him feel calm.

Ruth was coming home. They wouldn't be watching the clock then. They could ban clocks for as long as they liked, if that's what she wanted to do. It wouldn't be easy for him, but he didn't want to do anything she didn't want to do. He'd be happy to sit on the *stoep* and drink tea. Ruth liked coffee. They could go for walks on the beach, when she was stronger. Her last flu had really made her weak, and she was so thin now. Still, better to be skinny. He could never stand fat chicks.

He'd been thinking that maybe they could go on a little road trip. He could ask Barney to help him.

'Hey, doll, only one more week. You've nearly done it, just the home run and you're done,' he said. 'Hang in there, be strong.'

'I know, I know,' she said, staring down at her hands. 'Hey, that's good news right?' he said.

She was silent.

'Ruthie, it's nearly over, so nearly over, and we need to celebrate, *ja*?'

She looked up at him, a very tired face with eyes that looked like they didn't ever sleep.

'Ruth? What? What's the matter? I thought you'd be buzzing, doll. Hey, I'm buzzing.'

She said nothing. He stopped talking. He was confused. He didn't know what was happening.

'Tick tock, tick tock,' he told her. 'It's kicking out time for me soon, any minute now. I won't see you again until release next week. But I'll be here, I'll be outside, waiting for you, okay?' he said.

'I don't know what to do,' she said softly.

'Huh?'

'I don't know what to do. I've been in here for two years. So much time to think about what has happened to us, to you, to me. I don't know what to do. I don't know who to be. Nothing's like I thought it was. I'm not who I thought I was. I don't know what happens next,' she said.

'Well, hmmm, well,' he said, 'Well, me neither. But that's not a bad thing, is it? See, we get to start again. Not brand new, but just again, that's all I want.'

'Dad, I'm scared.'

'Don't be, doll. I've got a plan, a sweet little plan. It's going to be great.'

She looked at him. 'What plan?' she said, in a voice that sounded just like his wife's. Women, women – jeez these chicks were always so suspicious, never giving a guy a chance to surprise.

'A little driving holiday, you and me. No newspapers, no TV, no wardens, no clock. Just lots and lots of space.'

'I like space,' she said.

'So how about it?'

'What?'

'You and me, a little road trip. What do you say?'

'Uuh ... I don't know. I mean ... well, where will we go?'

'Somewhere with a big sky.'

'Where? I mean ... what ... where would we go to?

'How about Beaufort West? See, I've been thinking – it's not far from here, about four or five hours away. We could have a real adventure, the two of us. '

'But that's so far away, in the middle of the Karoo,' she said.

'*Ja.*'

'Why would we go there? To the Karoo?'

'The stars,' he said. 'Stars twinkling like diamonds.'

She was silent. Maybe she didn't want to be with him. He hadn't thought about that.

'Of course, you might have other plans. You don't have to be with me if you don't want to, I just thought, I hoped ... I ...'

'Dad, yes, I'd like that. I'd really, really like to do that with you.

Thank you, really. Thank you,' she said.

He blinked his eye. Those tears. They always turned up like the unwanted visitor at the party. He didn't ever remember crying like a baby before, with his other eye.

'Great, great, that's really great, Ruth. I'll get Barney to help me. He knows lots of things. He knows how to make a holiday. Barney can help us.'

'It sounds great, Dad, thank you.'

'It's going to be a little warm I think. About forty degrees. It's always hot in the Karoo, you know.'

'I love the heat,' she said.

'Me too,' he said.

They sat looking at each other until the guard came over, to end the final visit.

'See you Thursday, three pm,' he told her.

'I'll be there,' she said.

'Me too,' he said. 'I'll be there also.'

'Bye.'

'Bye, doll.'

CHAPTER 41

He once drove fourteen hundred kilometres in eighteen hours straight, without his eyes closing even for a minute. That was the whole *blerrie* journey from Joburg to Cape Town. It was important not to stop because his wife hadn't liked the desert heat. There was no air-conditioning in those days, just blasts of fast, hot air if you opened the car window.

The air was hot, so hot it could dry you out, maybe even hot enough to fry an egg on the car bonnet. He had never done that but he'd seen it done in cowboy movies from the American West. He'd had great cars back then, great big American cars that flew along the roads. He'd loved the great big seats, soft like an old armchair, and that really bouncy suspension for speeding along those long, flat roads. A person could drive for miles without seeing another car. Some people didn't like that kind of thing, but he did. Those had been great days, really something. He had loved driving.

He hadn't done much one-eyed driving – apart from what Barney and he had done last week in Barney's little car. He couldn't expect Ruth to drive the moment she became a free woman. She needed to be treated like a queen, driven around a bit so she could relax. Maybe they could share the driving after a while, if she asked. But he wouldn't ask her to drive. That wouldn't be fair. She could drive if she wanted to, but not because he needed her to. He didn't want to need her to do anything.

Barney had helped him sort out the route, book the guest house. Together they'd organised the visit to the Karoo national park. It was all so new. He'd never been to a national park. They had always been in a rush. His wife had been in a rush – to get to the sea, to be seen. These days people seemed to have more time to relax, to enjoy the small things. He hoped it was going to be hot. He hoped it was going to be really hot.

He felt as nervous as if he was on a date. He had been anxious about parking with one eye and it had taken him a lot of sweaty backwards and forwards manoeuvres until he had the car finally in place. He was thirty minutes early. He sat waiting for his daughter. Ruth could rest in the back seat, she could have the whole back seat to herself. She could even lie down and go to sleep if she wanted.

He didn't know what she wanted.

At exactly 2.00pm she walked out of the prison gates.

'*Howzit*, doll. Your first steps to freedom. Here, some flowers for you,' he said.

'Thanks,' she said.

He took her bag and let her follow him as if he were collecting her from the airport, instead of prison.

'Uuh, I haven't got a vase with me,' he said. 'A vase for the flowers. They might die.'

'That's okay,' she said.

'I just wanted to give you something pretty, for now. We can buy more, later, if you like, when they die,' he said.

'Thanks,' she said.

He stopped in front of the car. 'Here we are,' he said.

She looked briefly at the car, fiddled with her handbag, and then looked back at the car in disbelief.

'You're joking, right?' she said.

He smiled. 'Get in.'

'Dad, seriously, whose car is this?'

'It's mine, it's ours, if you want.'

'Oh my God! I can't believe it. I haven't seen a Valiant for years. Can I sit in the back?'

'It's all yours, doll, climb in.'

She opened the door carefully and sat on the edge of the seat. She lay down across the full length and put her flowers on the floor.

'Oh my God,' she said.

'Let's go,' he said.

He pulled out of the space, nice and slow, like Barney and he had practised. This was going well, better than he had expected. He felt himself relax into his soft sofa seat. Just like the good old days. Barney, he was just the man for knowing how to do things, and who to know when a person needed something done. He knew a guy who knew a guy, is all he had said, and then he had turned up three days later with this *blerrie* Valiant. What a beast. Black and shiny-chrome body, and red leather seats. A car for a queen.

He drove very slowly, he had fragile cargo in the car, his daughter. It wasn't every day a man's daughter came out of prison.

Chapter 42

'Where are we?' she asked.

'I thought you'd never wake up. We're in Laingsberg. We've been driving for three hours. How d'ja feel now?'

'Can we stop? I need to stretch my legs and then I can sit in the front with you.'

'Sure,' he said. 'Do you want a drink? Do you want me to stop for the Ladies?'

'No, I'm fine. Just some water please.'

He pulled over, and she got out and fiddled with her hair and face. She looked tired and old, and reminded him of his mother.

'What food do you have?' she asked.

'Chicken sandwiches, dried apricots, red apples and chocolate cake.'

'Okay,' she said. 'I can eat that,' and she scrambled into the front seat, next to him.

'How about some music?' he said.

The song was his most terrifying, most daring idea, and he'd been saving it until just the right moment.

She nodded, her mouth full of food.

That song. It was as if it had been playing for all these years, and he had just forgotten to listen. He dared not look at Ruth. He just kept driving.

He liked long, flat, desert roads where a person could see for miles in front and miles behind. Now that was a road, just as it should be. But suddenly they were starting to climb; he had forgotten about the winding mountain passes with their sheer, steep drops. His damp hands gripped the steering wheel more tightly. This road, it just kept darting left and then right, and then left and then right, like a crazy cobra. This wasn't what Barney and he had practised. He didn't like this road, a person had no idea of what was coming towards him.

'Hey, Dad,' Ruth said as Paul and John and Ringo and George

moved to the chorus, their voices filling the Valiant. He couldn't speak a single word. Her pleasure was more than he had dared to hope for.

'*She loves you, yeah, yeah. She loves you, yeah, yeah, yeah,*' she sang.

He reached for his daughter's hand.

'I love you, Dad,' she said.

He turned to look at her through his tear-blinded eye. He couldn't see a *blerrie* thing.

Book Club questions:

General
1. What was your favourite part of the book?
2. What was your least favourite part?
3. Did you race to the end or was it more of a slow burn?
4. What scene stuck with you the most?
5. What did you think of the writing?
6. Did you reread any passages?
7. Would you want to read another book by this author?

Questions specific to *We Were The Newmans*
1. Do you think the title *We Were The Newmans* reflects the novel?
2. What do you think of the book's cover? How well does it convey what the book is about?
3. The author set out to write a book that explored the possibilities of forgiveness. Do you think she succeeded?
4. Do you believe it is possible to forgive?
5. Forgiveness is right and revenge is wrong – discuss
6. Being told to forgive might prevent healing – discuss
7. The TRC enforced enormous responsibility of forgiveness on the victims. How do you feel about this?
8. The story is told through several voices: Ruth, Constance, and Ivor. Why do you think the author chose to do this?
9. How do you understand Ruth's decision to end her relationship with José?
10. What did you think about Liz naming her son Jon-Jon?
11. What do you think happens to Ruth and Ivor at the end?
12. Fiction is inherently inauthentic because it is made up – discuss
13. If you got the chance to ask the author of this book one question, what would it be?
14. If you were making a movie of this book, who would you cast?
15. Have any of your personal views changed because of this book? If so, how?

Printed in Great Britain
by Amazon